About the authors

Asha Miró, born in India, was adopted by a couple from Barcelona at the age of seven. Her first book was the best-seller *Daughter of the Ganges*. Formerly a music teacher, she now collaborates on several cultural television programs and actively supports adoption organizations throughout Spain.

Anna Soler-Pont, born in Barcelona, studied Arabic Language and Culture and is the founder of Pontas international literary & film agency. She has an adopted daughter from Ethiopia.

Asha and Anna's life-changing experiences inspired them to write the novel *Traces of Sandalwood*. This novel was adapted into a feature film, released in Spain in 2014, and has been awarded several prizes, including the Audience Award at Montreal World Film Festival 2014.

About the translator

Charlotte Coombe is a British literary translator currently based between Morocco and UK. Her translations include *The Solomon Islands Witness* by Marc de Gouvenain, *A Single Decision* by Maria Paulina Camejo, and *Johnny Depp: Anatomy of an Actor* for Cahiers du Cinema. She is currently working on a collection of short stories by the Mexican author Rosamaría Roffiel. Her forthcoming translation for World Editions of Abnousse Shalmani's debut novel *Khomeini, Sade and Me* has been awarded the PEN Translates grant.

Asha Miró and Anna Soler-Pont

Traces of Sandalwood

Translated from the Spanish by
Charlotte Coombe

World Editions

Published in Great Britain in 2016 by World Editions Ltd., London
www.worldeditions.org
By Agreement with Pontas Literary & Film Agency

Rastros de sándalo © Asha Miró and Anna Soler-Pont, 2007
English translation copyright © Charlotte Coombe, 2016
Cover design Multitude
Image credit © Hollandse Hoogte/Magnum/Raghu Rai

The moral rights of the author and translator have been asserted in
accordance with the Copyright, Designs and Patents Act 1988

First published as *Rastros de sándalo* in Spain in 2007
by Editorial Planeta

British Library Cataloguing-in-Publication Data
A catalogue record for this book is available on request from
the British Library

ISBN 978-94-6238-057-8

Typeset in Minion Pro

Distribution Europe (except the Netherlands and Belgium):
Turnaround Publishers Services, London
Distribution the Netherlands and Belgium: Centraal Boekhuis,
Culemborg, the Netherlands

CONTENTS

To Iris, Roger and Jan Soler Pont,

to Fatima Miró,

to Asha Meherkhamb and

to Saku Jagtap,

for our shared childhood and everything that came after.

'Crossing borders is the true meaning of life. [...] There are many borders we also have to cross that aren't physical: those of culture, family, language, love ... '

RYSZARD KAPUSCINSKI, in an interview with Ramón Lobo published in *El País*, 23 April, 2006

This story is pure fiction, although it recreates personal experiences and many characters are inspired by people that exist or have existed. Any resemblance to reality may be due to real events or may be coincidence.

Note: In the novel, the old name of Bombay has been used when it refers to the city up until 1995, after which it came to be called Mumbai.

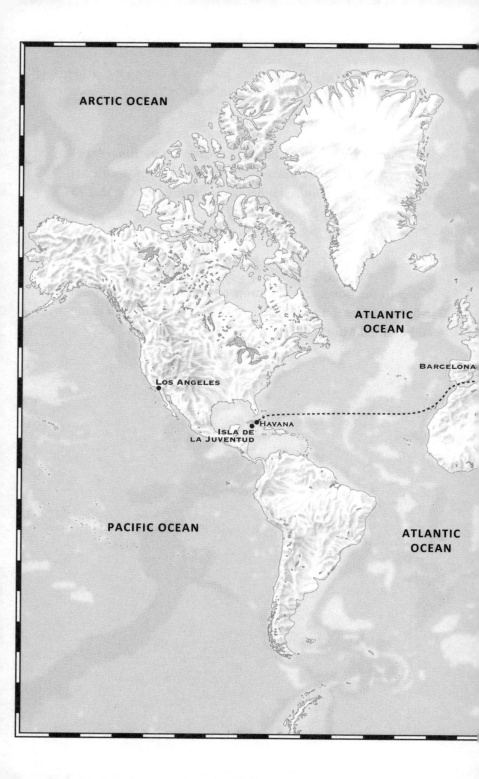

ROUTE OF THE BOAT AFRICA-CUBA

ARCTIC OCEAN

PACIFIC OCEAN

LAHORE

NASIK

MUMBAI

PONDICHERRY

ASSAB

ADDIS ABEBA

INDIAN OCEAN

PART ONE

Daybreak came quickly. As soon as the first faint rays of dawn appeared, the night immediately drew back its dark veil. Solomon sat on the windowsill gazing at one of the facades of the Entoto Mariam church, imagining the people inside the surrounding wall, all dressed in their white cotton clothing, crouching by the wall or leaning against tree trunks. There were always sick people around the church. Waiting. Most of them hoping that death would come soon. The smell of eucalyptus hung in the air. In the distance, far from the octagonal-shaped Orthodox Church, the shape of the city could just be made out through the dense fog. The hills around Addis Ababa rose up, three thousand metres high, cloaked in a leafy forest of eucalyptus trees. During the night, hyenas had been scrounging around for food next to the houses. They invaded the flooded, mud-filled streets trawling for bones, the remains of chicken carcasses, a stray lamb escaped from a pen or some old dog too crippled to fend them off.

'Come on Solomon! Get up! Get dressed and come and eat something, you're going to be late for school!'

'Has Dad already left?'

'Yes, he and Aster have both gone. It's just you left! Come on, up you get!'

Maskarem bustled around the house listening to the radio which was always on. The repetitive beat of military marches sounded out. They seemed to be on the radio a lot these days. Maskarem always had to make sure that there were embers burning in the small stone oven that their father had built, so that they could cook *injera** whenever they needed it. In one corner, on the floor between some large stones, was the fire that they used for heating water and cooking. Since their mother had died two years ago, Maskarem stayed at home while the others went out to work or to school. It was a small single storey house sufficient for the four people who lived in it.

At last, Solomon did as he was told by his older sister, got dressed and gobbled down a quick breakfast of *injera* with some *shiro wat* left over from the day before, using his fingers to tear off large pieces. He grabbed the cloth bag containing his notebooks and pen and ran out of the house, down toward the road to Shiro Meda, the neighbourhood which nestled at the foot of the Entoto hills, some five hundred metres below. Sometimes he would cut through the forest, leaping like a little goat so that he didn't slip. If he took the main road, he would run as fast as he possibly could. The road sloped steeply, with many sharp bends. There was very little traffic but there were a lot of people walking up and down it. There were also many donkeys carrying clay pots and plastic drums full of water, fastened tightly to their saddlebags with ropes. At this time of day, before it got too hot, many women were carrying bundles of firewood on their heads or tied to their backs, either going to sell it or taking it home. Others carried jars full of fresh milk. The smell of burning eucalyptus was all around.

When Solomon reached Sintayehu's house he didn't need to call for him. As soon as he drew near, his friend came dashing out clutching his schoolbag. His mother was busying herself with buckets of water and waved goodbye to him from the window. For most women, the morning was the time for water.

---

* Words in italics are explained in the glossary at the end of the book.

They either had to go and fetch it or wait for someone to bring it before they could start their cooking or cleaning. In that particular neighbourhood only a handful of the houses had running water. When Sintayehu caught up with him, Solomon slowed down and they walked side by side to school, which was still some distance away. They were both eight years old and in the same class at school. They both had brown skin and very short, curly dark hair.

'So have you asked your dad yet which day we can go?'

'No, not yet,' replied Solomon.

'What on earth are you waiting for? My dad says they're going to kick the emperor out soon. So if you don't hurry up we won't get to see the lions!'

'What do you mean they're going to kick out the emperor? My dad's one of his cooks!'

'I heard my dad talking about it a few days ago with my uncle and some of their friends who came to the house. I didn't really understand what they were going on about but they sounded really angry. I heard them saying that they've had enough of Ras Tafari and the time has come to throw him out.'

'Why are you calling him Ras Tafari when his name is Haile Selassie?'

A flock of goats grazed casually at the side of the wide road, nibbling the green grass, quite indifferent to the cars and buses rumbling past.

'Right now he's the king of kings; the lion of Judah; God's chosen one; but my father says that his name is Tafari Mekonen, that he's just a normal guy and he can't even read or write!'

'No way! You're always telling silly stories!'

'Well, believe what you like. But if my dad says that the

emperor never went to school then it's true!' replied Sintayehu, leaving Solomon lost for words. 'So can we feed them?' he insisted.

'The palace lions? Are you crazy? Only the emperor can do that!'

'Yeah, but maybe your dad can ask them to let us do it. Or at least let us see them in the cages in the garden!'

They reached the school. Dozens of boys just like them and little girls with their hair in plaits were making their way inside the building. Solomon and Sintayehu could hear a large group of people shouting, mostly young men. They were yelling slogans against the emperor. It was yet another demonstration by university students, moving slowly up the avenue and bringing the traffic to a standstill. The cars, small vans that served as collective taxis and buses were all beeping their horns. Demonstrations like this one happened often. If it wasn't students then it was farmers clamouring for their rights. Every time, more and more groups of different people came together wanting the same thing.

'*Meret le arashu!* Land to the tiller!'

'Down with the feudal regime!'

'*Meret le arashu!*'

'Give us back our land!'

'End the tyranny!'

The crowd repeated the same cries over and over. Solomon and Sintayehu watched them with curiosity and without the faintest idea what was going on.

Some of the men doing the shouting were red in the face with anger and looked like they might kill the next person who got in their way. There were some soldiers amongst the students too.

18

Everywhere you went lately, there seemed to be more soldiers than ever.

'Come on, everyone inside! Hurry up!' a teacher told them.

'Do as you're told, or there'll be trouble!' The school guard gripped the gate railings, ready to close it once all the children were inside. Then it was just him standing by the railings and the flagpole with the Ethiopian flag rippling in the morning breeze.

The school day usually started with all the boys and girls lining up in the playground to sing the national anthem while the headmaster raised the three-coloured flag. But when there were protests like that morning, the children went straight into the classrooms. There was no lining up, no national anthem, nothing. They took their seats and the teachers immediately went round closing the windows overlooking the street. It was hard to concentrate, both for the students and the teachers. There were days when the noise outside made any other activity other than copying out of textbooks absolutely impossible. Text after text, copied diligently into their notebooks, while the teacher watched what was going on in the street with interest.

'An end to hunger!' shouted the protesters, their voices rising above the din of car and taxi horns.

'*Meret le arashu!*'

Other times, the protesters were taxi drivers, complaining about the price of petrol. Without taxis, Addis Ababa was a ghost town. But it was even worse if the Ambessa bus workers decided to join the protest too, demanding a pay rise that never came. Then it was complete and utter chaos.

'Which land are they talking about?' Solomon asked Sintayehu.

'Which land do you think? Ours of course!'

19

Solomon definitely didn't understand what was going on; why so many people were shouting in the streets; why everyone seemed so on edge.

'Quiet!' said the teacher.

Solomon knew that things were happening that he didn't understand and no-one would explain to him. He didn't play much. He went to school early in the morning, made his way back up through the woods for his lunch, went down to the city again for his afternoon classes, slower and quite tired when they finished. He was a good pupil just as he had promised his mother he would be, before she died. She had barely been to school. She had spent her childhood in the mountains of Tikil Dingai, between Gondar and Dansha. The mountains were known for their "well-placed rocks" which were unusual shapes. When she became a city woman, although they lived in the Entoto hills, her main concern was that her children should study. At last year's prize-giving ceremony for the school's best pupils, Solomon had won his class prize. More than one child received lashings and punishments from the teachers, using all kinds of whips. Solomon had never been punished either at school or at home. He was possibly the only one who had never been punished. He did his homework every day at the wooden table in their house and helped out as much as he could. He had no reason not to. Before he went to primary school, he went to a small school run by Orthodox priests, next door to the church. There he had learned to read and write, monotonously repeating the syllabic alphabet out loud. *Ha, hu, hi* … It seemed more like a singing recital class than anything else. Anyone who made a mistake or fell behind was hit with a wooden stick or a whip. Striped whip marks on their skin were a common occurrence.

Ma, mu, mi … The parents didn't complain; quite the opposite in fact. They would often beat their children even more for having angered the teachers.

They were going to the Entoto Mariam Church as they did every Sunday morning. Solomon's sisters wore long white dresses and their hair covered with a *netela*, a white cotton cloth with a single blue-coloured border around the edge. Small silver crosses strung on black wool hung round their necks. As well as the cross, Maskarem also wore one of her mother's necklaces, made from some pieces of old silver from her northern homeland.

'*Salam*, Biniam!' said Solomon, seeing his friend on the steps of the church.

'How are you?' asked Maskarem as she came up the steps behind him. Without saying anything else, she discreetly slipped him a few *birrs*. Biniam stuffed them into his pocket immediately, looking down at the floor.

'Thank you, I'm fine.'

Biniam was slightly older than Solomon and lived alone on the streets. They had known each other a long time, since before Biniam's parents had become ill and died, one after the other. He had some relatives in a town in the north, near Lake Tana, but all of his close relatives were dead. They used to play together, making shoes out of empty cans so they could see the world from a few inches higher, but now Biniam just did what he could to survive. He shined shoes on the city's streets, carrying his father's old wooden box full of brushes and polishes and an empty paint can that he used as a stool when his customers sat down on a low wall.

'Do you want to come with me this afternoon? I have to take some sheep and goats out to graze.'

21

'Okay! Where are you going?'

'Not far. There's fresh grass everywhere. I have to collect Getasseu's sheep from near your house so I'll come and call for you after that. Then we can go and get the Denberus' cow and two goats from their neighbours. When it gets dark I have to take them all back to the stables.'

'Do you graze them every day?'

'Yes, I do now. They don't pay me very much but I prefer being out around Entoto with the herd than going down to Shiro Meda with my shoe polish box.'

'I think I'd prefer to stay round here too.'

The men and the women entered the church through different doors. Before taking their shoes off and going inside they spent a few minutes standing in front of the walls of the main facade; they kissed it and then kissed the ground. The doors were painted with brightly coloured angels, dressed in red, their almond-shaped eyes lined in black. The people would not leave the church until at least two hours later, sometimes more. Biniam always said that the thing he liked most about going to church was that it was the only place where he felt calm and protected. The church was filled with the strong smell of incense and sandalwood that a monk was burning in a copper bowl full of smouldering charcoal. A huge painting of Saint George, the patron saint of Ethiopia, riding a white horse with a sword in his hand, dominated one of the walls. Biniam also felt at home in Solomon's house, where he spent many hours and sometimes stayed the night, sleeping in a corner to keep out of the way.

'Come round for dinner. My father has cooked some *doro wat* and you know he makes really good *injera*,' Solomon said to him, before he started singing.

By the time he got home it was already starting to get dark. His father was listening to the radio, Aster was embroidering a piece of cotton fabric and Maskarem was sitting by the window sewing buttons onto a little dress. Maskarem had found work in the house of an American family living in Addis Ababa; she looked after their two blonde-haired children, cooked and did sewing for them as needed. It was a good job and was a chance for her to practice her English; she had learned it at school and spoke fairly well.

Peter Howard had moved to Addis Ababa four years ago with his wife Jane and their two children: Sarah, who was eight years old, and Mark, five. He was a paleoanthropologist working on various research projects. Occasionally he had to spend whole weeks in the Danakil region in north-eastern Ethiopia, directing various excavations. He was fascinated by the Rift valley, the geography of Ethiopia and its history, culture and language. He had learned Amharic and his team included students from the University of Addis Ababa who were working with him. Jane Howard was a cheerful, easygoing woman who adapted easily to any situation. She had travelled to many different countries, following her husband wherever his excavations and research took them, and she liked discovering new ways of life and particularly learning new recipes. She was English but when she met Peter she decided to go and live with him in the United States and so their two children had been born there.

Maskarem and Mrs Howard talked at great length about Ethiopian cooking, about the secret to making a good *injera*, the exact amounts of different spices to put in each dish and the cooking times for vegetables. Sometimes, the Howards had guests over and they asked Maskarem to stay and carry out the coffee ceremony.

She placed the coffee cups on a tray full of eucalyptus leaves. Sitting on a low stool, she roasted the green coffee beans on an iron grill with sandalwood smoking at her feet. When the beans were fairly blackened, she ground them, while everyone watched, crushing them in a small wooden mortar. She poured boiling water into a ceramic jug containing the ground coffee. Then she filled all the cups. Then she filled the jug with more water to serve a second round. Once everyone had left their cup on the tray she served one more round of cups. Each time the coffee was smoother.

Maskarem liked teaching her customs to these pink-skinned *farangis*; foreigners who showed a genuine interest in her country. But she didn't like having to stay over and sleep at the house when it got too late. She had told them this, so they would drive her home, up the road to Entoto. The Howards had hired an older married couple as servants because they didn't like the idea of being working parents, although this was quite normal for the foreigners who lived in Addis Ababa. The couple did the cooking and housekeeping. They told Maskarem that lately, all the Howards and their guests had been talking about was the country's drought and the government's failure to do anything to prevent more people dying of hunger. That, and the intentions of the military. On the radio they never said anything about that. Families lived their lives with their radios blaring out; their radios that didn't tell them what was really happening.

It was raining. It had been raining continuously for weeks and the streets, very few of which were tarmacked, had become muddy tracks. In the rainy season everything slowed down. Donkeys' legs sank deep into the mud making it hard for them to walk; bicycle wheels ran aground; cars skidded. People walked more slowly too, beneath their umbrellas, looking carefully where they were going, dodging puddles and mud so they didn't slip, and taking care not to dirty their shoes more than necessary. In the city it was frowned upon to be seen in gum boots like the peasants in the mountains, even though some streets were as bad as those in the villages.

Sintayehu was still insisting on going to see the lions the emperor kept in cages in the palace gardens and Solomon continued to assure him that it would be impossible. Apparently, the palace servants prepared meat on silver platters which the emperor would throw to the animals through the bars of the cages.

'Meat on silver platters? When I tell my father about that he'll be furious!' said Sintayehu.

'Why?'

'Don't you know that thousands of people are dying of hunger? They're dying next to huge storage barns full of food because the wealth is so poorly distributed!'

They reached Sintayehu's house and after barely mumbling goodbye, Solomon continued walking on his own up the road to Entoto. Sintayehu was talking like the grownups; he repeated everything he heard his father say. Solomon never knew what to say back.

Solomon kicked off his muddy shoes at the front door. 'What do you think will happen?' he heard Maskarem asking their father, as he came into the house.

'I don't know. I really don't know. Everything's moving so fast ... '

Solomon sat down at the wooden table listening with interest to the conversation between his father and sisters. Outside the rain was still pouring down.

'Have they let any of the servants go?'

'I don't know … Why would they have to do that? We're just palace workers, nothing more than that! We *sera bet* are the emperor's best cooks; we make the most exquisite delicacies … We haven't done anything wrong!'

'What's moving fast? What's going on?'

'Palace things, Solomon, just palace things … '

'What things, Dad?'

The man looked at his little son. He wasn't that little any more.

'The army are arresting ministers and dignitaries and the emperor isn't doing anything about it … ' replied his father, who seemed tired, dog tired, and older than he actually was. 'If only you could see what things are like inside the palace. There are dignitaries who have taken refuge there and are sleeping all over the place inside!'

'And no-one says anything to them?'

'Who would say something to them? They are dignitaries, and if his Highness allows it … Sometimes there aren't enough plates or food for everyone. Then they get angry; they call the servants and the cooks and ask us if we're taking orders from the rebels; they say we aren't serving them properly!'

The three children listened intently to their father. When he fell silent for a few seconds, all they could hear was the sound of the rain beating down on the tin roof.

'Sometimes there's too much food … and then the dignitaries argue with us because they say we haven't portioned out the food properly. It's a nightmare. I don't know how it will end.'

Mornings in early August were always misty and cool. But that August the mornings seemed colder and mistier than ever before. Thick fog hung over everything until well after daybreak and crept back again before darkness started to fall. You could hardly see the sky or the city at the foot of the mountains, at any time of the day. Water had flooded everything, running in great rivers along both sides of the main road and bursting out into wild streams in the forest. When Solomon left the eucalyptus forests and the leisurely grazing herds behind him and went down into the city, life seemed to be carrying on as normal. People were going to the market to buy and sell things, children were chasing each other around and some were playing football, without a care in the world, their bare feet caked in mud. There was no school; they were on holiday. But nothing had been the same since a minister, furious at not being served the food he had ordered, had gone into the palace kitchens and thrown out any staff that were in there at the time. His father was among them.

Student demonstrations were taking place more often and in larger numbers; now they happened practically every day.

'The country is drowning in corruption!'

'End the tyranny! We're sick of promises!'

'*Meret le arashu!*'

There were daily demonstrations that were noisy and violent. Students threw stones at the windows of official buildings and celebrated every time the army arrested one of the emperor's inner circle.

'Is this your brother?' a very tall, well-built man with blonde hair and blue eyes asked Maskarem as they stood at the entrance to a house surrounded by a garden. There was a swing hanging from a tree. Solomon had never seen a man with eyes that colour and he looked at him curiously. He had also never seen such a garden; it was so neat and full of flowers.

'Yes, this is Solomon,' replied Maskarem.

'Hi, Solomon. My name's Peter,' the man said to him, shaking his hand. 'I hear you're very good at drawing. It's a shame Jane and the children aren't here. I'm sure they would have loved to meet you. Please come in. My wife has left some clothes for you to mend, Maskarem; I'll go and find them. Would you like anything? Some water? *Kolo*?'

'No thanks, I'll just get the clothes and then we have to go.'

Peter Howard disappeared through a door.

'Why are his eyes blue? Is he ill?'

'Ssshhh! Don't talk so loud!'

'But has he always had blue eyes, or have they turned blue since he's been here?'

'*Farangis* have eyes of all different colours! It's the way they are!'

'Really, have you seen them? What colours?'

'Blue, green … I don't know Solomon, just be quiet, okay?'

The house was filled with all kinds of objects - masks, rugs, ceramic jugs and wooden sculptures. At one end of the room there was a bookshelf that covered the entire wall. There were books and photo frames everywhere. In one black and white photograph, a smiling girl and a boy with golden hair were sitting on a donkey. The boy was in the front and the girl behind, with both her arms round his waist.

'Here are the clothes. Jane told me there's no rush,' said Peter Howard cheerfully as he came into the room holding the bundle of clothes. 'Look, Solomon, I wanted to show you something. Do you know what this is?'

Solomon saw he was holding a stone in his hand. But from the way he was showing it to him, it was obvious it wasn't just any old stone.

'I found this fossil when I was eight - your age. At my school just outside Houston, in Texas, they were doing some building work to extend it and whenever I could, I would go to the site where the bulldozers were working and spend a long time looking for fossils like this one. I found so many! Do you know what it is?'

'No, sir,' Solomon said hesitantly.

'A bison bone! A fossilized bison bone. Do you know what a bison is?'

'No, sir.'

'I thought you might not, don't worry! Bison are … Hang on …'

Peter Howard went to the bookshelf at the end of the room and took down a book.

'Look. This animal here is a bison,' he said, showing him the book which he had opened at a page with a full-colour illustration. 'In my country they've always had them, but now they're becoming extinct …'

Solomon left the Howards' house with a bison bone fossil in his pocket and a book on American flora and fauna in his hand. He felt like he was carrying two treasures of immeasurable value.

'Can I come back another day?'

'I don't think so.'

'But why not? He said I can come back whenever I want!'

The eleventh of September was drawing near; the Ethiopian new year according to the Julian calendar. Everyone was more anxious than usual. Yet it wasn't the usual excitement of the holidays or the preparations for one of the most important celebrations and festivals of the year. It was something else. The hyenas also seemed more restless than usual. They roamed between the houses of the Entoto hills looking for anything they could eat. Everyone was scared of the hyenas. Men lit fires around the church and spent the night there, endlessly chewing *chat* to stay awake. They wanted to protect the ill people who were waiting for death in that holy place; to prevent the hyenas turning them into their prey. No one who had heard the terrified cries of someone being attacked by ravenous hyenas would ever want to hear that sound again. *Chat* wasn't just a stimulant; it also kept hunger at bay.

The fields were covered in a carpet of *adei abeba*, the wildflowers that heralded the coming of the new year after the rainy season. They had sprung up everywhere in a burst of bright yellow.

' ... *at the age of eighty-two he is incapable of fulfilling his obligations ... His Imperial Majesty Emperor Haile Selassie I is hereby deposed on 12th September 1974, with the Provisional Military Administrative Council taking power. Ethiopia first!*'

'Please turn off the radio, Maskarem!'

Maskarem, who was sitting sewing next to the radio, did as her father told her. A weighty silence descended on the room.

Time seemed to stand still.

'How can they say that they've overthrown the emperor because he was too old to go on ruling? How dare they! There is only the emperor under God, that's why he's lived so many years in good health!'

Their father's cries broke the silence. The three children didn't know what to say. They couldn't remember ever seeing him as worked up and angry as that day, the day after the eleventh of September. They didn't know what to think either. Why were so many young people spending so much time shouting in the streets and holding up the traffic, claiming their land for those who worked on it and begging for no more people to die of hunger, if the emperor was as good as their father said?

'It's a coup! They say they're loyal to the crown, but the military just want power; they aren't loyal to anyone!'

'It's lucky you weren't at the palace … it's a good thing they threw you out before!'

'How can you say that, Maskarem? It would have been an honour for me to serve the emperor to the end! He abolished slavery, he brought us electricity … He was a brave man! He stood up to Mussolini and nobody colonized us. The Italians tried but they couldn't!'

Outside, dogs were barking.

'I can look for work,' said Aster suddenly. 'Two of the girls in my class don't come to school any more because they have gone out to work.'

'No, darling. Your mother made me promise that you and Solomon would study. She wouldn't want you to do what she did … leaving school early … I'm the one who has to find work wherever I can.'

After that day, Solomon never saw his father smile again. The death of his mother had turned his father into an unhappy, serious and untrusting man, and now he was overwhelmingly so. He spent hours sitting in front of the framed black and white photo of his wife. Solomon knew every last tiny detail of that picture as well. He had also spent long moments sitting in front of it, talking to her without speaking. He had never known any other woman like his mother. Quiet and observant; her presence had filled the house. It filled everything with life and energy. He had also never seen another woman with a tattoo like hers on the forehead; it was a cross inside a circle. She had explained to

31

him that her mother had done it with a fine needle when she was very little. She didn't remember it, but had always been told that she hadn't cried one bit. In the mountains in the north of Gondar, nearly all the little girls were tattooed on the forehead. Each tattoo had a meaning, a symbol of beauty and relevance to the family. Some women also had their necks tattooed – they would tattoo one another when they came of age – so it looked as if they were wearing three or four blue necklaces.

During the first months of the revolution the streets of Addis Ababa were the scene of mass demonstrations. Some in support of the new military government, and others calling for it to be removed. There were also people calling for the fortunes of the emperor to be made public and shared out among the people.

Solomon didn't walk to school with Sintayehu any more. He ran down on his own from the Entoto hills and continued running through the streets of the city until he reached the school in the Shiro Meda neighbourhood.

'It's your fault that I never got to see the emperor's lions!

'I don't want to be your friend any more!' Sintayehu angrily blurted out.

'It's not my fault! Anyway, your father is in the army and so is your uncle! I don't want to be your friend either!'

Sintayehu used to get in a lot of fights, both at school and in the streets. For a moment, Solomon thought that he might hit him, scratch him, kick him and rip his shirt like he had seen him do so many times to other children. But Sintayehu just looked at him and said nothing. He turned his back on him and walked off in the other direction.

When he got home from school, Solomon would often find his father in the same place he had left him when he said goodbye. Sitting by the front door, just staring out.

'They've murdered him. I'm sure they've murdered him,' his father kept saying. 'I don't understand why they had to kill an old man who was so admired and respected by everyone.'

Lately there had been talk of nothing else but the death of Haile Selassie and more than fifty officials. Solomon couldn't imagine the country without its king; surely it would be impossible for Ethiopia to survive without an emperor. In his neighbourhood, life appeared to go on as usual. The women still got up early to fetch the water and firewood, just as they did every morning. At daybreak the roads and paths from the Entoto hills were filled with women of all ages carrying jugs of water and bundles of firewood tied to their backs or balanced on their heads. Then they would sit at the entrance to their houses, grinding chickpeas and lentils with one stone against another larger, bowl-shaped stone; crushing the dried legumes with slow, steady movements. Others would grind grains of wheat in wooden mortars with sticks that were taller than them. But everything was different; everyone was afraid. Solomon had heard the neighbours talking about some boys who had disappeared, all of them students from the university. A nephew, a cousin ... The military patrolled at all hours of the day and night in soft-top jeeps, armed with machine guns mounted on the passenger seat. They always cruised round very slowly. At night they would stop outside a house, a pair of men would get out, kick down the door, drag the suspects or members of the former regime out of bed, barefoot and without their documents and whisk them away with such force that the family wouldn't dare to protest. They just watched the jeeps roar off into the night. The dogs barked, but people no longer heard them.

The authorities ordered everybody to be registered. Everywhere. For any reason. Everybody was suspected of being the enemy. The registering was constant, as was the threatening feeling that hung over them. Solomon didn't understand what torture meant. Women spoke in whispers when they mentioned the word and he could never catch the end of the story.

'They had him hidden in his house for three weeks, and I'm sure they only came looking for him because some old friend turned him in; if not, I don't understand how they found him ... '

'They must have sent him outside the city, to some relative or other, or further, to Bahar Dar or to Gondar.'

Everything was in chaos. Everyone was telling terrifying stories: stories of young people hiding to avoid capture, or being tortured and killed; stories of families torn apart by the anguish of having to hide one of their children; the pain of losing a child, or more than one.

Every morning there were corpses lying in the streets. The families of those who hadn't come home the night before roamed the city, looking to see if any of the lifeless bodies were theirs. Official trucks collected them and took them to the morgue. Families queued up to pay the twenty-five *birrs* that the military demanded in exchange for releasing each body so they could be buried with dignity. Forty-eight hours after each night-time crackdown, if nobody had claimed the bodies or paid the twenty-five *birrs*, they took the bodies to the outskirts of Addis Ababa and dumped them, leaving them for the hyenas and vultures to feast greedily on.

Even though the arrival of the Ethiopian New Year had brought many changes, at school everything was the same, although they no longer sang the anthem of the flag in the playground before lessons started. One day, as there was no school in the afternoon,

Solomon stayed to help his father run some errands on the other side of the city, in a neighbourhood he didn't remember ever having been to. They boarded a bus full of taciturn people carrying parcels and packages. The women's heads and half of their faces were covered with white *netelas*. Many of the men also wore white *gabis*. Everyone was eyeing everyone else suspiciously. They managed to find two empty seats at the back. A herd of donkeys laden with sacks was crossing the wide avenue, probably on their way to the Merkato to sell their goods; flour or *teff*, or perhaps Afar salt which would have arrived in Ethiopia by camel caravan. Solomon was watching two young shepherds trying to guide their donkeys across the street without being mown down by the traffic, when suddenly the bus stopped and he bumped his head on the window glass. The driver opened the door and three men in sunglasses jumped on. They were brandishing sticks. From the front of the bus they scrutinized the faces of the silent passengers as if they were looking for someone.

'You! Get up! And you!' one of them shouted at two well-dressed passengers. He was wearing sunglasses. Waving his stick around imperiously, he pointed to their pockets and made them empty out whatever was in them. The men took their money, documents and watches from them, then got off the bus as arrogantly as they had boarded it. The driver moved off as if nothing had happened. Checks like this had become a frequent occurrence. No-one knew exactly who had the authority to check and register people, they might be military or police, or they might not.

'At least they didn't hurt anyone,' whispered an elderly man sitting opposite Solomon. 'The other day they made all of us get off the bus and those who wouldn't hand over their money were beaten severely with sticks. I think they killed one of them right there and then.'

Solomon was shaking with fear.

Most of the people who worked in the palace and all those with links to the emperor had been shot. Of those who hadn't been imprisoned, some had been able to flee the country, and others were hiding out in the mountains in the north or disguised as monks in monasteries. The few that had stayed in Addis Ababa avoided the military surveillance and checks as best they could.

'It's lucky that angry minister threw you out of the palace kitchens!' Maskarem would say to her father sometimes, although she knew he didn't like to hear it.

Solomon and Biniam were sitting at the top of a very high rock. Below them, through the forest of eucalyptus trees, they had an impressive panoramic view of the city. The sheep, goats and cows that they had brought up with them were grazing close by. From up there, in the silence of the Entoto hills, three thousand metres high, it seemed as if nothing was happening. Life seemed calm and peaceful.

'Here, take a look at this,' said Solomon, showing Biniam the bison bone fossil.

'How do you know it's a bone? He could have made it up!'

'Not you as well! Sintayehu said the same thing!'

'Well, you see. Now there are two of us who think the *farangi* has tricked you! How is this stone meant to be a cow bone?'

'A bison!'

'Same thing … an American cow!'

'Because Peter Howard told me it is … and his job is finding fossils in the Afar.'

'But he told you he found it when he was eight, right? How did he know it was a bison bone when he was eight?'

The radio was almost always on in the house, the volume turned down very low.

'The Howards are leaving; they're being thrown out,' said Maskarem, leaving the clothes she had been mending in the basket to one side.

'They're being thrown out of Ethiopia? Who by?' asked Aster.

'The military government, the Derg. I don't know why exactly, but they're finding any excuse to throw out lots of foreigners who work here,' replied Maskarem.

'Where will the Howards go?'

'To London. They don't want to go back to the United States and Mrs Howard's family are in England.'

Nobody said anything. Solomon and Aster sat at the table doing their homework and their father carried on transferring the *teff* flour that he had fetched from the mill, into jars. He didn't even look up.

'But I still have a job, don't worry,' Maskarem added.

Her father looked at her, still pouring the flour through a funnel made out of newspaper.

'They've asked me to go to London with them.'

Solomon looked up from his notebook full of sums.

'They'll pay me a good wage; I'll have my own room in their house. I'll carry on looking after the children, taking them to school, keeping things tidy. They'll sort out all the passport and visa formalities. In fact, they've been doing it for a few days now, everything is almost ready ... I couldn't find the right moment to tell you ... '

Her father sealed one of the full jars, slowly screwing the lid on.

'It's an opportunity we can't afford to turn down!'

'When do they want to leave?' he asked, as if it was a trivial question, concentrating on what he was doing. There were still two jars left to fill.

'Really soon. They've got sixteen days ... They've already bought the plane tickets. I'm sorry. It's something I have to do, I'm sure Mum would understand. I can send you money ... '

Aster closed the notebook she was writing in and sat very still at the table, looking at her sister as if she had just realized what this meant for her. She knew that Maskarem would go through with it. She would leave. And Aster would become the only woman in the house. She could feel herself growing older with every second that passed. The weight of responsibility that was about to fall directly on her shoulders.

Solomon jumped up, tipping over his chair, and fled from the house, leaving the door wide open. He ran down the street, taking no notice of his sisters who were calling to him to come back. A dog ran along after him until it grew tired and gave up. At sunset, the same intense smell of burning eucalyptus filled the air as it did first thing in the morning; it pervaded the air all around. He ran and ran blindly toward the city. There were many armed soldiers around, on foot or in trucks. He ran until he heard a voice calling his name; it was Biniam, blocking his way.

'Hey, Solomon, where are you off to? What's wrong?'

Biniam was walking up the main road, helping a blind monk who sometimes paid him a *birr* to accompany him from one place to another. He carried a huge silver Orthodox cross in his right hand. With the other he clutched Biniam's arm.

'You'd better go home, there are soldiers all over the place, and we heard shots ... '

'I don't care, let me past,' he said, panting.

'But Solomon, wait!'

Solomon tried to move past them, to carry on running down the road, when suddenly the wrinkled old man spoke out from beneath his white shawl, in a deep voice.

'Listen to your friend, my boy. Go home.'

The three of them walked slowly back up the road. They said nothing more until they reached the surrounds of the Entoto Church. A few people approached the monk, knelt in front of him and kissed the silver cross, waiting to receive his blessing. Before he went home Solomon also knelt in front of the blind monk, who placed his hand on his short, curly hair and rubbed the silver cross on his shoulder. Like all Ethiopian children, Solomon had been brought up to respect and obey his elders without complaining. Even more so if they were holy men.

'I don't know what you were running from, my boy. But nothing can be solved by running away downhill. Life is an uphill struggle. You have to be strong.'

Jane Howard sat on a kitchen chair in tears. Maskarem was folding the clothes she had laid out in the morning, piling them on the table, not knowing quite what to say. The house was full of cardboard boxes filled with books and objects. The library was now just a wall like any other; Peter Howard's study, which had always been in disarray, with mountains of papers, books, fossils and tools all over the place, now sat empty. Only the desk, lamp and chair remained. Peter Howard pottered in and out of the room, occasionally saying things to his wife to try and console her. They were speaking in English and so quickly that sometimes Maskarem couldn't understand what they were saying at all. But she understood enough to know that Mr Howard was very angry with someone. With someone who wasn't Ethiopian. With some other *farangi* who did the same thing as him and that it had to do with the discovery of that strange ancient skeleton that everyone had been talking about for months now.

'They're the ones who want me out of here! They've managed to get the Derg to throw me out; they've badmouthed me to the military! They're annoyed – they want to be the only stars of the show! They think they own the Afar!'

'But we have to go, Peter! Whoever it is, they want you out. And you'll be in danger if you stay,' Jane pleaded. 'Please, do it for me and the children. I'm scared. I want to go home. I don't want anything to happen to you!'

'I'll go for you. Just for you. And because we've already got our tickets and we can't afford to waste them … '

When Maskarem went, she left a huge void. Their mother had died too young of a disease that took her from them very quickly, and the absence of both women could now be felt immensely. Father stayed at home or went to the market; he went to fetch *teff* from the mill; and he took care of their clothes as best he could or asked the neighbours to add them to their own piles of laundry. Most of the time, however, they would never accept even a *birr* from him. They had been friends of his wife and they missed her too. Washing her family's clothes was the only way they could honour her memory. He prepared *injera* and various dishes to order; his reputation as a fine cook had spread throughout the city, particularly among the families closest to the emperor and those who were most nostalgic for the old days.

'Sintayehu always says that cooking is women's work. I don't know any other men who cook at home. You're the only one.'

'That Sintayehu … Come on, grab that knife and help me peel the potatoes. I've got a lot of work to do. In a few hours they'll be coming to collect their order. And they'll be coming up here by car, so it had better be ready!'

'Couldn't you have found work in a hotel?'

'What, you think I haven't tried that? Come on, get those potatoes peeled or I'm going to go and get Sintayehu to help us and then there'll be three men in the kitchen!'

Aster smiled as she plucked the chickens she had just plunged into a bucket of boiling water, so that the feathers would come off more easily.

In the kitchen there were always large jars full of *teff* flour mixed with water that, after resting for a few days to ferment, turned into a whitish liquid ready for making *injera*. Using a small jar, their father took small amounts of this liquid and placed it on the round earthenware grill which was kept hot over the wood fire in the oven. He wiped a cloth soaked in sesame oil over it, then let the liquid pour slowly onto it, drawing a spiral shape which started in the middle and became larger to form a circle which thickened as it came into contact with the heat. Then he covered it with a hat-shaped lid. Using a wooden spatula he lifted up one edge of the injera which was now cooked and taking care not to break it, lifted up the whole pancake with a round fan made of woven straw. It could take hours before all of the liquid had been made into mountains of *injera*, which was the foundation of all their meals.

The radio was constantly playing music which sounded like *fukera*, used many centuries ago by tribes preparing for battle, to strengthen their morale and frighten their rivals. Mengistu Haile Mariam's military government had composed a song in the style of *fukera*, called 'Yefiyel Wetete', to announce the names of all those who had been executed the night before or that day.

'Sshhh, the song's starting!' said father, turning up the radio volume. As soon as the first notes sounded, people all over the country would stop what they were doing to listen out for the names of the dead. Mengistu had started a campaign of widespread execution to eliminate those who were opposed to the regime. Those who survived fled into exile.

In the streets there were more and more people begging or rustling through rubbish heaps for food scraps. More and more young or adolescent girls were finishing school, and still in their uniforms, would make their way to the hotels in the centre of the city to sell themselves for less than a dollar.

'Why is it 1975 in the rest of the world, but here we're still in 1967?' Solomon asked his father.

'Ethiopia is a different country … '

'But why can't we follow the same calendar as the rest of the world? Why does our year have thirteen months, and why does it start on the eleventh of September?'

'Because we're different … '

'But I don't understand why we have to be different and tell the time in a different way. Why, when it should be ten o'clock in the morning, do we say four o'clock?'

'You carry on studying and then you'll understand.'

'Studying, studying … The more I study, the less I understand what's going on … Do you think they'll close down our school too? Sometimes boys come and throw stones at the windows … '

Neighbouring Somalia claimed more than three hundred thousand square metres of Ethiopian land in the Ogaden region. It tried to unite all the Somalis of Somalia, Ethiopia, Djibouti and Kenya into one territory, to create Greater Somalia. The Ethiopian military had already started fighting to prevent the borders being changed, in the hope that some countries that were allied with the Derg government would send reinforcements. If this didn't happen, then defeat would be assured.

'As if the war in Eritrea wasn't enough, now we're also at war with Somalia.'

The radio was always on. Military marches continued to be heard very often and news of what was happening in the country was relayed covertly, with very little detail. People lived in a state of absolute uncertainty and fear.

'Have you heard?

'Heard what?'

'They're calling for all men who are not in the military but who want to serve their country to enlist in the army. They get paid a lot.'

'Do you want to go to war, Dad?' exclaimed Solomon. 'But you always said you didn't like the army!'

'I don't like them ... But I have no choice.'

His father didn't say much more on the subject. A few days later he went to the training camp. He had become very introverted and secretive. It was hard to talk to him or to know what he was really thinking. He went away leaving Solomon and Aster alone in the Entoto hills.

'But what did you do as a job? You don't know how to shoot a gun and you're totally uncoordinated!' an official asked him, exasperated with this man who definitely didn't have the makings of a soldier.

'I worked in the house of some *farangi* diplomats, sir,' he answered, so as not to give away the fact that he had been a cook in the emperor's palace.

'What did you work as? A gardener taking care of their fancy flowers?' mocked the officer.

'No sir, I worked as a cook.'

'A cook? Well that's just great! Women's work. Say no more!' the officer and two soldiers who were listening to the conversation couldn't control their laughter.

'Sir, I wouldn't want to speak out of line, but the Ogaden detachment has only got five cooks; five old women to feed so many mouths,' said one of the soldiers.

The officer looked at Solomon's father with contempt.

'Well that's settled then. Since you used to do women's work, now you'll make food for all of us! And you'll be in trouble if you're lying and your *injera* isn't any good! I'll send you to the front line, to entertain the Somalis!'

Everything was foggy. The forests of the Entoto hills were covered in a thick mist hanging between the tall trunks of the eucalyptus trees. The stacks of damp chopped wood all around gave off a heady aroma. Solomon walked. With no father, no mother, no older sister. He walked in a daze, like so many other children who walked countless miles every day. He walked and he ran, unaware that further upheaval awaited him beyond the fog.

KOLPEWADI, INDIAN STATE OF
MAHARASHTRA, 1974

Muna walked along the edge of the field, her feet sinking down into the hot earth. The mud houses roofed with palm leaves were still a long way off. The spindly trunks of a few tall palm trees broke the monotony of the flat landscape. Everything was silent; just the sounds of her footsteps and some vultures feasting on the remains of a dead buffalo. The monsoons were late this year and the weather was swelteringly hot and muggy. Oxen with long pointed horns were dragging a plough through the field. Muna was returning home from the well along the ploughed fields, with a large brass container of water balanced on her head, holding it sometimes with one hand, sometimes with no hands at all. She walked with her back nice and straight as she had been taught to do ever since she was very young. Muna thought that she must be eleven years old but she didn't know for sure. She wore a *salwar kameez* that had once been pink but was now a non-descript faded colour. Her black hair was tied back in a ponytail that hung down her back. The dust clung to her damp sweaty skin, forming a dark crust as it dried.

As soon as she had dropped the water off at the house, she set off again carrying a huge pile of *saris* and dirty clothes down to the river. Sonali, the wife of her uncle Suresh – one of her father's younger brothers – was waiting for her there, to wash the clothes together. Muna had lived with them and their son – who was only a few months old – since the child had been born. Her work consisted of fetching water, finding fresh grass for the cows to graze on, washing clothes in the river, collecting firewood, lighting the fire and making sure that it didn't go out so that they could cook, and tending the oil lamps when darkness fell … She was always kept busy. She woke up at first light and slept when it was dark, lying on a rug on the floor in the small adobe house with its glassless windows, on the outskirts of Kolpewadi. She was eleven years old and she was exhausted.

As she walked barefoot over the warm earth toward the river with the bundle of clothes balanced on her head, Muna couldn't stop thinking about Sita. Her beloved Sita, sitting on the lap of a woman strangely dressed all in white, with a sort of small turban on her head, in a jeep driving away down the dusty road. Everything had happened so quickly. Sita had left without realising what was happening. The jeep disappeared and Muna was left standing there crying, watching as the cloud of dust that was whipped up gradually disappeared as well, leaving the flat, dry track deserted once more. She had never seen Sita again. It must have been three years ago now but she remembered it as if it had just happened. Hot tears sprang up when she thought about her little sister, of the hours she had spent looking after her since she came into the world.

She remembered perfectly the day Sita was born. Her mother screaming as she lay propped up on the floor of their house with her legs open, two women holding her by the arms and another at her back, talking to her constantly to soothe her, while other women brought buckets of hot water and towels. There were endless towels stained with blood.

'Ritu, work a bit harder, push hard!' cried one woman.

'Come on, just a little more Ritu. Ritu, you've got to do what we tell you!'

Muna had watched it all from a corner of the room with a mixture of fear and concern. A terrified five-year old girl who didn't know what was happening to her mother, who was emitting loud howling noises. She was also surprised to see how people were born in more or less the same way as cows. Not long before she saw her sister being born, she had witnessed the birth of a calf.

Although she was young, Ritu was in very poor health and she didn't recover from the birth of her second child. After Sita was born, she fell ill with an extremely high fever and spent her days lying on the bed in their small house which had only one room. Her husband didn't pay them much attention; neither Ritu nor her daughters. His name was Anjaney and he had never overcome his sadness at the death of his first wife. He had been madly in love with her. He had always been grateful to his parents for finding him a woman like her, his Namrata. For him, life without her had little meaning.

He had worked hard looking after the cows and fields to put enough food on the table for his five children and Namrata. But when he became a widower and his children were all gradually married off, the time came for him to find another wife, as he couldn't go on alone. He was contacted by a family with a daughter who was very beautiful but in poor health. They were prepared to offer a considerable dowry to anyone who wanted to marry her. Her name was Ritu and she was the same age as his oldest daughter. It was too good an opportunity to miss. Anjaney and Ritu had a child immediately: Muna. Ritu has spent her whole pregnancy wishing for a boy, like all women in India. Nine months imagining the parties and celebrations to announce the birth of an heir; nine months praying to the gods that it wouldn't be a girl. The birth of a girl was always a disgrace; some believed it was a bad omen for the family. Relations and neighbours came sorrowfully to the house to wish them "better luck next time". A girl was a burden on the family until they could be married off. Ritu didn't fall pregnant again for a long time. Finally, five years later, Sita was born.

The prayers and *pujas* to the gods were all in vain yet again: another girl was born. A neighbour who had helped with the birth suggested drowning her in a bucket of water straight away. In rural areas, many newborn baby girls were sacrificed within a few minutes: it was better for everyone that way. But Nadira, the eldest daughter of Ritu's husband, wouldn't let it happen.

Nadira and Ritu had become very close friends. Nadira didn't care that Ritu was her stepmother but was the same age as her; and Ritu didn't care that Nadira was the daughter of Namrata, her husband's first wife, who everybody missed so dearly. Nadira had given birth to a son, Raj, two months before Sita was born. The two friends' bellies had grown big at the same time.

Ritu's health was failing. Muna would hug her mother, who now hardly left the house, and then take her sister in her arms to stop her crying. Ritu's milk was drying up and little Sita was weak and thin.

'Nadira,' Ritu said to her friend, 'I think I'm dying … '

'Don't speak, Ritu, try to rest … ' answered Nadira, scooping up the tiny Sita, who was lying on the bed next to her sick mother.

The emaciated baby started wailing inconsolably in Nadira's arms. She was hungry.

'I'm not strong enough. I can't take the pain any more … '

Sita was still crying and Nadira didn't think twice. She sat at the foot of Ritu's bed, lifted the short blouse that she wore under her *sari* and put the child to her breast. Sita immediately clung to her as if she knew that she wouldn't have many opportunities like this to save her life. Ritu watched from the bed.

'Nadira ... If I die, please take care of my children, I'm begging you ... '

That evening Ritu died with her head on Nadira's lap, while the two babies, Sita and Raj, slept soundly in a corner of the house. Although she was only five years old, Muna was very aware of what was going on. She entered the house softly and sat down next to Nadira. Looking at her mother she asked, 'Is she sleeping?'

'Yes Muna. Your mother has fallen asleep, but this time I think it's forever.'

Muna became her little sister's protector. She carried her, strapped to her back with a strip of cotton fabric, while she helped out with all the housework. When Sita was hungry and cried, she would hurry to wherever Nadira was so that she could breastfeed her. Nadira was full of life and had a good, kind and happy husband, Pratap. The two of them did everything they could so that their son Raj, as well as Muna and Sita, wanted for nothing. They worked in the fields and sold the milk from their cows to neighbours who didn't have their own cows.

They lived in a very humble way but they were happy.

Shortly after Ritu died, Anjaney fell ill. His legs swelled up and he could no longer stand up. Luckily, Nadira and Pratap lived very close by; there was only one field to cross to reach their house. Anjaney grew weaker and weaker, until one day when Nadira went to take him some rice and vegetables, she found him lying dead in bed. They cremated him in the same field where they had cremated Ritu a few months earlier; and where they had scattered Namrata's ashes a few years before that.

'Don't worry Muna,' Nadira said, stroking the girl's cheek. 'From now on, you and Sita will come to live with us.'

Nadira and Pratap were very young and thinking about the future was a struggle for them. But they had adopted these two little girls and they would love them as if they were their own children. Nadira had also promised her friend that she would take care of them.

The adobe house was very small and inside it was practically empty. They all slept together, lying on the floor next to one another. Muna's main activity was looking after Sita, from the moment her little sister woke up hungry in the morning until the last lullaby at night. She washed her, fed her the meals prepared by Nadira and carried her everywhere strapped to her back. She copied Nadira's every gesture, becoming Sita's mother. A child became a mother. She watched how Sita quickly grew and changed; how she learned to walk.

Almost three years passed. Life wasn't easy. The rains were late and in the fields the crops were failing. Nadira was pregnant again as well; she was about to give birth.

One day, Pratap's father showed up, ready to alter his son's plans. He was an authoritarian man and was accustomed to being the head of the family and deciding what was best for everyone.

'But can't you see how thin Raj is?' he roared at them.

'Thin? He's a healthy little boy!'

'That's enough, Pratap! What are you thinking? The gods have blessed you with a healthy boy and you're risking his health by making him share the little food you have with these two intruders? Don't you know how hard it is to be responsible for four children? You know that one day you will have to offer a dowry for these two girls? Where are you going to get two dowries from? Eh?'

'There are quite a few years before that, father, we'll be alright, you'll see … '

'I'll see?' replied the man growing increasingly irritated. 'I won't hear of it! I will not have it! Have you gone mad? One thing at a time! You're too young to look after four children at once. Not to mention if you have another girl!'

The discussion between Pratap and his father – as well as Nadira, who dared to intervene a little – was a long one. Or at least it seemed so to Muna, who listened to them as she sat on the floor in a corner of the house, her back against the wall, paralysed with fear.

'Enough! I said that's enough! Those two girls are a nuisance; they can't carry on living in Shaha with you. It's high time we found a solution. End of discussion!'

There was nothing that Nadira and Pratap could do. Pratap's father found the solution in the house of a catechist in a village not far from Shaha. Every Monday a chaplain and a nun from a catholic convent in Nasik went there to hold mass, bring medicine and visit sick people. The nun was a nurse. Pratap's father told the catechist about the two orphan girls living with his son and his wife, a couple who were too young and without sufficient means to bring up three children, and with a fourth on the way. The catechist listened intently. He could ask for help for an individual case, but for two girls it was a bit much. The younger girl seemed to be the most fragile. The older girl was now eight years old, strong and independent; she could look after herself. So between that man and Pratap's father, it was decided that the following Monday, the chaplain and the nun should take Sita away.

'But why do they have to take her away, Nadira?' asked Muna, uncomprehending. 'I'll look after her; I'll make sure she doesn't break anything or make a mess!'

'I know it's hard to understand. But Pratap's father is the head of our family, he makes the rules and we can't go against his decisions. That's just the way it is.'

'It's impossible not to do what he says. The elders are always right; they always know what needs to be done. He knows that we love you both very much and that I promised your mother I would look after you, but he's made us realize that if we really want to take care of you, we have to find another place for you to live. I'm sure Sita will go to a much better place than this god-forsaken land where it never rains … She'll have chicken and lots of fruit to eat … Muna, here we can't offer you much and she isn't very strong. You don't want her to get sick, do you? If she got sick we wouldn't be able to treat her and she would die.'

Muna listened to Nadira and the mere thought of seeing her sister die made her stomach turn.

'Muna,' Nadira went on, 'do you think that these people who come every week to our villages to bring medicines and tell us so many things are bad people? If they were, they wouldn't do everything that they do for us; I mean we don't know them and we aren't their family!'

And so the dreaded day came. The day she had to say goodbye to Sita. The day that Muna grew up. She was eight years old, but that day she suddenly aged and could no longer look at Nadira in the same way. She had let her down. Early in the morning they made a *puja* at the small altar in a corner of the house. They made very few because they couldn't afford to buy the oil for burning, the incense and fresh flowers. But that day was special. Pratap jingled his little bell, while with the other hand he drew circles with the smoking incense in front of a faded image of Ganesh and sang prayers to the elephant god who solved problems and removed obstacles from daily life. They painted a *tikka* on Sita's forehead so that the gods would protect her: first a drop of oil, followed by the red powder. Sita disappeared in a jeep down the dusty road, sitting on the lap of a nun all dressed in white.

Now Muna was walking barefoot toward the Kolpewadi River carrying a huge bundle of dirty clothes on her head. She was eleven years old and she was responsible and well-behaved. But she was fed up of being docile and obedient! An old, faded bus was making its way over the bridge. It was a bus like the one that had brought her here from Shaha, stopping at all the villages, crossing the flat landscape of the sugarcane fields along roads full of holes that made you jump out of your seat when you were least expecting it. She saw Sonali and some other women washing clothes and exchanging gossip. Two neighbours folded *saris* together; taking one end each, they pulled the seven metres of cotton clothing taught between them and moved toward each other with each fold. Sonali's baby was sleeping under the shade of a tree, next to the calm waters of the Godavari.

'*Namaste, mausi*,' Muna greeted them before putting the bundle down on the floor.

'Muna, what took you so long? I thought you weren't coming!'

'I'm sorry, *mausi* Sonali. I came as quickly as I could.'

'Come on! Get the clothes in to soak before the baby wakes up. We have to get it hung out quickly if we want to come and collect it this afternoon.'

The days, weeks and months rolled by. Muna's life continued to revolve around the firewood, the fire, the pots on the fire, the water from the well, the grass for the buffalos, the buffalo milk, all the *chapattis* she had to make, the clothes she had to wash in the river ... For how long? When would this routine that wasn't hers come to an end? Sometimes, when she went to the village to buy things at the market she saw other girls dressed in school uniform and she looked at them enviously. She saw the white, well-ironed shirts, dark checked skirts and red ribbons in their plaited hair. She imagined herself dressed like them and daydreamed that she went to school too. The boys wore the same uniform but with shorts instead of skirts. In the morning they sat in groups of seven or eight boys and girls, in bicycle *rickshaws* that took them to school and picked them up in the afternoon. Their backpacks and bags hung together on each side of the vehicle. Sometimes, one or two of the children had to get down from the *rickshaw* to push and help the *rickshaw–wallah* get going again, as it was hard work for him carrying such a heavy weight. When the rickshaws crammed full of boys and girls in uniform went past her, Muna couldn't keep walking and she stopped to watch them. Why could she not go to school? She wasn't sure how, but she was going to learn to read and write. She would have dresses too one day.

Very close to where the women washed their clothes, there was a small island with two palm trees. There were always little boys clambering up them and jumping into the water from high up. The smallest ones took off all their clothes, the older ones jumped in fully clothed. Their raucous shouts and laughter became the usual background noise to their afternoons of laundry. Muna watched them while she scrubbed clothes against the rocks with a huge bar of soap. Some of them went there to swim after school. Others looked as if they had come from the fields where they worked with their parents. It must have been fun to jump off that little island, trying to touch the leaves with their hands and jumping into the water. That part of the river was fairly deep and it took a few seconds for the children's heads to bob up above the surface of the water. Why were there never any little girls jumping from the little island with the two palm trees? Why were there never any girls shouting and laughing freely like the boys from the village?

Muna sorted the lentils, picking out dozens and dozens of stones before cooking the *dhal*. The smell of drying cow dung pervaded the air and could be smelled everywhere, more or less pungently, depending on the direction the wind was blowing. She was also responsible for collecting the half-dried dung and arranging it in rows on the ground so that it dried out completely, or sticking it to the lower part of the house walls, and later, when it was dry enough not to smell any more, stacking it up next to the stable. Dried cow dung was the fuel that burned most efficiently and ensured that the fire turned to embers and didn't go out.

Sitting on the ground outside Suresh and Sonali's house, while she picked through lentils, she could hear them talking about her. It wasn't the first time. She heard them saying the names of villages she had never heard of; names of families; men's names. But that afternoon she realized what they were talking about: they were looking for a husband for her! A little while ago they had all been invited to the wedding of a girl not much older than her. She didn't know her; she didn't even talk to her. After the wedding she went to live far away and Muna never saw her again. She would never forget the scared look on that girl's face as she sat on the floor in front of the flames of a small fire, dripping with jewellery and dressed in a garishly yellow *sari* edged with a red trim, a necklace of flowers, her eyes elaborately outlined in black *kohl* and her lips painted like a sculpture in the temple of Ganesh. She stared blankly, with a large red *tikka* painted in the middle of her forehead and the parting of her hair also painted with a red line of *sindoor*. The groom was ten years older than her, or perhaps more, and looked equally unhappy. He was sitting next to her in front of the fire, wearing a garland of flowers round his neck like the girl. Both families, on the other hand, were ecstatic. Everyone was dancing and laughing. The women were dressed in their finest *saris*, their hands painted with *henna* drawn in elaborate and intricate patterns, their dark, well combed hair decorated with jasmine flowers, jangling their colourful glass bracelets that were bought specially for the celebration. They also wore ankle bracelets – fine silver or brass chains that jingled with every step they took. The men were elegantly dressed in white with their *kurtas* and *Gandhi topis*, the white hats that they wore to make them feel important. The tables were overflowing with food and flowers.

To Muna that wedding seemed like anything but a celebration, however many garlands of orange flowers had been hung from the ceiling and walls, however much music they played.

Now Suresh and Sonali were looking for a husband for her, just like that girl. She was sick and tired of other people's decisions that she didn't understand. She got up off the floor with the aluminium bowl full of lentils and padded barefoot and determined into the house. Her uncle instantly stopped talking. Sonali looked at Muna with a sly smile and started peeling onions in the corner where the kitchen was. But Muna couldn't say anything. What could she say? What could she do?

The fields of wheat grew taller. Muna carried on with her routine, day and night; with the sticky heat of the dry season, the dusty roads, the hot earth of the fields, hours spent washing clothes in the river, carrying them back and forth, hours selecting lentils for the *dhal* and sifting the rice full of stones ... However much of a misfortune it was for Suresh and Sonali, she was happy that they no longer had any buffalo because it meant less work for her. They had been forced to give them up before they were taken ill by a strange epidemic that was affecting buffalo in the region, which led to them producing less and less milk. They didn't eat the meat. Hindus don't eat meat from cows or oxen. Whenever they could – which wasn't very often – they ate chicken or lamb.

She was returning home one day carrying a load of firewood on her head when she noticed a car parked in the dry street, just in front of Suresh's house. Some chickens scampered out in front of her, nearly tripping her up and making her drop her load of firewood. There were hardly any cars in the village. She drew closer, intrigued. She set the firewood down next to the small stable, now empty of buffalo. She tried not to make a sound ... but they spotted her at once.

'Muna, we've been waiting for you!' said Suresh, coming out of the door holding a lit *bidi* in his hand. He never normally smoked.

'Oh yes? I didn't know!'

Behind Suresh came a man with a black moustache, dressed in a light blue shirt and trousers that were not like the ones any men in the village wore. Sonali also came out, cradling her son in her arms.

'This is my niece. As I've already told you, she is obedient and hard working. She helps us with everything here.'

The man with the moustache looked her up and down while Muna busied herself, pretending to stack the firewood into a pile.

'I can't give you more than a thousand *rupees*. That's the most we can offer. A thousand *rupees* and I'll take the girl to Bombay.'

Muna froze.

'To Bombay? What for?'

'Muna, please don't interrupt grownups when they're talking!'

'But if I have to go, I need to know where I'm going, don't I? Who do you want me to marry for a thousand *rupees*?'

'No-one,' said Suresh seriously. 'We don't have enough money for your dowry. We can't find any family who wants you for one of their sons. You're too young and you don't have a large dowry. Mr Patil is visiting all the families in the village to offer us a loan … We need to buy buffalo for milk again; we have to make repairs to the house which is falling down. I'm sorry, Muna, but this is our only solution.'

'And why do I have to go with him to Bombay? Can't he give you the money and you pay him back when you can? *Mausi*, why do I have to go?' she asked Sonali, who just looked away.

'It's been decided,' Suresh replied in a firm voice. 'The agreement is that he leaves us the money and you go to the city to work in the house of a family. I'm sure you'll be able to go to school … '

'To school?'

Mr Patil didn't say anything. He just looked at them.

'And when will I go?'

'Right now,' the man from Bombay finally said, touching his moustache. 'We have to get there today and it's a long way.'

Muna had no belongings apart from the *salwar kameez* she

was wearing that had once been pink, some worn-out plastic sandals and the red glass bracelets that had remained intact since the wedding of the frightened-looking girl. For that wedding she had borrowed a *sari* from some friends of Sonali who lived close by. Muna had nothing and nobody keeping her in Kolpewadi. She said a hurried goodbye to Sonali and Suresh – who had already stuffed the thick wad of a thousand *rupees* into his pocket after counting all of the notes while sitting on the only bed in the house – and got into the back of the car, as naturally as if she had done it all her life. It was the first car she had ever been in: the car that would take her far away. She didn't cry. What would be the point?

Mr Patil didn't have a particularly kind face, but then again Muna didn't find any adults' faces kind. Nadira and Pratap stopped having kind faces on the day they separated her from her sister. As they were leaving the village, they stopped in front of a house with a buffalo tied up at the door under a canopy of dry branches. Mr Patil got out of the car without a word and went into the house. Muna sat silently in the back of the car. Close by, a man was sharpening knives on a spinning stone rigged up to his bicycle. A few minutes later a girl perhaps a year or so older than her got into the car next to her. Her eyes were full of tears and she was staring at the floor. They didn't say anything to each other. As the car started to drive off they heard the terrible cries of a woman behind them:

'Nalini! Nalini! My Nalini!'

The girl turned and knelt on the seat to look out of the rear window but the road was full of dust and she couldn't see anything. She stayed there for a long time, kneeling on the seat, with her hands on the glass, as they crossed the bridge over the river Godavari and drove away from Kolpewadi.

Mr Patil drove in earnest, swerving now and then to avoid a cow, or a bicycle, or a lorry driving too slowly the wrong way up the road, a pothole that the car might get stuck in or the clothes that women laid out along any slightly better tarmacked stretches of the road, which seemed to be the best place they could find to do it. The landscape was immensely flat. The two girls looked at everything out of their respective windows, in silence. Muna had heard about Bombay. She knew that it was a big city; a huge city. She looked out of the window and thought about those boys leaping into the water from the little island with the two palm trees while she washed clothes. Surely they felt something similar to what she was feeling know; that lurching feeling in their stomachs before they fell in and splashed all the others. She was hungry. It was already midday and she hadn't eaten anything apart from a *chapatti* and a small amount of *dhal* at dawn. They turned off suddenly down a narrow, dry road that seemed to lead nowhere. The car drove on and on, swerving around holes and bumping over rocks until in the distance they finally saw a cluster of small adobe houses with plaited palm roofs, like the ones in Shaha. Mr Patil stopped the car and before getting out he turned and stared at the two girls.

'You two stay where you are, or you'll be sorry.'

He was back in no time at all, accompanied by a boy of around eight or nine with short, inky black hair and a hungry look in his eyes, who sat timidly next to them in the back seat. The car pulled away, bouncing its way back up the narrow road full of potholes they had driven down to reach the tiny village.

'That's all of you. Now we're off to Bombay,' said Mr Patil, his moustache twisting into a slight sneer. None of the children said anything. They went on looking out of the windows in a strange silence. A necklace of slightly withered jasmine flowers hung from the rear view mirror. It swung to and fro with every bump in the road. They passed a herd of emaciated cows with long horns. The boy herding them, who was wearing a tattered shirt and carrying a stick, waved.

After more than two hours of travelling in silence through an unchanging landscape, Mr Patil stopped the car at a petrol station which also sold food and drinks. He let the three children get out of the car to relieve themselves behind a small building with a latrine in it, while he bought some bananas, *chapattis* and a cooked cob of corn for each of them. They ate them right there and then, standing up, not far from the car. A young boy brought them brass cups full of water on a tray. The people around were all men, and no-one took any notice of them. They were all too involved in their conversations and their work. There were a few lorries parked up; their drivers sat on *sarpois* outside them, drinking tea and smoking.

'My name's Vikram. What are your names?' whispered the boy when the three of them were alone.

'Muna.'

'My name's Nalini. I want to go home. I don't want to go to Bombay.'

Muna woke up as they were entering the city. Vikram and Nalini were fast asleep. It was still daylight but it wouldn't be long before dusk descended. It must have been nearly six o'clock in the evening already. Mr Patil had the window down and was smoking a *bidi* as he drive through the thick traffic, with all sorts of horns blaring out loudly all around them ... She couldn't believe what she was seeing. So many people coming and going in all directions. Small cars, big cars, lorries covered in black or blue plastic tarpaulin tied on with ropes, and others with their loads on show: sacks, huge canisters, cardboard boxes ... Buses full of people standing or sitting, some looking out of the slightly misted up windows, black *autorickshaws* with their noisy engines, bicycles, motorbikes with two or three people on them, zigzagging between the cars and lorries ... Men carrying sacks on their backs or balanced on their heads, with live chickens eyeing them suspiciously ... To Muna it seemed that on every street corner there were people frying, boiling, peeling or chopping vegetables, making juices from every imaginable kind of fruit. She had never seen as much food as in those streets, which were full of people, young and old, all dressed very differently to anything she had seen before. The houses were very tall and had lots of windows. She had also never seen a house with more than one storey and the ones in front of her now had five, six or even more. Some had clothes hanging outside, or electric cables that ran along the front of them until they reached a really high wooden pole wrapped in more and more electric cables. There was a cow ambling along in the road, grazing at its own slow pace, as if it might find something to eat on the tarmac. The cars, motorbikes, bicycles and all the vehicles that passed by swerved around it casually. On the front of the buildings were multicoloured signs with letters in all shapes and sizes that Muna didn't know how to say. The beaming faces of people on advertisement billboards smiled down at her.

After driving through street after bustling street for several miles across the city, they stopped in a narrow little side street lit by a small streetlamp. It was dark now. Vikram and Nalini had woken up and were also looking totally bewildered at the vastness of this city that this man had brought them to. He was now hurrying them out of the car. They entered a building that smelled strongly of paint and wet grass. It was dimly lit and it took a while for their eyes to adjust before they could see that there were boys and girls all around, sitting or lying on the floor, some eating rice with their fingers from aluminium plates. Out of the corner of her eye, Muna saw a man who also had a moustache handing over a fat wad of notes to Mr Patil. There must have been at least five or six thousand *rupees* there. A fat woman with grey hair tied back in a ponytail approached them.

'You three, come with me. Bye Patil, see you next week!'

She took them to a kitchen that was practically empty apart from some enormous aluminium pots and pans with lids, resting on top of a few stoves. Two boys were sitting on the floor, eating in silence. Another boy had already gone to sleep right there on the floor, without even a blanket to protect him from the damp tiles. A couple of beetles scuttled out from beneath the marble sink and ran down the wall. The fat woman, barefoot and wearing a *sari*, served each of them a dish of rice with a thick sauce and a *chapatti* on top. She wore rings on her toes that made a metallic clinking noise as she walked over the tiles.

'Find a space to sit and eat, then lie down where you can to sleep. If you have to do your business, go to that door where the light is on, at the back. Tomorrow morning I'll explain what you have to do. And I don't want to hear a word out of any of you or you'll be sorry!'

The three children each took a plate and sat close together on the floor like frightened caged birds. Nalini was trembling. A few large, glistening tears rolled down her cheeks as she chewed her food.

Her fingers grew accustomed to their new work before she did. Muna watched how they moved between the threads of white cotton attached to the loom and the threads of red wool that they had to weave, as if those fingers were nothing to do with her. She was sitting at a wooden plank on the third level of the scaffolding that rose up to the top of an enormous loom. The scaffolding had five levels. Five wooden planks with about ten boys and girls sitting at each one; some on the ground floor, some a few metres higher up. They were weaving continuously. She no longer knew if it was day or night. When it was daytime there was slightly more light in there than at night time. A weak shaft of light trickled in through a few cracks in the ceiling. The space was a huge industrial hangar with walls covered with half-woven carpets and rugs and scaffolding in front of each one, with three, four or five levels of planks with children sitting in front of them, weaving away with their tiny hands and their tired, fretful eyes. More than two hundred children were weaving away almost in silence. The sound of them speaking in low voices, barely whispering, was like they were reciting some sort of jumbled prayer. Muna and Nalini were sitting at the same plank. In between them there was a girl who knew the ropes well and had been put in charge of teaching them. She had a diagram on a crumpled bit of paper that she looked at from time to time.

'Here, Muna, tie the knot here. And now pass the knot underneath. No, underneath. Like that. Now count five white threads and pass the wool over the top.'

'And where do I put this blue thread?'

'Oh no, Nalini! You've lost count again. Now you'll have to undo it. First, two threads over three times and then five threads over four times, but with the other coloured wool! When you finish the row, you have to tie a knot. But you don't have to do a knot when you change colour, got it?'

'But it's just so difficult!'

'Then try a bit harder! If we don't do it right they'll punish us!'

Nalini looked at the hands of the other boys and girls and wondered how they got their heads and their fingers around that jigsaw puzzle of wool and coloured threads.

'How long have you been here?' Muna asked her in a low voice.

'I don't know. It seems like a long time. So long I can't remember! I've seen three rugs started and finished – big ones like these.'

'Do you know where we are?'

'In Bombay.'

'I know that, but where?'

'It's a carpet factory. I heard one of the people in charge say that we make copies of antique Persian carpets.'

'Were there already this many children here when you arrived?'

'Yes, but they weren't all the same ones. New ones keep arriving, like you, and others are suddenly taken away and never come back. Those who get very sick are also taken away. One day they took a dead girl away. I saw her! She was so pale.'

Nalini started to cry and her hiccupping sobs grew louder and louder until she could hardly breathe. The girl who was teaching them put a hand over her mouth.

'Be quiet! Do you want them to beat us with the belt? Anyone who makes a mistake or doesn't work hard enough is beaten in front of everyone!' she said firmly, gripping Nalini's arm, without hurting her and without shouting; just enough so that Nalini listened to her. She took her hand away from her mouth.

'I want to go home … I want to go back to my mother … '

'Well then the best thing you can do is to learn to weave well, and just keep on weaving … Then perhaps you'll get what you want.'

There were so many flies. Big, bumbling flies that buzzed around the children's faces. And fleas that bit them all over, causing them to scratch furiously.

The daily routine and heavy-handed guardians made any chance of escape from that dark, dank place impossible. It was a jail where innocent boys and girls were imprisoned without any explanation. You could smell the fear inside. Why did the adults who delivered the multicoloured wool not say anything? Why did they act as if they couldn't see them? Maybe all those children had become invisible? What kind of person would abuse vulnerable children like that?

They carried on weaving and unpicking, day after day, their little fingers passing the wool over and under the threads of white cotton that hung vertically in front of them, following the instructions that the girl gave them; sitting at that plank with others who were doing the same. On one side of the scaffold there was some steps made from wood and ropes, which the children used to go up and down when they finished work. They worked for hours and hours; long hours. Muna, who was used to doing a lot of walking, now found that her legs hurt from sitting down for so many hours. They went to sleep, and when she had to stand up they hurt her a lot. Once she had learned to weave mechanically and safely she let her mind wander, thinking of the flat landscapes of Kolpewadi and how she used to walk briskly from the house to the river, from the river to the fields, from the fields to the well …

She remembered the hours she used to spend walking,

hoping that just by remembering, her legs would feel better.

Sometimes they bumped into Vikram who was stationed on another scaffold, weaving another carpet just as huge as the one that Muna and Nalini were weaving. Vikram's face was always sweaty and he greeted them with a slight nod of the head, without saying anything. It was incredibly hot in there. The boys wore very little: white cotton braces and shorts; the girls all wore a *salwar kameez*. They were all barefoot and very dirty, with their hair full of lice so they scratched their heads constantly. They were aged between six and fourteen. They all had the same haggard eyes.

The shouting of the angry foremen was terrible. There was one who always shouted at the same boy.

'What's wrong with you, huh? Don't you understand what I'm saying to you?'

While one of the men held him firmly, the angry foreman beat his legs from behind with a wooden stick. The boy closed his eyes and grimaced in pain but didn't shed a single tear. This seemed to irritate the foreman even more and he furiously beat the boy's legs, again and again.

'Right, get back to work! And if I hear any more complaints from you, the next time it won't be just a tickling like that. You've been warned!'

The whole room was silent. The hands of the terrified boys and girls on the scaffolding moved, trembling, between the threads and wool. It was torture. It was unbearable, but they bore it. When one carpet was finished, it was taken down, rolled up and the loom was prepared for another new one.

One morning like all the others, Muna was sitting at the third plank of a scaffold, starting to weave a small square with red

67

wool, with that empty, hungry feeling in her stomach that she had known for weeks now.

'You there! The one from Kolpewadi!'

'Me?'

'Yes, you, you heard me! Come down here!'

The little girls sitting at the same plank looked at her and she shrugged; she had no idea why they were calling her. She made her way down the ladder as fast as she could. Her legs had gone to sleep and she had to move carefully so as not to fall down the scaffolding. From above, the girl who had taught her how to weave was watching her. She waved goodbye. Muna followed the grey-haired woman down a dark corridor that she had never been down before. All she could hear was the sound of the woman's toe rings jangling against the tiles. She opened a door at the end of the corridor. The light that flooded in through the window hurt Muna's eyes and she covered them with her hand. They were in a small office containing a desk and some shelves filled with files and folders. A fan revolved slowly on the ceiling. It had been days since she had felt air moving around her. She found it hard to get used to the light. A man came in and shut the door immediately with a thud. She had seen him once before. It was the man who had given the wad of notes to Mr Patil the day they arrived. Both men looked alike: scrawny, with a large black moustache.

'You're leaving right away. You're going to work as a servant in the family home of an engineer. You'll be responsible for cleaning the house, washing clothes, shopping and meals: everything they ask you to do, understand? I don't want to hear any complaints.'

'Mr Patil said that I could go to school,' Muna dared to reply. It was as if the daylight had suddenly woken her from a nightmare.

'To school? Well Mr Patil got it wrong. Do as you're told or we'll find you a more unpleasant job, do you understand me? Atul!'

A young boy with very dark skin, dressed in baggy trousers and a shirt like the man with the moustache, heard his name being shouted and came in through another door next to the window. Through the window, Muna could see an empty courtyard. He must have been sitting outside waiting for them to call him. His mouth was completely stained red from chewing *paan*.

'Atul, take this one to the address written on this piece of paper. Right away. And give this envelope to whoever greets you there. They're expecting you. Then come straight back here!'

'Yes, sir.'

'And you, you heard me; I don't want to hear any complaints!'

Atul crossed the deserted courtyard with Muna following a couple of steps behind. It had been a long time since she had felt the heat of the earth on her feet. On the other side of this flat space with the sun beating mercilessly down on it, Atul opened a small iron gate and they went down a few stone steps that led out onto a bustling street. From the gate Muna had already heard the noise of cars, motorbikes, people's voices ... and she felt saved. At the bottom of the steps, Atul's black *autorickshaw* was parked up. Muna got into the seat of the small doorless cab while Atul started the engine, with its distinctive loud rattle. Then they were off, racing through the traffic of the city. Two months shut away in that inhumane factory had left Muna very weak. Crossing the courtyard and going down the stone staircase in the midday heat had seemed like a long, exhausting journey. Now, sitting in the back of an *autorickshaw* for the first time, the hot air rushing in through the open sides of the tiny black vehicle brought her back to reality. She thought about

Nalini and the girl who taught her to weave and about Vikram and the others inside; locked up, forced to make carpets by the dim light of the bare bulbs, eating very little and sleeping badly, with shouting and beatings for those who complained. There was so much life out here in the streets, so many people, so much activity. The dismal images of the carpet factory were being left behind; she wanted to blot them out but they remained as if they were woven into her very being. All around her she could see hawkers selling fruit, clothes, newspapers and flower garlands, women dressed in beautiful brightly coloured *saris*, lorries and bicycles competing for space in the crowded streets, signs, tall buildings with square windows, fabrics draped everywhere, clothes hanging from wooden balconies ... A policeman was trying to direct the traffic at a crossroads while a motley assortment of vehicles honked their horns repeatedly; wagons pulled by oxen, bicycles, *rickshaws*, motorbikes and idle cows moved along as best they could, not taking any notice of the people waving wildly at them. A few men were pasting up a soap advertisement on a very high scaffold using paint pots and brushes.

Atul had to stop and ask for directions four times in order to find the address written on the piece of paper. After a few laps, twice passing the same Krishna temple with its fresh flower wreaths at the entrance, they finally turned down a tree-lined street full of low houses. Atul slowed down until they entered the garden of the biggest house that Muna had ever seen. Two men, their backs completely bowed, were trimming the grass borders with scythes. There were huge piles of grass around them. They looked up from the ground to watch the *autorickshaw* entering the garden, then carried on with their work. Atul stopped in front of a veranda that had four wooden recliners, a rocking chair and a low table decorated with a large candle inside a lantern and a flowerpot with a bunch of red roses in it. The roar of the city's traffic was far away. Here it was silent apart from the sound of the birds. The flat, verdant garden was pleasantly shaded by the trees. Just then, an elderly woman – or perhaps she wasn't that old – came out to meet them. She was wearing a green *sari* and drying her hands on a cloth. Her grey hair was tied back and she wore a gold stud in her nose.

'Are you Atul?'

'Yes, I've brought you this girl and this envelope.'

The woman opened the envelope and peered at the note inside, holding it at arm's length.

'Can I go, Madam?'

'Every day they write things smaller and smaller. Go on, off you go! Everyone's in such a hurry these days!'

'Bye!' said Atul. He started the *rickshaw*'s engine and drove off noisily through the garden gates.

Muna stood there quietly. The woman looked her up and down, holding the envelope in her hand.

'So you're the one who's going to be helping me from now on. Well we're ready for you!' and she said something else in a language that Muna didn't understand. 'Come on, come with me, I'll show you the house. My name's Chamki and I make sure that everything runs smoothly round here. You'll also be in charge of making sure everything runs smoothly, you understand me, right?'

Muna moved her head from right to left in small movements to show that she understood.

'Where are you from?'

'From Godavari.'

'Where?'

'The Godavari is a river,' replied Muna faintly.

'Just what we need! Yes, yes the Godavari is a river, I know. Come on ... it looks to me like you could do with a plate of hot food and a big glass of milk. You can hardly stand up!'

And so it was that Muna ended up doing what Suresh said she would do in Bombay, according to the agreement with Mr Patil: working in a family home. He had also told her that perhaps she could go to school. This was what had made her accept her uncle's decisions without complaining; although complaining wouldn't have changed anything. But Muna had now been serving in the Raghavan family home for several weeks and she hadn't even heard a mention of school. She practically lived in the kitchen. She woke up when it got light and went to sleep well after dark. She was on her feet all day. She slept on a rug in a corner of the room next to the kitchen where they kept the clean clothes; the clothes she had to iron and mend. On a shelf was her old *salwar kameez* that had once been pink. Now she had two new ones: an actual pink one and a sky blue one. A little way from her spot, in a bed near the window, is where Chamkibai slept. She called her Chamkibai as a sign of respect. At night, Chamki drew a cloth curtain across between the two of them, to give them both a little privacy.

Chamki had been working for the Raghavans for many years. She was the rock of the household and this gave her great satisfaction. She was from Kerala, in the south of the country, and had been widowed at a very young age; so young that she hadn't even had time to try and have children. Her husband had died in a car accident. When she became a widow, she wanted to get as far away as possible from the short memories of her married life. Via some relatives who lived in Bombay she had been offered work in the Raghavan household. Life wasn't easy for young widows. Many still killed themselves practicing *sati* – burning themselves alive on their husbands' funeral pyres – although the practice was forbidden. Chamki had left her white *saris* of mourning in Kerala with the aim of starting a new life in Bombay. She came from a good family. She had gone to school from a young age and continued to study until just before she got married. Her parents had already died; they were very old when she was born. Apart from Malayalam – her mother tongue and the one she liked to mutter in and say all the things she didn't want people to understand when she got angry – she spoke Marathi and Hindi perfectly and she could read, and even speak a little English. Sometimes people came to visit her and she was free to invite them in to take tea or eat the leftovers in the kitchen; there were always leftovers. Very occasionally, she went to stay at her relatives' house on the outskirts of Bombay if she was invited to a celebration and the Raghavans didn't need her for anything in particular.

On Muna's first day, Chamki explained to her how the household was run and who lived in it. Mr and Mrs Raghavan had five children. The oldest was called Sanjay and was now studying medicine in England; at King's College, Cambridge. He was twenty-four and hadn't been back to India for two years now. Chamki had heard them saying that perhaps he would come back for the next *Diwali* celebration and that they had already received several proposals from renowned families for him to marry one of their daughters. Sanjay was the family heir and everyone hoped that he would turn out to be a famous surgeon or even the country's Minister of Health. Then there were three girls: Bani, Parvati and Indira. Bani was twenty-one years old and studying secretarial skills and piano, but would soon be giving all that up because they were about to find a good husband for her. In fact, according to Chamki, Bani only studied and played piano because she would then be more valuable in the eyes of her future husband's family (who she believed would be the son of that judge who came with his wife for dinner at the house not long ago). Parvati and Indira went to school every day and wore a uniform like the girls in Kolpewadi. Parvati was fourteen and always in a bad mood. Indira was eleven, like Muna. The youngest was Rajiv. He was six years old and also went to school. When he wasn't at school, he spent his time pedalling up and down in his pedal car; a red plastic car that he rode incessantly around the flowerbeds and lawns. Much to the infuriation of the gardeners, he frequently swerved and collided with the flowerbed, which was a wide row of yellow hibiscus and rosebushes with roses in all different colours.

Mr Raghavan's very elderly, white-haired mother also lived with the family. She spent most of the day sitting on the veranda at the front of the house or lying in her room with the curtains drawn tightly to prevent the heat and light getting in, gazing at the framed picture of her dead husband which was always covered in garlands of fresh flowers, an oil lamp burning underneath it. Sometimes she would talk to the portrait in a low voice. Grandmother Raghavan also spent hours in the room where they worshipped the family gods. At a small altar on the floor, surrounded by coloured cushions, were bronze figures of Ganesh, Lakshmi, Krishna and Shiva. There were always lit oil lamps and offerings of fresh, aromatic flowers. Muna's job wasn't just to dust the figurines and keep the room clean; she also had to prepare the cotton threads and sticks of incense for the *pujas*. The family would often gather in that room and recite prayers while Mr Raghavan rang the little brass bell.

The two gardeners lived with their families in two small

houses between the Raghavans' garden and their neighbours' garden. They also worked as guards at night and helped to do the shopping for the household. They went with Chamki once or twice a week to the market and were responsible for carrying the packages, bales and baskets or finding a *culi* or *rickshaw-wallah* to take them home. One of the gardener's wives was an excellent seamstress and sometimes Muna would take her a garment that needed mending. Other people also worked in the house, coming to take care of occasional jobs such as helping to cook and serve when important dinners or celebrations took place. There were always people coming and going.

Chamki was the chef; she was the one who decided how everything was prepared and cooked. She was very knowledgeable and Muna had simply to follow her orders for everything to turn out right. Her specialty was Keralan cuisine, which she said was the best in all of India. She had managed to persuade the Raghavans of this too and they were always asking her to prepare dishes from southern India where she was from, and they now formed part of the family's usual meals. As a result, Muna was soon sick and tired of grating coconut, because Keralan recipes always had grated coconut added to them, whether it was to make *curry* sauces or *sambar*, the most typical sauce in the south to eat with rice dishes. It was also used for making coconut *chutney*, a type of thick jam served with *masala dosas*, fried rice pancakes with pureed potato inside. Cutting, chopping, grating, frying lentil flour *pappadams* … In the kitchen, the frantic jangling of Chamki's bracelets could always be heard as she never sat still. Neither did Muna. The house constantly had the sweet aroma of coconut and fried onions drifting through it.

Mr Raghavan was an important man, Muna was sure of that. And he didn't seem like a bad person. He didn't shout very often and she had never seen him hit anybody so far. Everything in the house revolved around his activities and his schedule, when he came in or went out. He usually left the house carrying a leather briefcase; sometimes he would be picked up in a magnificent, gleaming black car. Every morning he would eat his breakfast on the veranda while reading the *Times of India* brought by the neighbourhood newspaper boy; a scrawny little boy who went from house to house on a bicycle that was far too big for him and a bag over his shoulder full of newspapers. Muna noticed the strong smell of the newspaper ink when she went over to bring a silver tray with *chapattis* and mango chutney. She served his *masala chai* – black tea with cardamom pods and black pepper – just the way he liked it. He barely looked up from what he was reading. It was as if she was invisible to Mr Raghavan. She never asked him if the tea had enough milk and sugar, because she knew it was just how he liked it. She also brought him the post that the postman delivered very early in the morning. She put this on a separate silver tray – which she made sure was always so shiny you could see your face in it – along with a silver letter opener. After this she served breakfast to the others and made sure that there were enough *chapattis* and tea for everyone. Mrs Raghavan only took tea with ginger; the children took their tea with milk and a lot of sugar; and little Rajiv had a glass of warm milk, with the skin that formed when you boiled it carefully removed. If he found even the slightest trace of this skin, he would kick up a fuss and cry.

'Chamki, aren't there any *idlis* left? Bani and Indira have eaten them all!'

'How could you possibly think there are no *idlis* left for you Rajiv? There are always *idlis* for you!' And Chamki would ask Muna to run to the kitchen to fetch the plate of *idlis*: cakes of steamed rice in little balls, typical of southern India.

Once everyone had left the house, Muna peeled potatoes and carrots, peeled and chopped a huge amount of onions, chopped coriander leaves, selected lentils to cook *dhal* – although they contained much fewer stones than the lentils in Kolpewadi; she noticed that someone had already partially sorted them before selling them. She also had to sort through the rice to check that no hidden stones remained. She also had to clean the floor tiles in the living room, on her knees, with a cloth and a bucket of soapy water. She washed the *saris* of all the women in the house, the children's school uniforms, the *salwar kameez* and shirts in the big laundry room and hung them out on the clothes lines at the bottom of the garden. The thing she hated the most was ironing. The iron was very heavy and adding the right quantity of charcoal to it wasn't easy. She was always frightened of burning the fabric if a piece of charcoal fell out onto it. She tried to get up slightly earlier or go to bed slightly later so that she could iron when the weather wasn't so hot. Chamki taught her how to iron the *saris* made from silk – the most risky fabric of all – and how to carefully fold them in half. In the mornings Muna woke up and tied her black hair back in a thick plait that reached down to her waist. Then she would go to greet the milkman who rang a funny little bell as he entered the garden, pulling his cart full of fresh milk up to the steps of the veranda. Muna immediately went out to meet him with a 3-litre container, which he would fill with the still-warm milk, using a wide handled ladle. He would tell her the same stories every day: why he no longer went from house to house with his cow, milking it there and then for his customers; how his father had always done things that way and his grandfather before him; and how the well in his village had dried up completely. Muna then had to boil the milk straight away so it was ready for breakfast. The smell of the milk as it boiled reminded her of her life in Kolpewadi. But she felt no sense of nostalgia for it. Parvati liked to eat the cream produced by the milk when it boiled, with a little sugar on top. This was one of the only times when she seemed to be in a good mood. Muna also had to wash the dishes, pots, china teacups and crystal glasses in the big marble sink, looking out of the window at the trees in the garden. She had to clean all the windows and sweep away the dried leaves from the veranda. She simply did what Chamki had told her: made sure that the household ran smoothly.

Sometimes Muna went to the market with Chamki. On those occasions she would put on sandals that they had given her so that she didn't have to go barefoot through the streets of the city. She only wore them when they went shopping in a taxi that came to collect them. The taxi driver accompanied them everywhere and helped to carry their bags. Muna looked out of the open window. The air was warm but it wasn't yet the hottest time of year. Thick, odorous black smoke also blew in through the window from the cars and trucks around them. One day they were stuck in a traffic jam and came to a halt in front of the gothic facade of the Victoria Terminus. Hundreds of people of all ages were going in and out of the train station, laden with suitcases and bundles, hawkers parked their carts around the main entrance, selling all kinds of food, drinks, fruit and sweets. Muna took it all in, watching every last detail of this huge throng of people. She followed the movement of the trays of *samosas*, *golgappas* or small steaming glasses full of tea with milk, the basket of mangos being sold by an old woman; she watched the *culis* carrying the suitcases of the recently arrived passengers on their heads, a goat chewing at a small wooden cart full of fruit belonging to a street vendor, or a man buying *paan* from one of the street stalls, who popped the whole thing into his mouth: a few minutes later, he spat out a red liquid like blood. Muna carried on watching out of the window until the car started again and they left the station behind them.

The market was full of people and stalls piled high with every kind of fruit and vegetable imaginable, all arranged perfectly according to colour. Chamki and Muna also stopped at the meat stalls that were always buzzing with flies. They gave off a strong stench but Muna didn't find it unpleasant at all. In fact it made her feel alive; alive in the midst of so much life. Chamki would have lengthy discussions with the rice seller about the different kinds of grain. Mostly they discussed the price per kilo for Himalayan basmati or for a rounder kind of grain that wasn't as aromatic.

'Where I'm from, Muna, rice is the symbol of prosperity ... That's life!'

Occasionally they would finish their shopping trip at a small *sari* shop run by an old friend of the taxi driver, and he would wait outside smoking *bidis* and talking with other drivers without moving far from his car and keeping an eye on all the shopping bags. They would be served tea with hot milk in glasses and Chamki and Muna would sit cross-legged while the shopkeeper and his assistants unfolded the *saris* that were neatly folded and arranged on the shelves, following Chamki's orders. Muna looked at the coloured fabrics unfurl like rivers of cloth around her. Orange, bright blue, green ... Chamki gently felt them with her fingers and discussed the quality of the cotton or silk with the shopkeeper.

'This one's for me. And now I need to choose one for Mrs

Raghavan to give her cousin as a present. Which one do you like best, Muna? The blue or the yellow? Touch them, go on … Feel how soft the silk is! It's silk from Kanchipuram.'

Muna smiled and stroked the different silks, not sure which one was the most beautiful.

'By the way, Kumar, remember that when the Raghavans' daughter gets married, we'll need a lot of *saris* from Kanchipuram and we'll be ordering them from you!'

'Don't worry, Chamkibai, I'll find you the finest silks in the country!'

Every week, Mrs Raghavan and Chamki sat at the large table in the dining room – an English-style rectangular table with ten chairs always tucked in around it – to go over the accounts for the week's purchases, which they wrote down in a notebook, and to make lists of various orders and menus that needed to be planned if there was a dinner with guests coming up. They had guests over often; the Raghavans had a busy social life. They regularly entertained ministerial secretaries, big business owners, judges and lawyers – with their wives or on their own –, university professors … The two women spent hours with their reading glasses on, because once they had gone over the accounts and drawn up all kinds of lists, they liked to pore over the clippings from the *Times of India* that Mrs Raghavan kept in a battered old sandalwood box. She cut out the announcements offering boys and girls as future husbands and wives. The two of them loved reading the descriptions of these potential daughters-in-law or sons-in-law out loud to each other. There were even advertisements placed by families living in England looking for Indian daughters for their sons; looking for an authentic Indian girl so that they didn't lose their customs and traditions.

Mrs Raghavan and Chamki liked reading those announcements, checking the most recent ones and commenting on each one, comparing the dowries they offered. The two women got on very well and although it remained clear that Chamki was an employee, she was very privileged to be considered one of the family. She was privy to everything that went on and her opinion was always taken into account.

When it rained heavily the electricity would cut out throughout the entire neighbourhood. The fans stopped turning and the house was suddenly swamped by the sultry weather. Muna would then have to help light all the candles they could find and make sure that everyone had light in their rooms. If the electricity went off early, before dinner, the whole family stayed in the living room where there were the most candlestick holders. They would finish off their homework, read or sew. Muna had learned how to mend mosquito nets and she would sit quietly next to a candle and carry out this task. There were always leaks in some corner or other of the room and she had to place buckets underneath them and dash about mopping up water with cloths.

During the monsoon season the streets could become like real rivers and the usual traffic jams seemed like a mere trifle compared to the chaos that then spread throughout the city. The water sometimes reached up to people's knees and they had to take their shoes off so as not to lose them, and balance the things they were carrying on their heads. Motorbike engines were totally flooded and unusable, like many car engines. Children amused themselves by splashing each other, with their tops off, lying down in the enormous puddles which were a mixture of rain water and sewage and gave off a terrible stench.

In the kitchen they had to seal all the food jars especially carefully or else the damp would spoil all their grains, lentils, potatoes and spices.

Chamki was responsible for doing all the women's hair in the house. She warmed coconut oil in a jar and then she would make them sit down on the steps of the veranda, between her legs, one after the other, and would gently smooth and massage the oil right through the length of their hair. As she did this, she sang or told stories about her childhood in Kerala. She said it was like a different country. She told them about the landscapes full of water and rice fields, palm trees laden with coconuts, and the forty hour train journey separating Bombay from Kerala ... And when there was too much oil – which was almost always the case – she would also put some on her helper Muna's hair. With her eyes closed, sitting on the ground, Muna enjoyed those moments. She had nothing else to think about but her hair.

'Chamkibai, do you know why they brought me here?'
    It wasn't an easy question for Muna to ask, but one day when the two of them were alone in the kitchen she dared to ask it. She needed to know why. Chamki was stirring a *sambar* sauce that she was making on the stove. She had a very particular way of stirring sauces and tasting them, placing a little in the palm of her hand and bringing it to her mouth. She didn't look up as she swirled the wooden spoon.
    'You know, don't you?' Muna insisted.
    'Yes. I know that you were working in a carpet factory. Someone that Mr Raghavan knows owed him a debt. When the girl who did your job before you received a marriage proposal unexpectedly and left, Mr Raghavan's acquaintance found out – I don't know how – that he needed to replace her, and offered

to pay his debt by finding someone to serve in his house. And so in a few days time you came along.'

Muna still had nightmares about the dark days she had spent in the carpet factory. She awoke in the middle of the night, her body drenched in sweat and trembling, remembering the faces of those slave children. Picturing herself, terrified, weaving without understanding what was going on, sitting for hours and hours on the scaffolding, with her legs numb, the sound of a child shouting out as he was beaten with a belt ... At the Raghavan house they didn't pay her. They gave her food, new clothes and a place to sleep. She worked hard but not much harder than she had in Suresh and Sonali's house in Kolpewadi. And in return, she ate better than she had ever eaten in her life; she had the finest *salwar kameez* and the most fun she had ever had. She didn't go to school but she was learning a great deal. She was learning and she felt appreciated.

Muna hadn't been out of the house for many weeks and to find herself sitting in the midst of so many people, seemed strange to her. The room was packed with people; there was a lot of noise and excitement. Indira grabbed her hand, smiling, and told her not to be scared. The Raghavans' oldest son had returned from London to celebrate *Diwali* and one day, he had decided to take his three sisters to the cinema. After they had eaten, Indira asked if Muna could come too, but Mr Raghavan didn't want to allow it.

'A servant is a servant!'

'But Father, she's just a girl like me and she's never been to the cinema!'

'Do I need to tell you again? A servant is a servant!'

Defiantly, dressed like an English boy, Sanjay looked at his father sitting across the table from him.

'As far as I know, a servant would receive some *rupees* for their work and this girl works all day long and doesn't get paid a single *rupee*.'

'Don't get involved, Sanjay!'

'How can I not get involved? I'm ashamed to belong to a family that owns a slave girl!'

'Sanjay, I told you to stay out of it! Who do you think you are? When you're a doctor then we'll talk, but in the meantime don't raise your voice to me!'

'You don't have to be a doctor to know injustice when you see it!'

Their voices were raised and could be heard all throughout the house. Muna listened to the conversation from the kitchen, with Chamki next to her. Her heart was pounding.

'I see that in England you've learned how to overrule your father, and disrespect him!'

'Yes, I'm learning a lot of things in England, not just medicine. Is it really asking too much for you to let her go to the cinema, seeing as you don't actually pay her anything?

'It wasn't enough for those Englishmen to colonize us! Now they have to change our way of thinking too.'

'It's not the English, father, it's common sense!'

The rest of the family listened to the discussion without daring to intervene.

'If a servant is allowed to go to the cinema, what will they ask for next? A servant is a servant, I told you! Do you want the neighbours to make fun of us? What family do you know that lets their servants go to the cinema?'

'That's your problem. All you care about is what others will say about you. Hypocrites! That's what you all are!'

A few moments of tense silence followed. Mrs Raghavan didn't say anything. She just gesticulated along with what her husband and son were both saying. From her gestures, it was impossible to tell whose side she was on.

'Chamki!' shouted Mr Raghavan. Chamki hurried from the kitchen to the dining room.

'Yes, sir.'

'Chamki, what do you think about all this?'

'She deserves it, Mr Raghavan. She's been working here for months and she does everything so well; I really don't have any complaints. Muna is the best helper I have ever had; the most efficient and the most intelligent. And what's more, tonight's dinner is ready. I don't think she'll ask for anything more from you. She'll go to the cinema and then she'll carry on working.'

So in the end, Muna went to the cinema.

Seeing all the people bustling here and there and the raucous atmosphere, it seemed impossible that everyone would finally end up sitting quietly and still in their seats for the three hours that the film lasted. However, once the lights went out nobody moved from their seat until the intermission. Keeping quiet was quite another matter, as from time to time the whole audience would erupt with laughter or shouting at the leading actors to warn them of danger, as if the actors and actresses could hear their shouts and cries from the other side of the screen! Indira had explained to her that it was a 'film'. Muna found it hard to imagine what this might be like. When the film finally started, however, Muna entered a magical world unlike anything she could have ever dreamed up. Those beautifully dressed women wearing *saris* she had never seen before anywhere, and ... Oh! The dancing! The music, the beat of the percussion instruments, the love story ... Each time the leading actor was about to give her a kiss the camera would pan out and the whole audience started shouting hysterically. In every song they all began to sing and clap excitedly. Some got up and danced until the people in the rows behind them asked them to sit down. Muna laughed and cried. She was enthralled, delighted and shocked ... During the interval, Sanjay went out to buy peanuts and sweets at one of the numerous stalls outside the cinema. They ate them all as they talked about the scenes in the film and tried to imagine how the story might end.

'Hey, it's starting again!' everyone shouted, rushing back to their seats.

The next hour and a half passed so quickly. When the lights went up again and the audience were getting up to go, Muna felt changed. She had never imagined that within reality there could be another reality; the one she had seen on the big screen. That film was her first contact with the world of fiction; and she knew she would like to live in that other reality forever. What Muna didn't know is that her first trip to the cinema marked a major turning point in her life. The five of them returned home, all crammed into a taxi. Parvati sitting next to Bani, Sanjay next to the driver, talking about their favourite parts of the film, the flamboyant songs and the colourful dancing, the women's *saris* ... Muna watched the lights of the city flash by as if they were also scenes from a film.

Night had fallen but everywhere there were people walking around, on bicycles, sitting in the doorways of their houses ... The hawkers lit kerosene lanterns at their stalls selling fruit, sugarcane juice or fried foods. Those lights gave an ephemeral feel to everything Muna glimpsed out of the taxi window, as it drove through the organized chaos of the city, the taxi driver honking his horn so as not to collide with a cow, an old woman or a man meandering along on a bicycle not looking where he was going.

Indira admired her older brother a lot and was always saying how she wanted to be like him. The last time that he had gone to England she had asked him for a special present. She asked him to write down his address at King's College Cambridge in a notebook and to leave her a box full of stamps so she wouldn't have to ask anyone for them. All the years he was away, Indira wrote him long letters telling him all about school and the family and keeping him up to date with what she overheard her parents saying about potential future wives for him. Indira was desperate to win the approval and complicity of her older brother. So in order to show him that she had listened to the discussion between him and his father about whether or not Muna could go to the cinema, she started to become closer to this girl who was like her, but who hadn't had the luck to be born into a family like hers. She would go into the kitchen under the pretence of fetching a banana or a glass of water or to ask if she could go and see what had happened to the fuses, as the fans had stopped. Then she would stay there talking to Muna and keeping her company while she peeled potatoes. One day she even sat down on the floor with Muna to help her sort the lentils, so that they could carry on talking.

'I've had an idea, Sanjay!' Indira said to him one day as her brother sat reading, leaning back in one of the reclining chairs on the veranda.

'Oh yeah? What's today's bright idea then?'

'I think that Muna should be taught to read and write. It's not right, at her age, that she doesn't even know how to write her own name!'

Sanjay, who was expecting a much more childish and trivial sort of idea, put down the book he was reading on the low table and stretched his hand out toward his sister.

'Come here, my little sis!' He hugged her tightly, moved by her suggestion. 'Do you know that's the best idea anyone in the Raghavan family has had for many years? How did I not think of it before?'

'Do you really think it's a good idea?'

'The best, I swear!'

'But do you think dad will let me?'

'I'll take care of that, don't worry. Seeing as they don't pay her anything and she works more than twelve hours a day, she can at least learn to read and write in this house!'

'And to add and take away, and multiply too. She doesn't know that either, and I learned that when I was six!'

'Of course! I'll talk to dad this evening.'

BOMBAY, 1974

The ceiling fans revolved endlessly, turning and turning, always at the same speed. The heat and humidity were stifling. Sita couldn't sleep. It was getting light. It wasn't quite dawn but the first sounds of the street could be heard already, the first hawkers, shouting, selling fruit, freshly fried *samosas*, fresh milk straight from the cow, cups of hot tea … She could hear bicycle bells, a car racing past, motorbikes … Lying on the floor, on the thin towel that served as her bed, Sita tried to imagine what was going on outside that huge room full of girls like her, but who, unlike her, were sleeping soundly. Why were the others not afraid of the dark or of the bars surrounding them on both sides of the room? Despite being surrounded by more than a hundred girls all lying on towels very close to each other, she felt incredibly alone.

Gradually daybreak came and as the first shadows started moving across the walls, it was finally time to get up. It wouldn't be long before they heard Sister Aline with her bell and her voice signalling that the night and nightmares were over. The noise of the city was building. Finally she heard the nun's footsteps in the hallway, just like every morning at the same time, when she opened the two wooden doors of the room where the girls slept beneath the fans.

'Good morning! Time to get up!'

Sita jumped up right away, folded her towel and made her way directly to the bathrooms which always smelled of disinfectant, to wash her hands before the others got there and used up all the water. It was Saturday and there were no classes today.

The Bombay Missionaries of Mary centre was divided into two large buildings. In one there was the convent, where the nuns and the orphan girls, like Sita, lived. The other building could only be reached by going down a set of stairs, and was a boarding school for little girls who had families. A large garden surrounded the two colonial-style buildings, painted dark grey, with huge picture windows. One of the facades was almost completely covered in bright pink bougainvillea that tumbled boisterously down the walls. There were two towering palm trees that could be seen from the street, before you crossed the iron gateway and entered the grounds along the dirt track. The younger nuns looked after the garden and tried to make sure there was always an array of multicoloured flowers.

Saturdays like that one were always emotional. After breakfast with all the other orphans, Sita ran to the garden and clambered up onto a stone bench to spy on the boarding school girls, looking at the beautiful dresses they wore and watching how some of the nuns helped them to do their hair in neat plaits, tying them with strips of well-ironed, brightly coloured fabric. The bedrooms in the boarding school were shared; each had two beds, two bedside tables and a big wardrobe. Sita stood watching intently, not missing a single detail as the families of the girls arrived to take them out for the weekend. Some of them were picked up by their parents. Fathers with moustaches, *Sikh* fathers with orange or red turbans. Mothers in turquoise or purple *saris*, their hair black and straight, or in a long plait down their back, with bracelets in gold or coloured glass that jangled with every movement. Other girls were collected by their grandparents, who were like the parents but had grey or white hair. Sometimes they turned up with younger or older children too;

brothers, sisters or cousins. On Sunday evenings before it got dark, Sita repeated the adventure of climbing up on the stone bench to watch the girls return to boarding school, accompanied by their families. It was then that she saw the scenes she liked best: a mother hugging her daughter, holding her close to her, staying still in that position for a few seconds. What would a hug feel like? Nobody had ever hugged Sita in that way before. As far as she could remember, no one had ever hugged her in any way before.

That Saturday, when she had been on the stone bench in the garden for a while, quietly watching until all the girls had left with their families, she heard someone calling her.

'Sita! You're up there again? Come on, come down, I've got something for you!'

'For me?'

Sister Valentina was the Mother Superior of the convent and the director of the boarding school. She always wore a white habit, her hair covered in matching fabric. A large silver cross dangled in the middle of her chest. She had a way of talking and looking at people that was different from the other nuns. Sita liked being around her. Sister Valentina took her by the hand and they went into the building together.

'Did you know that today is your birthday?' she asked as they went up the big spiral staircase to the Mother Superior's office. The stairs were wooden and Sister Valentina's sandals clacked against them with every step.

Sita was barefoot. She had never worn shoes; she didn't even own any shoes.

'My birthday? Really? How do you know?'

'Sit down on that little armchair,' she said, taking out a

package wrapped in dark blue paper. 'It's three years today since you arrived here, Sita. And as you must have been three when you came, we could say that today's your sixth birthday … what do you reckon? Take this; it's your birthday present!'

With a big smile, Sita started to unwrap it with a surprised look on her face – it was the first birthday present she had ever had. From within the blue paper she pulled out a dress, printed with little yellow flowers. It looked like one of the dresses that the boarding school girls wore. They wore them with white socks and shoes with buckles.

'Here, I'll help you put it on!'

'I love it,' said Sita, once the dress was on and her old dress lay crumpled on the floor. 'But when I get up on that bench to watch the girls, it's not because they're wearing new dresses and shiny shoes!'

'Oh no? Come here, I'll fasten it up at the back. It looks lovely on you … and it's big enough that you can wear it for quite a long time!'

Sita was very small for her age and although she was very thin, she always looked strong and healthy.

'Sister Valentina … '

'Yes, my child.'

'Could I have parents like the girls in the boarding school?'

Sister Valentina finished buttoning up the dress in silence. Sita was standing with her back to her with her slight frame and very dark, short straight hair. She didn't know what to say to her. She turned her round to face her, holding her by the shoulders.

'There we go! Now you've got a new dress! Happy birthday!'

'Sister Valentina … Couldn't I have some parents as a present, if I give you back the dress?'

The nun looked at Sita for a long time, as if searching the

depths of the dark brown eyes of the girl standing before her for the best way to respond.

'Oh Sita! If only it were that simple! That's what you want? Parents? Aren't you happy here with us? With me, Sister Niharica, Sister Juliette, Sister Urvashi, Sister Aline … With the other girls?'

'Yes … But I want a mother of my own!'

Sister Valentina took a deep breath. Those words, spoken in perfect Marathi, were hard for her to hear. Such astuteness for such a little girl. It had been three years since the day that Sita was brought to the Bombay Missionaries of Mary centre from the convent in Nasik, where she had been looked after by Sister Kamala and the other nuns. She remembered the telephone call from Sister Kamala asking her if she could take a three-year old girl; a bright, lively little thing who was eager to learn. The convent in Nasik was small and there were too few nuns to look after all the people who arrived there to die peacefully. They were not doctors, or even nurses, but word had spread that women could go there to die in peace, and not alone. Sometimes, dying women came with small children who were also very ill and even all the nuns' best efforts were not enough to save them. The nuns cared for them, gave them a place to lie down on the floor, tried to keep them as clean as possible, maintain their dignity at least until their final moment; they held their hand when they were suffering extreme pain; they brought them some comfort. Other times, women came to them with healthy children; it seemed more like it was the children that had brought them to the convent to die. The nuns looked after them until they became orphans and then continued to look after them until they managed to find a relation, neighbour or another family to take care of them. In truth, they would prefer not to have children there because they couldn't cope with them. Sometimes these children would end up falling ill after arriving there healthy, through being in contact with so much illness and infection, and so much death.

Sister Kamala had already done more than enough when, having recently arrived from Goa to run the Nasik convent, she had taken in that little girl from a nearby village because the family was poor and it seemed there was no one to look after her … She had done quite enough by baptising her in the Santa Ana chapel near the convent. The girl had survived so much hardship. But Sister Kamala thought that Sita would be more likely to succeed in Bombay, where the convent had the resources to give lessons to around a hundred orphan girls. Most of the nuns were also teachers in the boarding school that ran the institution. They ensured that the girls would receive the minimum basic education and therefore have a chance of a more decent future.

Sister Valentina sat down on a chair.

'So you want some parents … '

Sita's dark brown eyes met the Mother Superior's own. The girl's brown skin was emphasized by the light fabric of the new dress, which had short sleeves and hung down to her knees. Sister Valentina, who was now well over sixty, noticed that she was of the age where situations like this softened her more than they used to. She was no longer the harsh woman so often accused of being insensitive by the nuns, or the authoritative woman feared by the girls, whether orphans or not, poor or not so poor.

'It's okay, it's okay. Do you know what you have to do from now on? Pray a lot, Sita. Pray to God that he finds you some parents!'

'But if he doesn't find them, will you find them for me? It's just that if everyone asks him for things, I'm sure he won't be able to do everything!'

'You just pray, Sita. And I'll see what I can do, alright? Now off you go. Go on outside to play!'

'I'll keep the dress, but if you find me some parents, tell me straight away and if you want I'll give it back to you, okay?'

Sita left the office smiling and made her way barefoot down the spiral staircase, sliding her hand down the wooden banister. In the garden the girls were riding bicycles round in circles. They had just two rusty bicycles to share between all of them. While two girls rode around the whole paved area of the garden, the others waited, playing with a skipping rope or just chatting. Sita was a solitary child; she didn't belong to any of the groups of friends that existed in the orphanage. She liked to chase butterflies, or look for round white stones hidden in the gravel on the driveway, which she collected and hid in a secret place in the garden.

Sister Valentina remained sitting where she was, mulling over Sita's words. She had been running convents and orphanages for many years and in all those years, never had such a young girl asked her to find her some parents. Ensuring a good future for the orphans was one of her main priorities, but it wasn't an easy one. As they grew up she had to observe them carefully and decide what was best for them. Those who had more of a religious vocation – who liked to sing and sew, who were serious and diligent – would become nuns there in the convent or in another convent of the Missionaries of Mary, in India or elsewhere. For those who showed a motherly instinct from an early age – the ones who turned every object into a doll, or if they were lucky enough to get their hands on a real doll, half-broken and abandoned by one of the girls from the boarding school, would spend hours mothering it – she knew she must find them husbands who would accept a reduced dowry. Sister Valentina even arranged marriages with the fathers of teenage boys who were looking for a good wife for their sons and who thought it was a good idea for them to be educated in religious principles, even though they were not their own, but above all educated in austerity and obedience. Ultimately, she did what all Indian mothers did for their daughters: she found a suitable husband for them.

She got up and went to sit at her desk, her place of refuge. Behind that huge desk made from tropical wood, filled with books and piles of paper, she felt good; the time she spent there seemed all too short. She picked up the sheet of paper she had left half-written the night before. It was a letter to a Spanish couple who were in the process of trying to adopt a little girl … More often than they would have liked, the nuns found babies left at the gates of the convent. She couldn't say that these children were abandoned. No mother in the world abandons a child. In any event they are trying to give them a better future. If they were boys the nuns would take them to a centre run by Franciscan priests. They kept the girls at the convent. Adoption wasn't the normal way out for the little girls taken in by the Missionaries of Mary. Sister Valentina received letters from people recommended by priests or by nuns from all over Europe or the United States, offering to adopt an orphan girl. But she didn't have the time to reply to all of them or fill out all of the paperwork it entailed. It involved going to a judge to declare that the girl in question was really an orphan and didn't have anyone in the world who might lay claim to her; then going to the embassy or consulate of the potential parents' country to fill out form after form … And furthermore, she wasn't at all sure about giving one of her girls away to a couple that she knew almost nothing about and who lived far away. She was worried about doing the wrong thing and she was someone who liked to be sure she was doing things right.

This Spanish couple were different, however. From the outset she was able to write to them in Spanish, her own language. Sister Valentina was from Santo Domingo in the Dominican Republic. Her life had taken many twists and turns and she had lived in many different countries, but even though she had hardly spoken it over the years, the language had always stayed with her. In her library she had bibles and missals in Spanish, as well as the complete works of poetry of Saint Teresa of Avila and St. John of the Cross. And among the other books there was one very special volume that she had kept since her early childhood in Santo Domingo: a copy of *Don Quixote of La Mancha* that she had read many times and which had made her imagination run wild, when she was still young enough to let it.

Ramón Riba and Irene García had written to her for the first time over a year ago, on the recommendation of a nun from Santo Domingo with whom she had worn her first habit in her country, and who was now a nurse in a hospital in Barcelona. Her name was Guadalupe. She remembered her perfectly. A feeling of homesickness and nostalgia for her Caribbean island and the sound of her language made up her mind to try and make those friends of Guadalupe into parents. They had already exchanged several letters, which travelled slowly across the globe. The letters from Barcelona always arrived first, among other things because they always replied immediately. In one of them they had even sent a black and white photograph of the two of them. They seemed like good people. They would prefer

97

to adopt a baby girl; as young as possible. They were unable to have children and thought that they could make an orphaned girl very happy and give her everything she could want. She re-read what she had begun writing the day before. She grabbed her pen and finished the letter in one go. She wrote the address on the envelope. Barcelona.

One day she had looked for the city on the large map that hung on the wall when she was giving a geography class to the older girls of the boarding school. The Mediterranean Sea. From Barcelona she ran her finger along the coastline. Marseilles, Nice, Genoa, Naples … all the way to Istanbul, then she lost herself in the names of the Greek islands. She felt that over there, a girl could grow up to be a happy woman. And even more so with parents with such good references. He was a doctor in the hospital where Guadalupe worked. She was a school teacher. At that time, there were no babies at the convent. That is what she had written to the couple in Barcelona. They had either grown up and were now aged three or four years, or had become weak and died without anyone being able to do anything for them. Like the last girl that they had buried, who was a little over a year old. It was very hard to look after children so small. They fed them as best they could with lots of rice, vegetables, chopped up fruit and bottles full of tea with sugar. The babies were very weak and Sister Valentina hated seeing such weak and defenceless children fall ill. Sometimes, several little girls might catch a virus and they would all get ill, with unstoppable diarrhoea and fevers. Within the room that was used as a dormitory for all the girls, there was a small room with no door and a single bed for the child that needed it most at that moment. But when so many of them were ill, it created a real problem. Some of the nuns had a few basic nursing skills and they would prepare a large saucepan of a nondescript coloured liquid which tasted awful. The children had to line up to take two spoonfuls each. Very occasionally a doctor would come to give injections or to examine a girl who was very ill. Although she believed that everything that happened was the will of God, Sister Valentina preferred to intervene so that things went as she wanted them to.

She folded the letter. Just as she was about to put it in the envelope she had an idea. She got up and went to the bookshelf where she kept a series of brass boxes of various sizes, labelled with the girl's names. She took down the box with Sita's name on it. She took out some photographs, looked at them and picked one out. She unfolded the letter again and wrote a few final lines at the end. Perhaps doctor Riba and his wife might know of another couple who, like them, would like to adopt an Indian girl and didn't mind if she was already six years old, with a past, a strong personality and who only spoke Marathi. She folded the letter up once more and put it in the envelope along with the black and white photo of the smiling Sita. On Monday morning, she would take it herself to the post office to make sure that they put all the correct stamps on it so that it would reach its destination as soon as possible.

Since she had arrived at the convent of the Bombay Missionaries of Mary, Sita had become Valentina's favourite, her special little girl. Perhaps it was because of her assertive look and the way she laughed. Sister Kamala had wanted Sita to leave the Nasik convent so that she could go to school, but in fact she had never sat through a whole lesson; she couldn't follow any of it. Sister Valentina didn't seem to mind too much. She was the one who had decided that Sita should accompany her on her errands around the city. A taxi waited for them, parked up in front of the iron gates at the end of the dirt track. It was almost always the same taxi driver, a short man with very dark skin whose name was Layam. Sita and the Mother Superior got in the back. Layam started the car without saying a word, still smoking his *bidi* out of the open window. As if it was a special ritual, Sister Valentina would get an apple, a knife and a white handkerchief out of her bag. Then she began to peel the apple slowly, removing the peel in one go, and then cut the fruit into small pieces that she arranged neatly on the handkerchief spread out on her lap. Sita would eat the pieces of apple, looking out of the wide open window so that she didn't miss a single detail of what was going on in the streets. Bicycles, *rickshaws*, cars, people carrying all kinds of packages, a cow at the bus stop among a group of people that barely even glanced at it, motorbikes carrying three people, a truck loaded up with tyres, fruit stalls lining the pavements, piles of pineapples and mangos, food stands and others selling fabrics of all colours, heaps of shoes and sandals. When they were stuck in traffic, hawkers would come up to the open window offering papayas and bananas, a glass of water or newspapers, with the deafening din of horns providing the background music to the scene. A woman with leprosy begging with her stumps; or a child with six fingers on one hand; or a deformed child. How could there be so many children with such awful deformities? Sister Valentina often asked herself this, but she never showed any emotion. She already had enough to deal with, with her orphans.

Most days the nuns would make a tour of Bombay's most luxurious hotels. They would go in the back entrance which led directly to the kitchen and collect the leftovers that had been packaged up for them in parcels and bundles. Sister Valentina only went once in a while, to thank the people in charge. The kitchens of the big hotels were enormous and Sita always stopped to gawp at the skinned animals piled up on the worktops; chickens, lambs … She could never understand what those horrible looking animals were doing in the kitchen! The taxi driver then helped them to put everything in the car. While they were carrying and loading these packages into the car, one of the chefs from the kitchen would usually come up to Sita and give her a piece of cake or some other treat. The Taj Mahal hotel was the best place, not just because the building was spectacular, it was on the seafront, it had a different atmosphere about it and at any time of the day it was a special and magical place, but also because they always left there with pans full of all kinds of food, plenty of lamb *biryani* and chicken *massala*, that after a few days they returned to them clean and shiny. Sita always left there with a *samosa* in each hand, which she ate in tiny mouthfuls to make them last, and to savour all the flavours inside. The food they collected from the hotels was for the orphan girls and the nuns. The boarding school girls had their own meals. In the orphanage, the children were fed on leftovers from hotels that the nuns in charge of cooking would pad out with rice, vegetables and fruit. When they had plenty of meat from the hotels, the cooks would mix the sauces with rice and chop up the pieces of fish and meat into small chunks so that there was enough to go round.

That morning, after mass, Sita was entertaining herself by chasing one of the cats that often hung around the garden. She would run after it and catch it, only to let it go when the cat became agitated. Then she would chase it again. A group of girls who were getting ready to go to a lesson – some her age, some slightly older – were watching her, pointing and talking amongst themselves from a little distance away.

'Hey! Golden girl! Aren't you going out for a walk today?' said one of the older ones, coming up to Sita.

'Do you know why you don't go to class very often? Because you're good for nothing!'

'Yeah, that's why they take you out on walks, you good-for-nothing girl!'

'You don't even know how to hold a pencil. We've *all* learned to write!'

Sita was used to defending herself, to fighting. It wasn't easy being one of so many. The nuns couldn't keep an eye on all the girls; there were too many of them.

'I bet you don't even know how to write your name! Am I right?'

'It's because I don't need to know how to write!' Sita suddenly blurted out, looking at them defiantly with all her six-year-old confidence. The cat seized the opportunity to flee for good.

'Oh, no? What a smarty pants! She doesn't need to know how to write!'

'And why not?'

'Because soon I'm going to have parents to take me away from here, and you won't!'

'Stupid girl! How are you going to have parents if you don't know anything?'

The group was starting to close in around her, their words growing louder, more hurtful and violent. The girls knew how to hurt each other with words, and when words were not hurtful enough, they turned to blows. One of the girls kicked her; Sita kicked her back and the two of them ended up rolling around on the floor, scratching and pulling at each other's hair.

The other girl was called Sundari. Sita would remember her for the rest of her life because at that moment, as they lashed out at each other, amid the other girls' shouts, Sundari jumped on top of her and holding her down forcefully with her hands, she bit her on the cheek leaving a mark that would remain forever.

Sita's shrieking finally brought a pair of nuns running out to restore the children to some kind of order.

'What's going on here? That's enough!'

But it was too late. Sita's cheek was covered in blood and she was sobbing uncontrollably.

'You bunch of savages! Who started it? Never mind, I don't want to know. Everyone inside, now!' shouted Sister Urvashi, doling out a few slaps on the back of their necks. 'We have to dress the wound immediately! Come on, up you get, come with me Sita.'

The nun didn't know who to be angry with, and Sita looked so wretched that she ended up shouting at her more. She took her by the hand and led her to the medicine cabinet.

With her face half covered by the bandage that Sister Urvashi had placed on it, after cleaning the bite wound with a liquid that made Sita scream, Sita headed resolutely for the spiral staircase. If Sister Valentina had come to fetch her to go and run errands then the fight would never have happened. But there weren't always trips out in the taxi; sometimes Sister Valentina had other things to do. The doorknob was too high for Sita to reach, and she couldn't open the door. She knocked a few times but no one answered, so she sat dejectedly on the top step of the staircase to wait for the Mother Superior. She was hungry. Her breakfast of tea, banana and two pieces of dry bread seemed a long time ago and the fight with Sundari had taken a lot of energy out of her. She was thinking about the *samosas* and sweets that the chefs gave her in the hotels when suddenly she heard the stairs creaking. She looked between the banisters and smiled. It was Sister Valentina.

'Sita, what on earth happened to you? Don't tell me that a crow pecked your face! There's just no way to keep those black beasts out of those trees!'

'Sundari bit me.'

'Oh dear … Well I don't know what's worse! And what are you doing sitting here then?'

'I wanted to know if you have found me any parents yet.'

Sister Valentina panted as she came up the stairs. She was carrying a bag full of books in one hand and clutching the banister with the other.

'No, Sita, I haven't found them yet, but I've started looking for them. Have you been doing what I told you to do? Have you prayed to God a lot to find you some parents?'

'Hmmm … A bit!'

'So pray, Sita, pray a lot more!'

Sister Valentina went into her office with Sita trailing behind. She felt devoted to the little girl who was so different to the others. Or perhaps she was just like them. But to her she felt special, and seeing her suffering hurt her deep in her soul. She didn't want to imagine the fight in the garden. She had seen many fights from her window and she didn't need to imagine it. The lives of girls in an orphanage like that were governed by the rule of survival of the fittest. She always hoped that one of the nuns would hear the shouting or see them, and run out to break it up. But if she had seen Sita in the middle of the ruckus, she would immediately have run out herself to rescue her.

'So, Sita, do you want to tell me why Sundari bit you?'

'All of the girls keep telling me I can't write or anything and that's why no parents would want me.'

'Of course there are parents who will want you! But perhaps it is about time you learned to read and write, like the other girls. You know that if you learn, your life will be better? Learning is very important and you're getting older now!'

'But it's so boring!'

'Sita, from now on you will go to lessons every day. You have to learn so you can be strong!'

'And I can't go with you to the city?'

'Yes, but only if you go to Sister Juliette's lessons in the afternoon and you show me what you've learned!'

Since the biting incident – the wound had healed, but she was left with a scar on her cheek – the days, weeks and months were so similar that they seemed to blur into one another. Every morning, after breakfast and daily mass, Sita went up the spiral staircase and sat out of the way, waiting for Sister Valentina. Every day she asked her the same question and the reply was always the same. Sister Valentina was still looking for parents for her, but she had to keep on praying. After the interrogation, Sister Valentina would go into her office, pick up her bag and possibly some letters or documents. Then they left the building and made their way down the dirt track to the big iron gates. Layam would be waiting for them there, smoking a *bidi* and leaning against his taxi which was parked by the entrance, and they would set off to run their errands. In the afternoon Sister Juliette would teach her the meanings of some symbols that seemed unpronounceable to her. The most commonly spoken language in the orphanage was Marathi but the nuns also wanted to teach them basic Hindi and English. The classes contained girls of all ages, divided between several nuns in different classrooms. The nuns who worked as teachers worked very long hours as they taught both the girls from the boarding school and the orphans.

One morning, Sister Valentina made the taxi stop outside the post office. It was a magnificent colonial building. Sita held her hand tightly as they went inside. There were a lot of people everywhere. Sister Valentina had told her that this enormous place with lots of people coming and going was dangerous and that if she let go of her hand and got lost, she would certainly not be able to find her again. There were extremely long queues at each counter window, of people sending letters and parcels, or collecting them, as well as at the phone booths where people were talking on the phone or sending telegrams. It was so hot. Sita was absolutely fascinated by this place. She couldn't yet read or write but she knew that if she did, she would be able to send letters and large parcels like those people too. She watched the elegantly dressed men wearing ties, sticking stamps on huge piles of letters, and the *culis* loading up parcels onto a cart to deliver them. What could be in those enormous packages? Clothes perhaps? Or packets of tea? Or perhaps tins of paint like the ones they used to paint the orphanage's chapel? As they waited in the queue to collect a letter, Sita stood there, open-mouthed, watching everything going on; admiring the colours of the women's saris against their coloured glass bracelets and gaping at the large quantity of fans there were on the ceiling. Some of them turned; others seemed to be sleeping. When her turn came, Sister Valentina exchanged a piece of paper she was carrying for a letter and they went outside again, avoiding the crowd.

'Did you know that letters like this one travel for many days?'

'Where is this one from?'

'From very far away! One day I'll teach you how to travel on a map!'

Sister Valentina put the letter away in her bag and noticed that her heart was beating fast. She was torn between wanting to read it and being afraid to. In the end she decided not to read the letter in front of Sita, so she took her by the hand and they made their way back to where Layam had parked the taxi. Layam had just spat out the remains of some *paan* and his mouth was stained completely red as if it were bleeding.

In the middle of the night, the wind tore through the palm trees in huge gusts. The noise of the palm leaves slapping against each other and the tree trunks woke Sita up. It was very late at night. Only a slither of moonlight slipped under the door, which creaked in the wind. The ceiling fans turned, moving the air around the room, but Sita found it hard to breathe. The other girls were sleeping as usual on the floor in rows next to each other. Sita was cold, despite the sweltering heat. She tried to move closer to the girl closest to her, to feel the warmth of her body. The sound of the palm trees – as if they were fighting each other – and the banging of a plant pot or a piece of wood as it rattled around in the wind outside the building, were unbearable. Sita was so afraid that she didn't even dare get up to go to the bathroom. She looked for the slither of light but the darkness had swallowed it up. Without realising, she fell asleep again until Sister Aline's bell rang to wake them up. It was daylight. Her towel was soaking wet; like so many mornings before after a night of wind, noise and nightmares. The girls all had to take their towels to the courtyard to air them out before they went to breakfast.

'Sister Urvashi … My towel is wet … '

'Sita! Again? How is this possible?'

With that, the nun gave a short, sharp slap on her cheek, where her scar was.

'Give me your towel, I'll wash it and hang it out. What a pain you are, child! Go on, get out of my sight!'

Sister Valentina had memorized the letter from reading it so many times. Sitting at her desk the first time, with the door closed, she had felt emotional. Seeing Sita's face in the black and white photo had completely changed the couple's plans. From the moment they saw her they couldn't stop thinking about her and, although they were concerned about becoming parents to a slightly older child, they felt like this little girl had come to them and they couldn't turn their back on her now. So they told Sister Valentina that they had decided to start the process of adopting Sita and given up on the idea of adopting a baby. The process wasn't an easy one. From what the couple had told her in their letters, Spain was different to other European countries. The procedure to follow was relatively unclear to everyone. The doctor and his wife said that they already had some information but that there was still a lot of official paperwork to be filled out, a considerable pile of documents that needed to be authorized by the Spanish authorities as well as in India; and that this would take longer than a week to complete. Sister Valentina thought that it was too early to tell Sita yet. But she did tell the other nuns, in confidence. It didn't seem right to keep the decision of agreeing to Sita's adoption to herself. She felt a knot in her stomach; a combination of happiness and deep sadness. She definitely felt older and wearier.

It was Saturday. Like the other girls, Sita was sitting on a wooden pew in the chapel, a small church next to the convent grounds. She still didn't understand what mass was, or what it was for. She knew all of the songs and sang them in a steady, tuneful voice. There was a brightly coloured stain glass window above the altar and the mass was long enough for Sita to observe how the light reflected the colours on the walls, or the floor of the aisle. If God was all around, then perhaps he was in those colours too, so she stared at them intently and said to herself:

'Please, God, find me some parents to take me away from here!'

After church she ran out once more to clamber up on the stone bench in the garden to watch the families arriving with the girls from the boarding school. During the week they wore a uniform of a white shirt, navy blue skirt and white socks. They all wore the same, whether they were older or younger. When their families came to pick them up they were all dressed differently; some in a *salwar kameez*, others in short-sleeved dresses like the one Sister Valentina had given her. Sita watched the happy faces of the mothers and fathers as they were reunited with their daughters. She didn't understand why they left them in a boarding school for so many days if they loved them so much. She also didn't understand why some girls had parents and others, like her, didn't. The nuns had told them that all the girls in the orphanage once had a mother and father but now they don't. Some because they had died, others because they thought that their children would have a better life if they left them there. Sita didn't know what had happened to her parents; nobody had ever told her anything about it. Her earliest memories were of the convent in Nasik, with Sister Kamala and the other nuns. As hard as she tried, she couldn't remember anything else; it all started in Nasik.

She recognized some of the boarding school girls from seeing them playing in her part of the garden or at special masses when a priest from far away came, or if it was a particular day of celebration. Then, all of the girls from the centre of the Missionaries of Mary, both those who had families and those who didn't, sat side by side on the wooden pews in church and sang all the hymns together. None of the girls were her friends. In fact, Sita didn't have any friends; she did her own thing. It had been months since the first time she asked Sister Valentina to find her some parents and since then the ascending spiral of the wooden staircase had become a symbol of her search. Sita was obsessed with the idea of having a family, perhaps because she sensed that her life wouldn't end here, that she would enjoy a fuller, freer life. She received affection from Sister Valentina and another nun who fussed over her, but it wasn't a great deal of affection. She wanted someone to look at her every day with the look of happiness that she saw on those mothers' faces.

The place where they did the laundry was one of Sita's favourite places in the convent. There was always some distraction or other to keep her entertained. The older girls from the orphanage would help the nuns wash the coloured *saris*, sheets and towels, *salwar kameez* and other fabrics. There was so much dirty laundry! Particularly on hot days, it was nice to get your hands wet in that cool shady part of the garden. The large grey stone sink was filled with soapy water, and there was always someone there, scrubbing away at the clothes with a huge bar of soap, a brush, a piece of coconut coir or just their hands. Then they rinsed the clothes in a metal bucket full of water and hung them up on the ropes that they used for washing lines. Some days, if the colours of the fabric might run, they separated them out by colour. Sita liked those days the best, when she could play at hiding among a forest of red, fuchsia or turquoise *saris*…

Hidden among the clothes hanging on the line, she heard two young nuns who were washing clothes, their white habits rolled up at the elbows, talking about a long journey to a place far away called Barcelona. The name sounded exotic and hard to pronounce.

'Poor little thing! So small and it's such a long journey!'

'Tell me about it.'

'Do you think you could live far away from here, in such a cold place?'

'Poor little girl, sending her to live with complete strangers!'

'You're right! If it were me, I wouldn't go! Don't they think she can grow up well here and be happy?'

'Would you like to go so far away?'

'Oh, no! I wouldn't leave here, not for all the tea in China!'

'Not even to see what it's like?'

'No, not even for that!'

'Well, I'd like to go … I want to know what the world is like on the other side of the ocean … '

The next time Sister Valentina took Sita out on their tour of the hotel kitchens, as she was sitting in the back of the taxi eating slices of peeled apple prepared by the nun, Sita asked one of her unpredictable questions:

'Sister Valentina, can I go to Bar-si-lona?'

'Oh, Sita! You don't miss a thing do you?' For a moment, Sister Valentina noticed how fast her heart was beating. 'And what have you heard about Barcelona?'

'Um … nothing! Where is Bar-ce-lona?'

'Barcelona is a city thousands of miles from here. They also have the sea there, but it's a different sea.'

'And could Layam take us there?'

Layam smiled, showing the holes in his decaying teeth, and looked at the girl in the rear view mirror as he drove. He didn't know where Barcelona was either but he presumed it was very far away.

'Yes, we could go by car, but it would take many, many days!'

Sita carried on eating the slices of apple with her hands, which were as always slightly dirty, but not as filthy as her bare feet. She was wearing the dress with the yellow flowers. She hadn't grown that much and it still fit her well. In the streets of the city, Sita also saw a lot of girls like her who didn't go to school and sold all sorts of things at the stalls like the adults did, or begged. They were also barefoot like her, but much dirtier. Their hair dishevelled, their eyes painted with *kohl* and their clothes ragged. But perhaps they had parents.

The Christmas celebrations were over and it was already a few days into the New Year. Some of the girls had helped the nuns to carefully take down the nativity scene that they put up every year in the convent's hall. It was a cave made from dried palm leaves and a few large ceramic figures that someone had given to Sister Valentina a long time ago; they were her treasured items. Now the hall was back to normal with the two leather armchairs and the low table for any guests that Sister Valentina was expecting to visit, and the large painting of the founder of the order of the Missionaries of Mary, a French woman with very pale skin.

Sita went to lessons every day but she didn't learn much. She barely knew how to write her name and a few other words, and she recognized numbers with some difficulty. She found it hard to concentrate; she wasn't interested in anything the nuns explained to her in front of the blackboard, nor did she have the patience to try and understand adding and taking away.

One February morning, on a day that started like any other day – the same heat, the same dash to the toilets and the dining room for breakfast – Sister Valentina came looking for Sita, who was still dunking a piece of bread into her sugary tea, slumped on a wooden bench at a wide table full of girls all sitting side by side.

'Good morning, Sita!' she said, standing behind her. 'When you finish, come up to my office, I've got something for you!'

Sita turned to face the Mother Superior, stuffing the remaining piece of bread into her mouth.

'Finished! Can I come up now?'

They went up the spiral staircase together in silence. Sita hurried in front, still chewing her bread. The nun behind her, more slowly. Before she even told her to take a seat in the small armchair in front of the desk, Sita was already sitting down; her little legs dangling as her feet didn't reach the floor. Sister Valentina sat down in her chair and looked for the envelope edged with the blue and red stripes of airmail letters, which were not the same as ordinary letters. She picked it up and pulled something out of it.

'What have you got for me? It's not my birthday today is it?'

'No, Sita, it's not your birthday. I've finally found you some parents!'

'Really? Real parents?'

'Yes, here they are.' She handed Sita a black and white photograph.

Sita gazed in awe at the faces in the picture. Real parents, smiling, sitting in two chairs surrounded by plants. She was lost for words. She looked at them closely. The mother had long, very dark hair; she was wearing very wide-legged white trousers and sandals. The father wore glasses and had curly hair.

'They're from Barcelona, Sita. They live very far from here but they want to be your parents. Although they still have to do some paperwork and fill out lots of forms, okay? Lots of printed documents! And then, in a few months, you can go to Barcelona and start a new life ... '

'Barcelona is that place where Layam can take us in the taxi, isn't it?'

'I'll show you where it is.' Sister Valentina got up and took an atlas off the shelf on the other side of the room. She opened it to the page showing the map of the world. 'Look, we're here,' she said with the book open, resting it on a chair and pointing out Bombay to Sita with her finger. 'And here is Barcelona,' she went on, moving her finger across the map from right to left.

'And can you go by train?'

'No. By car it would take too long and the journey would be very difficult and by train it's even harder. You'll go in an aeroplane.'

'An aeroplane? How do I go in an aeroplane?'

'By flying, Sita! You'll see! It's just like going in a bus that flies. And you'll be there in just a few hours!'

'And will they be my parents forever? How do you know they will?'

Sister Valentina closed the atlas and put it back on the shelf, then sat down again in her chair across the desk from Sita, who had never been so still.

'What did they say to you?'

Sister Valentina had never experienced a moment as emotional as that. Telling a seven-year-old girl that she had found parents for her wasn't something she did every day; in fact it was the first time she had ever been in such a situation. Despite her apparent coldness she was a sensitive woman and she felt very strongly about this little girl, who was now asking non-stop questions with her bright, alert look. She loved her very much. She realized that the countdown had begun to Sita leaving forever and that she was going to miss her terribly.

'What did they tell me? Lots of things. When you first asked me for parents, I had already written to the people you see there in the photo. Their names are Irene and Ramón.'

'What?'

'Irene is the name of the woman who will be your mother; your father will be called Ramón.'

Sita couldn't take her eyes off the photo.

'One day I put your photo in a letter, so that they could help me find you a family and now they've decided that they want to be your parents.'

'And will you come with me?'

'I don't think that will be possible Sita ... You're more grown up now and you can go on your own. In the aeroplane there will be people who'll look after you and keep you company for the whole journey.'

Sita was still sitting in the chair, staring at the photo. Sister Valentina would have given anything to know what she was thinking at the moment. The moment she had so longed for.

'Can I keep the photo?'

'Yes, of course!' Sister Valentina smiled.

Before they left the office together, the nun stopped in front of Sita, taking her face in both hands and looking at her for a few seconds as if she was trying to remember those dark eyes forever.

'Good luck, my child. Now we have to start preparing for your journey!'

BARCELONA, 1974

Irene walked from her house to the school and waved amiably at the handful of children who were waiting at the entrance. It was just before nine o'clock in the morning. Their parents had dropped them off on the way to work. It was a chilly winter morning and the children were wrapped up warm with gloves and scarves, prepared to spend a little while waiting outside. She had only been a teacher at the school for a year, and she taught the fifth year: students of ten or eleven years old. Teaching was her vocation. She couldn't imagine doing anything else. She had also worked for four years in a nursery school uptown. A house that was covered in purple bougainvillea from spring, when the good weather came, until the autumn. To get there she had to go all the way across Barcelona in her white Seat. The nursery school had a very friendly atmosphere; the classes were small and it was a real luxury to be able to give one-on-one attention to the students, cutting out shapes or helping them to learn their first letters. But she was keen to work in a bigger school. It was also a special school in that it was committed to its ideals and advocating the freedom that wasn't yet fully a reality in the country.

Now she could walk to work and Ramón took the car. It took her less than half an hour, walking briskly, which helped her to keep fit. She went up the stairs to the first floor where her classroom was. Two large windows looked out onto the street, the grey painted iron gates and the entrance courtyard, where more and more children were gathering with their schoolbags on their backs, waiting to go inside. Just in front of the school was the main entrance to the Park Güell and from the windows you could see the two round shaped houses that, to the children, resembled something from a fairy tale. She hung up her coat and began taking the exercise sheets she had prepared at home and some notebooks out of her bag. She sat down in her chair facing the two long lines of small, individual desks, two per row, where her thirty-two students sat and listened to her. She liked to arrive with enough time to prepare her lessons and above all, to gather her thoughts before the day started. Lately, her mind had been thousands of miles away from that classroom. She found her diary and took a black and white photo out of it. A girl stared back at her, smiling; a girl with brown skin and dark hair in two plaits with bows. This would soon be her daughter. Soon, after so many failed attempts, her dream of becoming a mother was going to become reality.

For Irene, the eight hours at school passed quickly. From dictations to maths exercises, from history lessons to science, to French class (which she also taught), to music, (which a colleague taught), with break times, games and songs, lunchtime, arts and crafts … She enjoyed it and generally the pupils were well-behaved and didn't exhaust her as much as they did the other teachers, perhaps because they were older than her. They often commented that when they got home they didn't have the energy to do anything else. At thirty-five, Irene felt she had plenty of energy and was looking forward to Sita's arrival so she could give it her all, as a person, a mother and a teacher. She and Ramón had prepared the girl's room. They had decorated the walls with large, bright flowery wallpaper and had put in a wooden bed that some friends had given them as a present, to match the low round pine table and four small wooden chairs.

She wondered if this little girl from India would feel at home in that room. Sometimes she wondered if perhaps they were going a bit over the top. She didn't know anyone who had gone through the same thing as her. It made her feel very insecure and isolated on her adventure. Sometimes she felt very lost. She knew some couples who hadn't been able to have children and who had given up on the idea, but she wasn't ready to do that; she desperately wanted to be a mother. She had also heard about a couple, friends of friends, who had adopted three orphan children, all three born in Barcelona.

They were living in strange times. Revolt had been in the air for years now. The dictatorship was unbearable and there had to be an end to it, but it was taking too long to arrive. Since they had begun the first step in the process to adopting Sita, Irene had stopped going to the teacher meetings to discuss the need for a more open and stimulating method of teaching; one that was less repressive and doctrinarian than the one that had prevailed until then. She had also stopped going to the neighbourhood meetings, which were becoming more political and demanding in nature. She needed to focus on herself and on getting ready for the arrival of the girl who would be her daughter. Every day, more and more people were taking part in the fight against the dictatorship and this eased her guilty conscience somewhat over stepping back from it.

'Is that her?' asked Pilar, Irene's childhood friend who lived in Paris and who had come round for dinner. She had taken down the black and white photo of Sita from a shelf.

'Yes, that's her. The director of the orphanage in Bombay sent us that photo in one of her letters, asking us if we knew of a family who might want to adopt her,' replied Ramón. 'We've had the photo up in the dining room for months now, as you can see!

Practically everyone tells us we're crazy to adopt an older child! But we don't care; we want to do it.'

'How old is she?'

'Five or six ... in this photo. When she arrives she'll be seven, or even older.'

'She's so cute!' sighed Pilar, looking at the photo.

'Yes, very cute! But who knows what she's been through. And what language she speaks ... And what she's thinking. And what education she's received. And what illnesses she might have. And her genetic inheritance!'

Ramón's sister Rosa wasn't at all convinced about the idea of adopting a slightly older child of unknown genetic inheritance from an orphanage in India. They had spent hours at dinners like these, around that very table, discussing Irene and Ramón's decision. Being a doctor, Rosa placed a great deal of importance on genetic inheritance; on everything that was passed on from parents to children without people realising. She had two children, aged four and five, and she had the theory that from day one they looked like her husband and her; like two peas in a pod. Not just physically, but in all their gestures and their character.

'But doesn't it worry you that you don't know where this girl comes from? Who her parents are?'

'We've explained it you a thousand times, Rosa,' said Irene. 'No, it doesn't worry us. We think about it and we've discussed it a lot but we aren't worried about it. She will have her genes and she will look like some parents that we don't know and we won't know why they abandoned her, or what they died from. We want to be her parents, give her everything we can, a better life than the one she has as an orphan in Bombay. An education, all the love we can, just being with her every day ...'

'Yes, what you're doing is very commendable, but perhaps you don't fully understand what you're letting yourselves in for! A child is for your whole life! If it's yours, you can cope with it, but if it's not yours and it doesn't turn out well, what then? Will you also be able to deal with it your whole life?'

'Rosa, we're perfectly aware that a child is for life. And our daughter, whatever she is like, will be ours forever!' replied Ramón, puffing on his pipe. He never appeared to be fazed by anything but inside, his blood was boiling.

'Have you thought about a name for her?' asked Rosa's husband David.

'What do you mean a name for her? She already has a name! She's called Sita, you know that!'

'But Ramón, don't tell me you're going to call her Sita, just like that; she'll be the only Sita in Barcelona!'

'It's her name, it's one of the few things she has! It's part of her history ... Someone chose it for her one day and who are we to erase it? Anyway, Sita is a beautiful name from Indian mythology,' replied Ramón, gripping his pipe.

Pilar, Rosa and David finally left. Irene was already tired of explaining to family and friends all the time. She felt as if she was constantly explaining herself. She understood that the people who loved her were concerned. What they were about to do – become parents of an unknown little girl who would arrive on her own from far away, who had lived seven or more years in a country they knew nothing about – was unusual. It was especially unusual in a country as closed as theirs. A friend of Ramón's had cut out an article from an American newspaper about the adoption of Korean children in the States, and that little slip of paper had made them feel slightly more normal.

In the United States, thousands of boys and girls had already been adopted over the last twenty years. They were tired of being questioned and even criticized by those closest to them. After clearing the table and washing the dishes together – one at each sink, as they liked to do, chatting about the discussions at dinner – they went to bed. They had known each other for ten years. Every day they told each other that being together was the best thing that could have happened to them. They wanted children to share this togetherness with.

All that was left on the dining room table were the presents that Pilar had brought them from Paris: a Ravi Shankar record that she had told them they must listen to in order to get to know India, and a big hardback book of photos of Indian children, in colour and black and white. They would sit and listen to that Ravi Shankar record and look at the photographs in the book over and over again.

The cafeteria of the Hospital de Bellvitge was on the ground floor. It was a place where relatives and friends visiting patients mingled with doctors, nurses and various members of staff. The bustling din of the room contrasted with the calm atmosphere of the rest of the building, which was twenty floors high and separated from the world by its location on the outskirts of the city, near the airport. The clinking of plates, cups, spoons and coffee pots mixed with the shouts of the waiters and the conversations of so many people who were desperate to have a chat and a smoke. Ramón made his way down from the floor where he worked to meet Gabriel as he did at the same time every day for breakfast. He was intending to ask him the question that had been going round and round his head. In the lift he bumped into a couple with a little girl; they were both holding her hand. He looked at them intently, trying to work out how old she might be. Five? Maybe six?

Gabriel was waiting for him, queuing at the bar and jostling slightly with those around him, carrying four croissants and a bottle of water that he had picked up from the self-service counter. The room was filled with cigarette smoke and the smell of fried bacon.

'This is outrageous! The waiter's been looking at me for ten minutes and he's served everyone else but me! I hope you want your usual white coffee, because that's what I've ordered you.'

They managed to find a table in a corner next to the window where there was less noise, so that they could talk without yelling at each other. Through the glass they could see an ambulance arriving.

'What a frightful place! It's simply unbearable.'

Ramón lit his pipe. The cafeteria was one big cloud of smoke. There was hardly a doctor in the hospital who didn't smoke.

'Gabriel,' he said finally, waiting until his friend was eating a croissant for his chance to ask him, 'When Clara was born did you feel like she was your daughter from the very first moment?'

'What are you talking about?'

'Exactly that; from the first moment did you know that she was your daughter? Did you love her from the first day, as soon as you saw her?'

'You're acting so weirdly lately … What's going on with you?'

'Nothing, I just want to know if when you were in surgery and you saw Clara being born, or after, in the hospital room when she started to breastfeed and you were watching her, mesmerized, if you already felt like she was yours, like she had come from inside you…?'

'Man, from inside me and from inside Luisa, yeah, sure!'

'But did you feel like she belonged to you, I mean *really* belonged to you?'

'Ummm, well I don't know!'

'And now she's two years old, do you feel like she's yours and yours alone?'

'Well, I suppose so, I don't know ... I haven't really thought about it to be honest ... Why? Where are you going with this Ramón?'

'It's just that I've been thinking that, in some way, all men adopt their children. They're born from inside the woman after a physical process of many months, one that the men haven't experienced in their own bodies, and when they come out they adopt them, they have to accept them and believe they are theirs. You see?'

'Yes, I suppose so ... What you're trying to say is that, for a man, waiting outside the operating room for a child to be born could be the same as waiting for a child to arrive by plane from India, right?'

'More or less.'

'Honestly, it's not the same thing. But what you're saying is interesting ... I've never thought about it before!'

Ramón looked out of the window. The ambulance had dropped its passengers off and there was less activity around the A & E entrance.

'Do you know what's worrying me most lately?'

'Coming from you, it could be anything!' exclaimed Gabriel.

'I'm worried about all the time that Sita will have spent in a convent full of Catholic nuns ... about everything they've drummed into her ... '

'No big deal, man!'

'How is it not a big deal? Haven't you had enough of catholic repression in this damn country? I'm sick and tired of priests and nonsense! I've had enough, I swear!'

'Well it's a good thing you erased it from your life then, isn't it?'

'Yeah, renouncing my faith is one thing that has made me feel better in recent years … '

'Why did you do it?'

'Because my in-laws wanted us to get married in a church – you know what staunch Catholics they are and how many obstacles they tried to put in the way of me and Irene living happily together. I've never been the son-in-law they wanted for their daughter. They threatened not to speak to Irene ever again if we didn't get married. Obviously the only way I could avoid getting married in a church was by renouncing my faith … If I was no longer officially a catholic, I couldn't get married in a church; I could only do it by civil ceremony. It wasn't a very pleasant experience … I still remember the face of the priest. I could tell he was already imagining me burning in hell … '

Gabriel listened to his friend with an amused expression as he fumbled around for a lighter in the pockets of his white coat.

'I'm sure the nuns who've looked after Sita all these years are nothing like you imagine, with the situation like it is here … '

'I hope you're right.'

'You don't know anything about her past.'

'You said it. I don't know anything about her past and it scares me!'

Ramón held his pipe in both hands and looked at his friend. Neither of them spoke again until they had finished their coffee and Gabriel stubbed out his cigarette in the glass ashtray. Then they took the lift back up to the floor where they worked.

During the months that they were preparing for Sita's journey, from time to time the tour of the kitchens of Bombay's hotels would extend to visiting some shops and markets. Sister Valentina always got Sita to accompany her, and in the shops, which were often second-hand clothing shops, she looked for girl's winter clothes – something that wasn't easy to get hold of in Bombay. Whenever they came across some, possibly from England, Sita would try on jerseys and wool skirts, overcoats or raincoats and waterproofs in all different colours; garments that clung to her skin and itched her. She found it strange to think that there was a place where people wore clothes that were so thick. Sister Valentina helped her, making the initial selection, but in the end she asked Sita to decide what she wanted to wear. Little by little they were accumulating a selection of clothing that Sita would take with her to Europe, where Sister Valentina told her it was very cold and the rain wasn't like in India, where it fell heavily on the hottest days during certain months of year. In Europe, she had explained to her, with the illustrated atlas wide open on the desk in her office, the rain was much finer and colder and it could rain at any time of year. And it snowed too. To explain what snow was to Sita, Sister Valentina had to use an old calendar that a friend in Austria had sent her, full of pictures of the Tyrol in the Alps and the streets of Innsbruck blanketed in crystal white snow.

One day, Sita put on a pair of shoes for the first time. Sister Valentina walked purposefully into a shoe shop, eager to buy a pair of strong, hardwearing shoes for the little girl going so far away. The shopkeeper, a plump woman dressed in a red *sari*, her wrists swathed in gold bracelets with little jingly, put a pair of socks on Sita. This was also the first time she had worn socks. Then she started the adventure of trying on one pair of shoes after the other. With laces, with buckles, without laces or buckles … it was impossible. Sita's feet were used to being bare; she didn't understand the feeling of pressure on her feet caused by wearing shoes and she said that all of them hurt her. After trying on many pairs they left the shop with a bag containing some dark blue closed toe sandals with thick soles and a buckle on the side. Sita wanted to stay barefoot for the moment.

All the while, she was becoming aware that her life was about to change. With every week that went by, every hour of lessons, every night lying on her towel with the ceiling fans swirling above her head, she was getting closer to her dream of having a mother and father. A vague, childish fantasy that had taken shape when she had spied on the boarding school girls leaving for their holidays. The photo that Sister Valentina had given her went everywhere with her. It was gradually becoming more and more crumpled in the pocket of her dress or the only pair of trousers that she owned. In her solitary leisure hours, she no longer chased butterflies but stayed in a corner, looking in close detail at the black and white photo of these two people who were her family and, who, if she understood it correctly, were eagerly waiting for her arrival.

The other girls tried to take the photo from her once. But just once. Sita gathered all the strength of her small, slight frame, kicking and scratching and shouting as if she were possessed. She lashed out so loudly and viciously that even before a pair of nuns arrived to see what was going on, the group of girls had fled, leaving Sita alone once and for all, sitting quietly with her crumpled photograph.

Another day, Sister Valentina decided that Sita needed to take a present to her new family. Spending *rupees* when they usually didn't have enough to buy milk or meat wasn't easy, but the Ribas had sent some money to cover the costs of preparing for Sita's journey, the plane fare and the final documents that needed to be obtained – an Indian passport which would then be sent to the Spanish embassy in New Delhi for them to provide the visa – and everything they might need. They had also said in a letter that they were sending more money than was necessary, by way of a donation to the orphanage. Sister Valentina had already decided that the money would be used to carry out some important repairs to the building where the nuns and orphans lived, where last year's monsoons had caused serious damage. So it seemed only right that she should buy them a little something. In one of Sister Valentina's old friends' shops full of artisan objects from all over India, Sita chose some wooden dancing dolls from Rajasthan; when you tapped them, their whole bodies moved. These would be for her parents.

The wind shook the palm trees in the garden incessantly. It was a warm wind. In the city, the day had started in the usual way: the hawkers setting up on the streets, the boys and girls going to school in their uniforms, cars, lorries, motorbikes, bicycles, English double-decker buses full of people going to work, *rickshaws* and all kinds of vehicles following their own traffic rules, beeping their horns endlessly and avoiding pedestrians that walked wherever they wanted while managing not to be knocked down, dodging the odd cow here and there. But it was no ordinary day. It was one of the most important days of Sita's life. The day of her great journey had arrived.

After breakfast, Sister Valentina called all the nuns and girls of the centre of the Missionaries of Mary to the chapel. Once they were all seated on the wooden pews, the Mother Superior went up to the altar and made a small goodbye speech for Sita. She explained that she was going very far away and asked everyone to say the Lord's Prayer and to pray for good luck for Sita. Sita, sitting in the front row, stared at the window on the wall in front of her, looking at the colours and shapes, unable to think about anything or concentrate on any kind of prayer. When they left the chapel, some of the nuns, quite choked up with emotion, waited for Sita to come out. They gave her a kiss on the cheek and told her to take care of herself.

When Irene and Ramón had given up on the idea that it was better to adopt a child as young as possible and decided to adopt the one who had been looking down at them from a photograph on the shelf, Sister Valentina hadn't found it easy to convince the other nuns of the advantages of Sita's adoption. They had never experienced it before; they didn't understand it. It wasn't an option that featured in their educational approaches. The girls in the orphanage were like their daughters and in their own way they loved them, so letting one go was hard for them, even though they knew that they were offering them a better life.

At the door of the church, girls of all ages also came up to Sita to say goodbye. It couldn't be said that these girls were her friends, but she had taken turns on the bicycles with them and shared games in the garden, desks and wooden pews in church or in the dining room, not to mention sleeping next to each other on the floor of the dormitory.

'Hey, wait! Sita, wait!'

Sita turned round. She was walking toward the convent building alongside Sister Valentina – who seemed different that day, anxious – and she saw Sundari running toward her.

'Sita … will you be coming back one day?' she asked, panting.

'I don't know; I'm going very far away.'

'Sita, do you forgive me?'

'What for?'

'For biting you! Look! You can still see the mark!'

Sister Valentina, who had stopped next to Sita, continued walking toward the building.

'Don't be long, Sita! We have to go to the airport!' She had to hold back the tears that welled up as she turned her back on the two girls standing in the middle of the lush tropical plants of the garden.

'Of course I forgive you, Sundari! And the mark on my cheek will help me to never forget you!'

'Do you know where you're going?'

'Not really … Want to see the photo of the people who are going to be my parents?' she said, pulling it out of her pocket. 'Look, there they are.'

Sundari looked at the black and white photo. She didn't know what to say. Sita looked at the girl who had always been so cruel to her, who had so many friends and ordered everyone around. She didn't say anything either.

'Will you come back one day?'

'I don't know.'

'I hope to see you again.'

'Me too.'

Sita put the photo back in her pocket and said goodbye to Sundari, who ran off in the opposite direction as Sita hurried into the building. Her little suitcase was already waiting for her in the hallway. She had bought it with Sister Valentina on one of their trips round the city. The dress with the yellow flowers, which was now a bit small for her, along with another garment of hers, would be left behind in the drawer of the communal changing rooms. They would be used by the younger girls when they got a bit bigger, or if a new girl came to the orphanage. Perhaps she would use her towel to sleep on too.

'Sita, come on, you have to put your socks and shoes on before you go! You can't go the airport in your bare feet!'

She hadn't tried them on since the day they had bought them. Sister Juliette sat her down on one of the armchairs in the hall and helped her to put the knee-high white socks on, followed by the shoes. Sita didn't pull any funny faces. That morning, Sister Juliette had helped her get dressed in her new clothes. She had put her in a red shift dress with a dark blue long-sleeve cotton jersey underneath. Draped over the other armchair were a brown coat and a school satchel, ready to take with her.

The moment came when she had to go to the airport. Sister Valentina and Sister Juliette would go with her. The other nuns stood on the steps at the entrance, under the porch, to watch Sita make her way down the dirt track through the garden, to the iron gates and then leave forever. It was as if she were going on a trip to the hotel kitchens and would be back in a few hours; but they knew she would not. One of the guards carried her suitcase to Layam's car which was waiting in front of the gate and the two men tied it to the roof rack. The boot of the car was filled with the clean pots and pans to be returned to the hotels. As the boot wasn't fully closed, they tied it shut with a rope as well. Sita and the two nuns got in the back of the taxi and it pulled away from the centre of the Missionaries of Mary. Sita did not say anything for the whole journey, just watching out of the window. She knew that very soon she would be leaving everything she knew behind.

The airport was a huge, charmless place; there were people everywhere – whole families going to say goodbye to or greet someone. The fluorescent strip lighting in the ceiling didn't emit much light. Sita held Sister Valentina's hand while Sister Juliette carried her coat and satchel. They made their way to the Air India desk, followed by Layam carrying her suitcase. When they arrived the queue was short. Sister Valentina didn't want to make herself more stressed than she already was and had ensured that they arrived early. Layam left the suitcase and said goodbye to Sita:

'Have a safe trip, little one! I'd better go and park the car up properly. I'll be waiting outside, ladies.'

When it was their turn, they were greeted by an air hostess dressed in the company uniform *sari*. She smiled when she saw Sita's passport and the ticket to London with a connecting flight to Barcelona.

'And where's the passenger who'll be travelling?'

Little Sita was hidden behind the high desk and the stewardess had to stand up in order to see her.

'Ah! Well we'll put you by the window so that you can see the view, okay?'

Her suitcase, with a large label stuck to it, disappeared on the conveyor belt. Sister Valentina's heart was pounding faster than ever. Sita watched the suitcase go with a grin, after the stewardess had told her that the belt took it to the aeroplane where it would be loaded on the plane along with the other passengers' luggage.

'Don't worry, Madam, the girl will be accompanied by one

of my colleagues at all times.' Sister Valentina wanted to make sure that everything was under control and kept asking the stewardess questions. The queue of passengers behind her had grown considerably. 'Yes, when she arrives in London she will be accompanied to passport control and then to the boarding gate for the Barcelona flight. We will also take care of her suitcase, which has to be picked up in London and checked in again at the Iberia desk for the flight to Barcelona.'

With all of her seemingly complicated questions answered, there was still quite a while to wait before boarding. The two women and Sita sat in the waiting room. It was very full and it wasn't easy to find three empty seats.

'Sita, you have to promise me that you'll send drawings and write to me when you learn how to. Your new parents have got my address, okay?'

'Yes, Sister Valentina.'

Around them entire families sat eating and drinking; a few children ran around chasing each other; a *Sikh* in a maroon turban who had taken his shoes off lay across four seats, snoring; and a group of businessmen in ties were having an animated discussion. Well before the agreed time, they went once again to the Air India desk, where they had arranged to meet the stewardess who would accompany Sita to the plane. It wasn't usual for a child so young to be travelling on her own to Europe and Sita was definitely the talk of the airline staff that day. They headed for the glass doors that separated the waiting rooms from the zone exclusively for passengers, passport control and the boarding gates. Sister Valentina and Sister Juliette couldn't go beyond that point. They hugged Sita like no nun had ever hugged her before and showered her with kisses.

'*Ay, mi niña, ¡Que Dios te bendiga!*'

Sita couldn't understand a word they were saying in their funny Dominican Spanish. Then a stewardess took her right hand and Sita took hold of her coat and bag from Sister Juliette. They went through the glass doors and the two nuns stood where they were, waving goodbye frantically in case the girl turned round one last time. But she didn't. Holding the stewardess's hand tightly, Sita felt a strange fluttering feeling inside her. She was so excited that she didn't feel scared or sad. She just looked toward the end of the walkway that would take her to Barcelona; that walkway marked her path and she didn't even think about turning back. At the age of seven, Sita knew that she was beginning a brand new life.

During the flight to London, Sita couldn't sit still in her turquoise Air India seat. She drew scribbles in a notebook with three coloured pencils given to her by the stewardess; she ate everything they put in front of her and spilled a glass of orange juice between her seat and the trousers of the man who was resignedly sitting next to her; she walked up and down the plane, with a stewardess or on her own; she visited the pilot in the cockpit ... Worn out, she slept for the entire flight from London to Barcelona. When they woke her up just before landing, she looked out of the window and saw the vastness of the ocean as she had never seen it before. Everything she saw out of the window was an intense blue, dotted with a few cargo ships and other much smaller boats; she could make out some white sails. The beaming rays of bright sunlight warmed her face. It was a nice feeling. She leaned her forehead on the window and gazed out, mesmerized at what she saw. The plane turned and she could then see a very long, empty beach of white sand. The horizon was filled with mountains; a row of gentle curves on the landscape. She hadn't had a chance to imagine what Barcelona would actually be like, but it would certainly never be quite as luminous as that first image she saw of it.

ADDIS ABABA, 1978

Solomon went over the house one more time, wandering through every room as if he didn't want to forget an inch of it. His luggage had been ready since the night before, waiting in front of the door. Aster had bought him a small suitcase to pack his clothes, soap, hair oil and a few notebooks so he could do drawings during the journey. They didn't know what he would need and it had been difficult to pack. Between the folded clothes, Solomon had slipped in a branch of eucalyptus leaves and a piece of sandalwood that he had collected from near the church. He had also packed the bison bone and the book that Peter Howard had given him as a present. He sat on the windowsill. He had grown a lot – he was now twelve years old – but he still fitted on the sill if he tucked his legs in tight. He looked at every detail of the green painted Entoto Mariam church, committing it to memory. In the distance, beyond the eucalyptus trees, he could see the city through the morning fog. He saw a boy go past with a herd of goats and three cows. He thought of his friend Biniam. One day he had disappeared and Solomon had never seen him again. That was before his father had died in Somalia. Why did he have to go to the front to work as a cook for the soldiers? Why hadn't he carried on looking for other work in the city's hotels instead of agreeing to join the war against Somalia? The Somali military forces were well-armed thanks to the help of Arab countries and had managed to get close to the cities of Harar and Dire Dawa. His father died in an ambush, just before the Cuban soldiers arrived to join the Ethiopian forces and finally succeeded in getting the Somali army to withdraw. Aster and Solomon were together when they received the news. They couldn't believe it. They sent a telegram to Maskarem in London. Their father's body never made it back to Addis Ababa. They were lucky to even receive notice of his death. Most often, people just presumed that the men who had gone to war had died, when their families stopped receiving news or letters via the lorry drivers who took provisions to the army.

Aster had finished her secondary school studies and felt she had fulfilled her father's wishes. Now she had no choice but to work. Fortunately she had found work in the library of the History Faculty. It had been hard for the two of them to get used to living alone in the house at Entoto, but they got through it and moved on. Solomon stopped for a second in front of the picture of his mother and looked at her face one last time, at the tattoo on her forehead; the strength she emanated. His mother would always be with him.

They had heard about it on the radio one afternoon: the Cuban government was showing support for the Ethiopians by offering scholarships to the youngest students to study in Cuba. Mengistu's government decided that these scholarships should be for children whose parents had died fighting for the country's revolution. Aster hurried to find out about it the next morning and put in an application for Solomon to go to Cuba to study.

'Cuba doesn't sound like the name of a country ... ' said Solomon, looking at the atlas that Aster had brought home from the library. It lay open on the table.

'Well I think it's a good name for a country. And particularly for an island where it's never cold!'

Solomon carried on studying the map, tracing with his finger the blue area that separated the African continents from the islands of the Caribbean.

When they published the names of those who had been awarded the scholarship, Solomon Teferra was on the list. Before going to Cuba, all the boys and girls who had been chosen, – orphans whose parents had died in combat – had to travel twenty miles from Addis Ababa to Tatek, to train and prepare. There was a former military training camp there. The previous year, thousands of soldiers had set off from that camp to go and fight the Somalis in the Ogaden region.

A neighbour in Entoto offered to go with Solomon and Aster to Jan Meda, a large open space in the Sidist Kilo neighbourhood, from where the children would travel by military coaches to Tatek. Then from there – they didn't know exactly when – they would travel to the port of Assab where they would set sail for Cuba. They put the luggage in the boot of the car and headed out on the windy, pothole-ridden main road toward the city.

'All that boasting about the train line between Addis Ababa and Djibouti and now it's closed! This war with Somalia has brought us nothing but bad luck,' grumbled the neighbour as he drove, talking to himself more than anyone. 'And now, the army in all its wisdom has decided that the best thing to do is send thousands of children by coach across Eritrean territory … whatever next!'

The camp at Jan Meda – where they say that the first plane landed in Ethiopia – was filled with rows of coaches and army trucks parked up next to each other.

There were a lot more buses than Solomon had ever seen in the bus station. There was still a long time to wait until all the vehicles started their engines but Aster and Solomon were anxious and had wanted to get there in plenty of time. The hawkers quickly flocked to the area. One man was selling sugarcane and it was one of Solomon's favourites, so Aster bought him a large piece. The two of them sat side by side on the suitcase, on the ground. Solomon peeled the cane with his teeth, spitting out the bits he ripped off and then chewing and sucking the soft pulp. His stomach was in knots and he couldn't even begin to imagine what his sister was feeling. She would be the one left alone in the house. Completely alone.

'I hope that you find a good husband soon. Please look for one, Aster, don't spend too much time on your own. I feel so bad about leaving you ... '

'Don't you worry,' smiled Aster. 'Everything will be fine.'

More and more children were gradually arriving; disorientated-looking children and teenagers with their mothers and relatives. The crowd gradually grew until it reached several hundred. More and more children with suitcases, more and more relatives accompanying them; until there were over a thousand people waiting. A man in military uniform holding a megaphone climbed on top of a pile of tyres and started giving instructions. The boys and girls began getting on to the vehicles as quickly as possible when their names were called. They handed over their suitcases before they got on. The soldier asked the families to start saying goodbye, in order to speed up the operation. Within minutes, all around there were scenes of mothers hugging their children and crying. Aster and Solomon didn't move from where they were, holding hands in the midst of that enormous farewell. Tears were rolling down Aster's face but she said nothing. She couldn't get the words out. Some girls not much younger than her were also going to Cuba. But Aster was taking on the role of mother without being one. She could have been a daughter but she was no longer one. The youngest children were around eight years old; the oldest, seventeen or eighteen.

'Solomon Teferra!'

Aster clutched him tightly to her, so tightly that Solomon thought she would smother him. She said something but he couldn't really hear it because her arms were muffling his ears.

'Go on, off you go!'

These were the last words he heard before he headed for the coach, clutching his suitcase. Once he had given his suitcase to the men who were placing the luggage on the coach roof rack by clambering up and down a rusty iron ladder, he turned round for a moment to look at Aster. His sister waved goodbye, crying. He said goodbye and boarded the coach.

The vehicles started their engines and left the station one after the other in convoy, beeping their horns among a multitude of mothers, sisters, brothers and relatives who watched as the youngest members of their family set off for a place that they found impossible to imagine. Sitting next to the window, surrounded by children who had now fallen strangely silent, Solomon waved goodbye once more to Aster. Both of them forced a smile.

'You! Don't you know that men don't cry?' shouted a soldier from the middle of the aisle. The shout was aimed at a boy who couldn't contain himself any longer and had broken down sobbing when his family were out of sight.

In the end there were one thousand two hundred students at Tatek. They spent two whole months there; two very strange months in a fenced off enclosure containing some houses with walls and roofs made from cement and corrugated iron. They were military barracks. In the makeshift dormitories, they had made very long rows of mattress bases from thin eucalyptus trunks, end to end, and on top of these they had placed mattresses side by side.

It was in Tatek that the militias had formed and thousands of men had been trained to go to war with Somalia. His father had gone off to war from there. Now in the encampment there were just children. All of the men were at war or had died.

They were woken at five in the morning, when it was still dark, and were made to run as if they were little soldiers. The absurdity continued as they were taught to march to the rhythm of military marches, boys and girls alike. The bizarre training left them practically no time for anything else, apart from a small amount of leisure time and meals consisting of *injera* and *shiro wat*, tea with sugar and *dabo*, a type of thick white bread. They always ate the same thing. There was no chicken, or lamb, or eggs, or even lentils … Only once did they kill some lambs that were grazing in the compound and they ate *injera* with a hearty meat stew. They had very few hours of lessons.

The day before they set off for the port of Assab they were given the uniform that they would have to wear for the long journey. The boys wore blue shorts and the girls wore skirts in the same colour. There were red jumpers and white socks, for both the boys and the girls. They were made to unpack their suitcases and leave them on the bed, then put all their things in small red plastic suitcases, all identical, which formed part of the uniform. Twelve teachers arrived to accompany them to Cuba and give them lessons in Amharic, as well as the geography and history of Ethiopia. An Ethiopian colonel would also be accompanying them as the head of the expedition. Thirteen Ethiopian men in charge of one thousand two hundred boys and girls.

They were woken up earlier than usual. It was still the pitch black of night and it was cold outside. Soldiers were unloading lorries that had brought food for the journey to Assab. Cooked chicken, *dabo*, oranges and a load of *kolo*, corn, peanuts and roasted chickpeas. There wasn't much else.

Still half asleep and carrying their small red plastic suitcases, the children trooped across the fields in front of the fenced off enclosure and silently made their way to where more than twenty coaches were waiting to take them toward the coast of Eritrea on the Red Sea. The vehicles had their engines running, their headlamps casting a ghostly light on the long line of children and teenagers boarding the coaches, following the instructions that the soldiers bellowed at them through megaphones.

'Come on, get a move on! There's room for sixty people on each coach, everyone has a seat!'

Solomon managed to get a seat next to the window. Next to him sat a dark-skinned older boy. The two of them sat clutching their red suitcases on their laps, in silence. Nobody spoke. A soldier got onto the coach to check that there were no empty seats left.

'No-one is to get off the coach unless we tell you to, got it? Even if the coach stops. When you get off, you must go straight to the food trucks and water cistern trucks and form a queue. The water is for drinking only; there will be no water to wash your faces.'

A few moments later, the coaches pulled away and started leaving the Tatek military enclosure. Although it was still very dark, Solomon could see that there were armed military jeeps at the head of the convoy. In Eritrea there were active armed guerrilla forces, so they needed to be escorted.

Gradually everyone fell asleep. Solomon slept with his head leaning on the window, bumping against it with every pothole they clattered over. They had been told that the journey would take at least three days and that they would sleep for those three nights on the coach.

The sun had been out for several hours. They had left Addis Ababa, Nazareth, Awash and Mile behind them.

'This highway goes to Kombolcha … ' said the boy next to him in a very small voice, pointing out a road that turned off to the left that they were passing by.

'How do you know?'

'It goes to Kombolcha. I know. That's where I'm from.'

Every one of the passengers on board those coaches had a hidden history behind the name of a city or a town that the others didn't know.

They talked very little and there was no music, not that they felt much like singing. So they passed the hours and miles watching the increasingly arid landscape out of the window. Sometimes the coaches stopped to fill up on fuel using hose-pipes from the cistern trucks. The children used these stops as a chance to hop off and do their business behind some bushes or rocks. The convoy driving all these boys and girls was very long. The highway was in a terrible state; an earthy, stony road. The vehicles were overloaded and every few miles they had to stop for some incident or other. Most often it was due to a flat tyre. The jeeps then moved forward to reach the coaches in front of them and make them stop. And so the hours passed beneath the beating sun. It was sweltering, and there were masses of flies.

Finally they stopped to eat and sleep. After forming long queues in front of the trucks to receive a bit of chicken, *dabo* and an orange; then in front of the cistern trucks so that they could drink a small amount of water, the children ate their food sitting on the dusty ground. Then they got back on the coaches to spend the night. The soldiers and drivers lit fires around the parked coaches and trucks. They chewed *chat* and drank *tella*, getting drunk and laughing. There were a lot of men sitting around fires, giving the makeshift camp a tribal feel in the midst of the darkness.

On Solomon's coach three girls were crying; the youngest ones. One had started and it had spread to the others. A little while ago they had all heard a soldier shouting at a boy on the coach parked next to theirs who had asked if he could get off.

'You piss and shit when it's your turn, not whenever you feel like it! Go, on then! But this is the last time!'

Two armed soldiers had taken him a little way beyond the fire. They were armed in case of starving hyenas that might attack any possible prey.

The driver of his coach hadn't got off to drink *tella* and chew *chat* like the rest of them. He had put his seat back and gone to sleep like his passengers. His name was Derriba and he was stocky, dark-skinned and with an intense look. He was of the *Oromo* people from Ghimbi, in the western province of Wollega. Like the rest of the drivers in that convoy, he had been made to do the journey to Assab in return for two sacks of *teff* flour and dried pulses for his family. The military government gave orders and people had to obey. The three little girls were still crying and now a few more had joined in. Wailing and sobbing could be heard all around the coach but it was hard to work out who was crying because it was so dark. Derriba got up and lit the fuse of an oil lantern. The sound of the match and the unexpected flickering light silenced the children at once.

'Now now, what's all this?' he asked loudly, lifting the lantern in the direction of the aisle between the seats. Nearly all of them shut their eyes at once, pretending to be asleep. But one of the girls went on crying; she was even more worked up now.

'What's the matter?'

'Please don't hit me!'

'Why would I hit you if you haven't done anything wrong?'

He went over to the girl and stroked her hair, which was plaited into neat little rows of braids.

'Who did your hair so nicely?'

'My mother … ' said the girl, starting to cry inconsolably once again.

'Come here, little one, have a good cry.' Derriba hugged her as if he were embracing his own daughter, who was also around five years old.

He hung the lantern in the middle of the coach, from a hook on the roof. It didn't shed much light but it warded off the darkness slightly. Then he began to tell them stories from his homeland; how he learned to ride a horse from a very young age, like a good *Oromo;* of the riding tournaments that were held in his village, with spears and shields to protect themselves, until, finally, one by one, the children all drifted off to sleep.

Being used to views of eucalyptus forests and the roads winding up and down the hills north of Addis Ababa, Solomon couldn't get used to that monotonous landscape. It was so flat and colourless. They passed through villages and saw very few people. A man walking along the highway, his donkey laden with firewood, was taken aback at seeing the never-ending procession of coaches, lorries and military jeeps with so many children. He waved to them as they went past. The children ate very little and were thirsty. They passed a refugee camp. There were army trucks there. Vultures circled over the desert land-scape, tracing indescribable shapes in the cloudless, blue sky. A group of people were queuing in front of a truck to fill up buckets of water. Every time they stopped, Derriba brushed his shoes and clothes off to get rid of the dust. He brushed off all the seats in the coach too and swept the aisle with a straw broom.

The last part of the journey was the hardest. A desert of sand and rocks that seemed endless. They were all exhausted. The unpredictable potholes seemed to join up and they were contin-ually being thrown about in their seats however much Derriba tried to swerve to avoid the rocks in the middle of the road, or the most obvious holes. Between Mile and Assab it was prac-tically all desert. From time to time a few acacia trees could be seen in the distance, casting their meagre shadows. The few plants they saw must have lived off air alone. It was just rocks and more rocks, dry earth; a land of bandits and Eritrean sepa-ratists. A land of camels. Some wandered alone, in the middle of the desert landscape. They saw caravans of just one or two cam-els, each one ridden by a man. And much longer caravans of up to ten camels, tied with ropes, carrying loads and moving along slowly, one behind the other, with a pair of men walking in front of them or riding the leading camel. Derriba told the children that he had done this journey several times. He had also been to Djibouti. They had attacked him when he least expected it. Armed men stood in the middle of the dry earth road and took everything they wanted from him: money, his load, the spare wheels ... 'You are hyenas, but we won't kill you,' they had told him and his companion. But now, with so many armed soldiers in the convoy, they wouldn't dare.

The stops were constant. The overloading and the high tem-peratures caused the tyres to puncture, first on one vehicle, then on another. Everyone had broken out in blisters on their faces and hands from the heat, sweat and dirt.

'It's mine! That orange is mine!' shouted a boy, violently kicking another boy.

'Liar! It's mine! You stole it!' the other defended himself angrily.

'Enough!' shouted a soldier, pulling them apart and giving each one a couple of slaps. 'Now the orange is mine!'

All of the scuffles started the same way. Anyone involved in them would always end up being hit by one of the soldiers. Solomon wolfed down all his food, just to be on the safe side.

Derriba pulled a bag out of his travel case and started sharing out a handful of *kolo* to each child, working his way along from the first row of seats to the back row.

'Eat it a little at a time; chew it well. Then I'll give you some water, I've got some for everyone. It will help you forget your hunger a bit. My wife makes really good *kolo*, you'll see.'

The driver had become the guardian of the boys and girls on his coach. He drove all the hours he had to and looked after the engine and the operation of the coach as if it were his own vehicle. Whenever they stopped he went out of his way to make sure that the littlest of the sixty passengers in his care would arrive in the best possible state to the port of Assab. He kept his conversations with the other drivers to a minimum; he kept himself to himself.

'I had a very hard childhood too,' Derriba told them on the last night of the journey, as they settled down to sleep, listening to his stories. 'My father died when I was six years old and from then on I had to help my mother and sister to get by. My family lived in the countryside. At fourteen, I left the village to work in

Addis Ababa as a truck driver's mate. I only spoke *Oromo* and in the beginning, I didn't understand a word of Amharic! I found it really hard to learn. By the age of eighteen I was driving trucks with trailers from one side of Ethiopia to the other.'

'And how old are you now?' came a boy's voice from the darkness of the coach, dimly lit by the lantern hanging from the ceiling.

'Twenty-nine.'

'And are you married?' a girl asked him.

'Yes I am married to Birhani…we have two daughters. My mother found me a good wife and arranged our marriage with her family, who were from our village. Birhani was eleven and I was sixteen. She had very light skin and I liked her straight away. For the first three years we were married, we didn't see each other much because I was working and she stayed in the village, at my mother's house. Then she came with me to the city.'

'And did she like you?' came the sleepy voice of a teenager.

'Of course! From the first moment she saw me! For her, I was a hero: I was going to take her away to the city. Our village is very poor and life in the countryside is very hard, both for men and women.'

The passengers fell asleep listening to Derriba's story. The lantern would stay hanging in the middle of the coach all night and would gradually putter out, before the convoy set off once again at dawn.

They finally reached the port of Assab on the west coast of the Red Sea after driving down an important-looking street, even though it wasn't tarmacked, with low houses standing side by side and painted blue and white with corrugated iron roofs. The coaches parked up next to each other on an esplanade full of cranes for loading and unloading coffee, salt and all the other products that Ethiopia exported by sea. The military jeeps also parked in the same place and the soldiers jumped down from them, armed and at the ready. Although who would attack a defenceless group of orphan children, and why? They heard the amplified voice of the muezzin calling out from a nearby mosque. *Alahu Akbar!* Once again, two soldiers with loud voices climbed up onto the highest point they could find, in this case an iron container, and started barking out orders. The children would get off the coaches when they were told, take their suitcases and in pairs would file down toward the boat that was waiting for them in the port. Anyone who didn't follow the instructions to the letter would be punished.

'Bye, little ones! Have a good journey and good luck!' Derriba said to them before he got off the coach. He stood at the bottom of the steps and shook their hands one by one. He was making an effort to hold back his tears.

The ship, the *Africa–Cuba*, was enormous. Solomon could never have imagined what it might look like because he had never been to a port. He had also never seen a boat before in his life. It was white with a huge black chimney in the middle that billowed out smoke. In Tatek they had told them that the boat was almost sixty metres in length, but he couldn't picture what those metres meant. Now he saw that they meant it was enormous. How could something that big and heavy not sink? The long line of children in uniform going up the gangplank two by two was an unusual sight, and all of the port workers and other passersby, or those with nothing better to do, gradually formed an impromptu farewell committee for them. There were not enough bunks for all the passengers on board. The Cuban sailors and the Ethiopian soldiers started putting mattresses in the gangways until there wasn't an inch of free space.

'The older ones must sleep on the mattresses in the gangways! Those over fourteen years old, sit on the mattresses that we're putting down and don't move until we tell you to! The younger ones will sleep in pairs in the cabin bunks, understand?'

One soldier was scurrying about the labyrinthine ship shouting orders at people. The allocation of cabins, bunks and mattresses was a complicated business. The boys and girls in uniform, red suitcases in hand, followed orders as best they could. They were disorientated and exhausted, being ordered this way and that. Those that had settled in the cabins were told to put their suitcases above one of the beds of the two bunks. Solomon was allocated the top bunk next to a small round window. The glass was very thick and pretty grimy, but through this slightly cloudy porthole he could at least see the docks and watch the men scurrying around carrying packages and loading them on board the ship.

'No-one is to move from their allocated place!' ordered a firm voice over the loud-speakers.

Solomon passed the time watching intently out of the window at what was going on outside.

'Let me see too! The window's not just yours!' said one of the other three boys sharing the cabin with him. His name was Siyoum. Solomon had never seen him before.

'Me too!' said another boy, Werret, who wasn't from Derriba's coach either.

Solomon moved away from the window to let them look out. The cabin's fourth member, whose name was Habtamu, lay on his bed coughing, his face turned towards the wall. Some of the twelve hundred children had arrived at the port of Assab in a poorly condition and no-one was looking after them.

Over the ship's loudspeakers the children were called out on deck to line up as if they were soldiers. They were made to sing the hymn to the flag, as the Ethiopian flag was hoisted up next to the Cuban one. A deafening siren sounded out and Solomon realized that his heart was pounding in his ribcage. The ship started to move off and the chimney belched out thick, black smoke. Despite their tiredness after the journey from Tatek, the children waved to the strangers who had gathered in the port. As they set sail, the activity in the port began to focus on another boat that had just arrived and which they were beginning to unload. A crane was setting down a huge container, and, on the docks, men carrying all kinds of packages struggled to push their way through the carts and the throngs of people.

They were leaving Africa, leaving the world they knew behind and going far away. As much as Solomon had tried to memorize the atlas, he couldn't get his head around the distance that separated the port of Assab from the port of Havana. The coast of Eritrea was fading into the distance as the *Africa–Cuba* set sail for the north of the Red Sea, toward the Suez canal. They passed by the Assab oil refinery. The workers waved to them merrily.

'The sea is like Lake Tana; I thought it would be different,' said Siyoum, one of his cabin mates, holding onto the deck railing.

'Have you seen it?'

'Have I seen Tana? I lived there!'

'Did you go on a boat?'

'Practically every day! My father built boats from papyrus reeds and we would go from the mainland to the islands to sell corn and other things that the monks and their families asked us to get for them. Before my father went off to war, I used to go fishing with him.'

As they went further and further away from the coast, the expanse of blue seemed even more incomprehensible to Solomon. The ship didn't move jerkily, like a coach, but it moved a lot. They were slow, constant movements that made you feel sick.

The first days seemed very long. On deck, the boys and girls sat on the floor and cried inconsolably. Many of them hadn't shed a single tear since they had said goodbye to their families to go to Tatek, but now the sensation of being on that imposing ship with its smoking chimney, a kind of floating building that was moving away from solid ground toward a totally unknown world, finally overcame them. Now there was no-one shouting at them and telling them that men don't cry. It seemed as if, suddenly, all of the adults had disappeared and left them alone, adrift in the middle of the water. The ship was packed to the rafters with children; no corner had been left empty. They were afraid. The older children consoled the younger ones. Some of the teenage girls took on the role of mother, singing songs and telling the most cheerful stories they could. But Ethiopia's legends and stories were not very cheerful unless they were modified a bit. After eating, vomiting was the most frequent activity; it couldn't be avoided. They went down to the toilets or vomited over the side of the boat as they gripped the iron railing. The skin on their faces was dried out from the sea salt.

'Have you heard? They've stopped the engines again!' a boy shouted.

Solomon was sitting with his back against a wall up on deck.

He felt sick. He was copying a bird from the book of flora and fauna that Peter Howard had given him, into one of the three notebooks that Aster had bought for him. It was true. The vibration he could feel up his back had disappeared for the second time that day. The engines had stopped. Sailors hurried from one side of the boat to the other, anxious and sweating. They had stopped in the middle of the Red Sea, surrounded by water. The engines didn't start again until well after it was dark and everyone had gone inside to eat. Something was happening because the *Africa–Cuba* changed direction. Nobody said anything and life aboard carried on as usual.

'We're in a port!' exclaimed Solomon when he woke up and looked out of the window.

'Let me have a look!'

'Me too!'

Solomon, Siyoum and Werret kneeled on the bed, their foreheads resting against the glass of the porthole. It was the port of Al Hudaydah, in Yemen. They heard the shouts of the fishermen returning from the inland sea and the muezzins' call to prayer from the minarets of the mosques. At breakfast time a teacher told them that the engine had a fault that needed to be fixed.

'We'll be anchored here for at least five days and we won't be getting off the ship. You can amuse yourselves by watching what's going on in the port from the deck. Meals will be at the same time.'

The sky was grey and the heat intense. On both sides of the ship there was a multitude of wooden boats painted white with brightly coloured stripes, their prows much higher than their sterns. When a boat arrived with a catch, a group of men with straight black hair would draw near and the fishermen would shout out to them, selling the goods before they unloaded them. Both on land and on the boats, there were children and teenagers working, helping the adults. They were just like the children on board the *Africa–Cuba*.

'Have you seen what they're wearing? The men are wearing long skirts!' Solomon said to Siyoum.

'Could you draw those boats? When I get home I want to show my older brother!'

'You've got a brother? Why didn't he come?'

'He's a lot older, he's twenty-three. But he is ill. He has deformed legs; he can't walk very well. He always has to sit down.'

'What does he do?'

'He weaves *netelas* and other cotton fabrics. He is always sitting at the loom, he spends hours doing it … He's really good at it.'

'Alright. I'll do some drawings of the boats.'

Solomon watched two men who must have been very old, their skin wrinkled and darkened by the sun, each wearing a white turban on their head, a checked cotton *sarong* rolled down at the waist and a white shirt. They were sitting barefoot on a mat made from plaited palm leaves, chatting casually among the nets, plastic containers and wooden boxes. Younger men were cleaning fish and throwing the remains back into the water, or were fishing off boats dotted around the port. The port had a different smell from the port of Assab. In Al Hudaydah it stank of fish, an odour that was very foreign to Solomon and his travel companions.

One day a boat came in with a shark in it, covered in blood and still half alive, thrashing about in its death throes. It took six men to unload it from the boat to the dock where they killed it, then began selling it off right there and then before they even had time to take it to the fish market. The enthralled children watched it all from the deck of the *Africa–Cuba*.

Solomon drew everything he saw from up on deck: the fishermen's boats, the green minarets and the carts pulled by mules, carrying fish … and above all, the camels. They were all over the port. Sitting gracefully waiting for cargo to be loaded up on their backs, carrying bags and walking in procession; he never grew tired of watching them. He also drew the chimney of the *Africa–Cuba* from various different angles and portraits of the boys and girls sitting round him … He had got over his first impressions of this enormous, leaden object floating in the water. He had grown accustomed to the booming sound of the deafening *foghorn*, the noise of the engine, the cries of the gulls and seabirds that circled overhead, the smell of oil and the thick, black smoke that enveloped them whenever the wind changed direction, like the fog hanging over the Entoto hills.

With the engine repaired they set sail once more for the north and finally reached the Suez Canal. On either side of the canal, which was a hundred and twenty miles long, the desert stretched out as far as the eye could see, in all imaginable tones of ochre. The canal was a strip of water – fifty metres across – that sliced through the yellow sand and the intense blue of the cloudless sky. Occasionally they would pass by small coastal villages where they saw women dressed in black from head to toe and children playing football, barefoot on the white sand that reached down to the waterline. In Port Saïd they stopped for a few hours to load fuel, drinking water and provisions. The cranes unloaded and loaded containers of all sizes onto the huge boats that had docked there, to save them from having to head back toward Africa. They entered the Mediterranean, a sea that did not have the various different blue tones of the Red Sea, or the coral islands that formed ring-shaped reefs surrounded by turquoise water that could be seen from afar.

'Look!' shouted a little girl with thin braids in her hair.

'There, there! Look at those big fish! Look at them jumping!'

'Those are dolphins! They're in my book!' said Solomon.

Hundreds of children leaned on the ship's rail and shouted and waved, exhilarated by the sight of those animals leaping playfully between the waves caused by the ship. Solomon went back to his spot to find that the notebook with his drawings, which he had left on the floor, had disappeared. All that remained were the pencil and rubber. Could it have blown away? If it was the wind then surely the pencil and rubber would have disappeared too. Somebody must have stolen it. Solomon started looking all around for it. Nobody had seen it. It was nowhere to be found.

'A boy took it … ' one girl finally told him, in a whisper.

'Who was it? Did you see him?'

'It was one of the big boys … '

'Well let's go and find him then!' cried Siyoum, determined.

'Really, there's no need … All they want is a fight, you know that!' replied Solomon. 'You've seen the way they're always looking for trouble. I can't take them on.'

'If you don't want to stand up to them, I will!'

'Are you crazy? They'll hurt you!'

'I don't give a damn! They've hurt me before. They've stolen my drawings of the boats in Al Hudaydah port!'

Siyoum recruited a group of boys who were slightly older than them but couldn't be more than fifteen years old. One of them knew where the older boys could be found. They liked to hang out at the stern of the ship; the furthest away they could be.

'Give us the notebook back!' shouted Siyoum defiantly, a scrawny little twelve-year-old squaring up to the older teenagers.

'Here come the *artistes*!'

'Give us the notebook back or it's war!'

'Oooh, I'm scared!'

Siyoum approached the boys and thumped one of them in the chest – the one who had spoken first.

'Give it back, it's not yours!'

'We'll do whatever we want, you bunch of monkeys!'

Suddenly, as if he was having some sort of fit, Siyoum flew at the boy who was nearly twice as tall and strong as he was and started punching, pulling his hair and kicking him. The rest of his gang also threw themselves at the older boy. The two gangs ended up fighting and shouting at each other with all their might.

'Pero *¡qué pasa aquí, carajo!*' shouted one of the Cuban sailors. '*¡Basta! ¡He dicho que basta!*' He waded into the brawl, throwing a few punches in the direction of the older ones to show them that they were not as tough as they thought.

Two more sailors had been alerted by the other children and ran over. So did one of the teachers. The four adults managed to stop the fighting. Some of the boys had bleeding lips and eyebrows, and were panting hard.

'From now on, all of you, the older ones, will have to wash down the deck. You will do it every morning. And then you will help in the kitchen, washing dishes and peeling potatoes or whatever we ask you to do! If a fight like this ever happens again, we will take measures. Do I make myself clear?'

Solomon retrieved his book and went with Siyoum to the infirmary so that they could dress his wounds. His lip was split and he had been punched in the eye; it was starting to bruise.

'Thank you … I did say there was no need … '

'I wanted my drawings back! And we won, you saw it!'

They crossed the Strait of Gibraltar and travelled many more miles until they finally reached the port of Santa Cruz de Tenerife. But they were not allowed to disembark there either. This was the final stop before they crossed the Atlantic. The endless days went on and on. Sometimes they were called up on deck to sing hymns or do some exercise, but without any routine or logic. The only things that were routine were their meals in the large dining room with wide tables and wooden benches on either side. These were announced by the sound of a siren. Everyone had dry, chapped lips and hair swarming with lice. Some lice were so big they could be seen with the naked eye, hopping between the boys' curls and the girls' braids.

'Do you think that we will never eat *injera* again, until we return to Ethiopia?' Solomon asked Siyoum. 'At home, *injera* was all I ate!'

'Me too!' said Siyoum.

'The food is horrible here,' said a boy sitting at another table.

'And why do they make us eat with these strange tools? I don't understand why they won't let us eat with our fingers, like we've always done!'

'Because this food is always hot and there's no bread or anything and because the pieces of meat are too big … '

'I want to go back,' said Habtamu, the quiet boy who also slept in their cabin and who, as always, hadn't eaten anything. His plate of food remained untouched.

'But we haven't even got there yet!' Solomon replied.

They passed a cargo ship. The two boats sounded their foghorns in greeting and some of the boys and girls ran up on deck to wave at the sailors, who looked surprised to see such a large number of African children, all dressed identically, in the middle of the Atlantic Ocean. The waves were strong and the ship swayed more than in the other seas they had left behind. In the Atlantic they saw very few dolphins; instead they saw sharks' fins following in their wake, particularly in the evenings when the cooks threw the kitchen waste overboard.

'Are you alright, kid?' asked one of the sailors.

Solomon was sitting on the floor in a corner of the deck, leaning against a wall, hugging his knees and looking out to sea. He had heard the question but he didn't know how to answer it and he didn't have the energy to try. In fact, he didn't move at all. He stayed still, looking at the sea and feeling the cool breeze on his face. The sailor crouched down and carried on talking to him until Solomon turned to look at him. He was a tall, well-built man, with very dark skin. He looked African but he was talking in Spanish.

'I've been sick a lot, I feel very sick ... ' said Solomon in Amharic.

'I don't know what you're saying but I can imagine. You're all very dehydrated. They must be mad to make you do this journey in such a state!'

The sailor gave him his hand and practically lifted him off the floor as if he was pulling up an onion from the soil. He was a well-built man with strong arms. Solomon let himself be led down a gangway to the ship's kitchens; he had never been in there before.

'What? Another one? Are you planning to save them all one

by one? You're not paid to do that … And we won't reach Cuba for days yet!' shouted one of the cooks, stirring an enormous pot, out of which wafted a smell that Solomon didn't like at all. The smell of beans, of stews…

'Let the guy from the infirmary look after him, that's what he's there for! So much for his white coat … We end up doing it all ourselves!'

'Leave me alone!' said the sailor, preparing a glass of water with sugar and something else that Solomon couldn't see. 'Here, sit down and drink this.'

Solomon sat on a wooden bench in a corner of the kitchen and the sailor sat next to him, watching him drink the concoction, which tasted bitter despite the sugar.

'You'll feel better right away, you'll see … Do you understand me?'

Solomon nodded.

'They've gone mad! They think that because they're Africans they can make them travel any way they want, like my ancestors when they left the coasts of Ghana to be sold as slaves!'

'What are you talking about, Oswaldo?' shouted another dark-skinned, stout cook. 'Our ancestors would've loved to travel like these children. I can assure you, they didn't get fed like they do or get to sleep in bunks with white sheets, even though I admit a lot of them are sleeping on the floor of the gangways!'

'This ship has a capacity of eight hundred and twenty-people … Do you know how many are on board?'

'I don't care! All I know is that there are a lot of sick children, and the guy in the white coat hasn't stopped for days; he has barely slept, or haven't you noticed?'

'Now you're defending the doc! Our ancestors were sick too

when they travelled! That's what I'm moaning about! How many died on the way from malaria and yellow fever, eh? How many?'

'Go to hell!'

Solomon was gradually beginning to feel better and was trying to follow the conversation which he couldn't fully understand, as they were talking in very rapid Spanish. When they spoke it sounded as if they were singing. Were the cooks Cuban or African? If the ship was called the *Africa–Cuba* and almost all of the crew were African, perhaps Cuba would be like Africa?

From that day onwards, whenever Solomon felt seasick he would go to the kitchen to ask Oswaldo for medicine. And if he saw that one of his friends vomiting more than usual he also took them to the kitchen, or told Oswaldo so that he could go and fetch them. Sometimes, even though he hadn't vomited, Solomon and a few other children went to the kitchen, sat on the wooden bench and listened to the cooks' stories. They talked non-stop. Gradually the children started to understand a bit better but it was hard for them to talk in a new language. The Amharic teacher – who was always reading – had also discovered the kitchen and went there to pass the time and practice his Spanish, which he now spoke quite well. Solomon took his notebook with him and carried on drawing in biro. He sketched portraits of the sailors.

'This ship was built in 1957 at the Spanish Society for Naval Construction of Sestao, near Bilbao. In fact they built two identical ships at the same time – twin ships! This one was called the *Cabo San Roque* and its twin was called the *Cabo San Vicente* … For many years they sailed the Genoa-Buenos Aires route.'

Oswaldo offered a glass of rum to the teacher, who had asked about the history of the boat. The sailor seemed delighted to tell him everything he knew.

'Put some water in it, will you? It's a bit strong!' spluttered the teacher after taking his first swig.

Solomon listened as he sat on the wooden bench, drinking the sugar and water remedy that Oswaldo had made for him.

'Last January it was in the port of El Ferrol and a fire onboard nearly destroyed it. It was severely damaged but a few months later a Dutch company bought it and decided to tow it to Greece, where it was repaired in the port of El Pireo and they changed its name to the *Golden Moon.*'

'*Luna de oro, chico.* Do you speak English?' interrupted one of the cooks.

'In Greece, once it was repaired, it was sold to the Cuban government who incorporated it into the Mambisa Shipping Company of Havana, who contracted it to us.'

'And they changed its name again,' said the teacher.

'Precisely.'

'I don't understand why they change the names of ships,' grumbled a sailor who wore a gold hoop earring, 'A ship should die with the same name it was christened with!'

'They called it the *Africa–Cuba*; I'm sure you can work out why!' the other sailor went on.

Solomon didn't know why, and he looked to Oswaldo for an explanation.

'This ship took Cuban soldiers to Africa, to fight alongside countries who were allies of Fidel Castro's regime ... '

The hours seemed eternal. Solomon was used to walking and running a lot and now he spent most of the day sitting still. His legs hurt. He drew in a corner for long periods of time. He had already filled two notebooks; he only had one left. He had copied all the details of the ship and was bored of doing portraits. The landscape was always the same. Sea. An expanse of dark sea in a non-descript bluish blackish colour. Violent, choppy waters. He felt weak and tired, like everyone else. There had been no fights for days now; nobody even had the energy to talk. One of the Amharic teachers read thick books and looked out at the sea, always sitting in the same place up on deck. The other teachers had disappeared, sometimes days went by without seeing them, even at meal times. They were probably eating with the captain and crew. The ship was like a floating prison. Whenever he could, Solomon made his way to the kitchen to listen to the adventures of the sailors who had travelled from one side of the world to the other, from Madagascar to Brazil, from Cuba to Hong Kong. Stories of slave trafficking and pirates, of deadly storms, of nights when the ship was tossed about by the wind, giant waves crashing onto the deck and near shipwrecks. One of the sailors, rosy-cheeked with long, greasy hair tied back in a ponytail, sang all hours of the day and night; the others sometimes joined in with his songs.

When it got dark there was no sound except the splish-splashing of the water, and sometimes, a few sailors drunk on rum, singing in the moonlight.

'Silence on deck!' roared the captain when the sailors were being too rowdy.

The drunken sailors would quieten down and stagger to their bunks, lurching and bumping into everything in their path.

He was coughing continuously. Habtamu had been coughing every night since they set sail from Assab. He didn't speak very much and had been ill since they started the journey to Cuba. He said that his chest hurt and that he wasn't hungry. He was always sweating but he felt cold. But that night his cough was different;

he was struggling to breathe. He was choking. Solomon woke up to the dreadful noise of Habtamu gasping for breath and coughing and he couldn't get back to sleep. All of the cabins had a small security light that was always on. Solomon looked at his companion, lying facing him on the lower bunk opposite.

'Habtamu, are you alright?' he whispered.

The answer was yet more coughing. Habtamu sat up and Solomon got up to sit next to him. He didn't look at all well; he was emaciated and covered in sweat. Little beads of moisture glistened on his brown skin. He had another coughing fit and, when it seemed he was on the point of choking, he spat onto the bed sheet. Solomon saw that it was blood and suddenly realized that the entire pillow was covered in large, dark stains.

'Siyoum! Werret! Wake up!' shouted Solomon, scared. 'Hey, Siyoum! Can you hear me? Wake up!'

'What's wrong?' replied a sleepy voice from the bed above.

'Habtamu is really sick!'

'We know he's been ill for days now, Solomon! I'm sleepy!' said Siyoum.

'There's blood coming out of his mouth and he's choking! And it looks like he's got a bad fever; he's burning up!'

'Like everyone else who's sick.'

'We have to tell someone! Today he's really bad,' Solomon got up and turned on the light. Habtamu coughed and spat, mumbling incomprehensible words.

'Is it time to get up?' asked Werret, half asleep.

'Werret, Habtamu is really ill. We have to tell someone.'

The boy's coughing and shouting suddenly roused Siyoum and Werret from their bunks. Solomon propped Habtamu up with a pillow behind him, but Habtamu had another coughing fit and couldn't breathe. Solomon slapped him on the back a few times, and out came a trickle of thick, bloody spit.

'I'm going to get the doctor, or anyone! Slap him on the back if he starts choking!'

The ship's corridors were silent and dark. The security lights offered only a dim glow. Solomon could vaguely remember where the infirmary was but he wasn't sure how to get there. He turned down one corridor and went down a narrow stairway. It was the wrong way. He retraced his steps back to the door of the cabin and followed the corridor down the other way. He turned right, went down another stairway and did a few laps up and down before he found it. He knocked insistently on the door until a bearded man wearing long underpants and a vest opened the door, his face full of sleep.

'What's the matter, boy?' he said in Spanish.

'My cabin mate is very ill; he's coughing a lot and spitting blood. He's burning up!'

'Oh god, another one!' exclaimed the doctor. 'Hang on a minute, I'm coming!'

Solomon waited in the corridor while the doctor got dressed and grabbed his doctor's bag. At night, the sound of the boat moving through the water was different. It seemed as if every sail, every railing, every wooden plank on deck rustled and creaked, as if they were complaining about the wind howling through them. The ship shuddered.

'Come on!'

They hurried through the corridors without saying a word. Siyoum opened immediately when Solomon knocked on the door. Habtamu's head was thrust back, against the wall, his eyes half closed. The doctor rushed over to him, took his wrist in one hand and placed the other on his forehead. The blood stains on the sheet were visible.

'My God! How long has he been like this?'

'We don't know … We woke up when he heard him coughing and choking … '

The doctor opened his bag and prepared a syringe. Sitting on the next bunk, Solomon, Siyoum and Werret watched him.

Habtamu coughed and looked as if he was about to say something but he couldn't speak.

'Hush, don't try to speak,' said the doctor. 'Breathe deeply. I'm going to give you an injection to calm you down. Your chest must hurt a lot … Do you understand me?'

Habtamu looked at him with his eyes barely open and his head lolling to one side. As if he was very far away.

'You! Come here and help me,' the doctor said to Solomon. 'Take his arm. Like that. I have to inject him. Stretch it out, with the palm facing up.'

He wiped a cotton pad soaked in alcohol over his arm and jabbed the needle in. Then he gave him water to drink, supporting his head.

'Is he really sick?'

'I'm afraid so.'

Habtamu started coughing again violently, choking; sometimes it sounded like he had stopped breathing. The doctor turned away from him. The boy's cries were dreadful. He was suffocating.

'What's your name?'

'Solomon.'

'Right, you're going to help me take him to the infirmary. He can't stay here, he's very ill. You lot go back to bed. You have to sleep and rest or you'll get ill too! And make sure you eat everything they put on your plate, okay?'

The doctor was very grave. He hauled Habtamu effortlessly

on to his back; he couldn't have weighed much.

'Grab a towel and put it here on my shoulder. If he coughs on the way, wipe his mouth; make sure nothing drips onto the floor. Now you can open the door,' said the doctor, with Habtamu riding piggyback, his breathing laboured.

They silently made their way back to the infirmary. It was still the middle of the night and they didn't meet anyone on the way. The ship's engines could be heard clearly, along with the waves breaking against the hull and the wind whistling. When they got to the infirmary Solomon opened the door, following the instructions of the doctor, who immediately lay Habtamu down on one of the two beds at the back of a small room separated by a door. Next to the porthole, away from the consulting table and the medicine cabinet with all the instruments and medicine bottles, was the corner where the doctor slept. On the nights when he managed to get any sleep at all.

'Thanks, Solomon. I'll take it from here.'

When they got up the next morning, Habtamu's bed was empty. There were no sheets, no blood, no pillow; even his mattress was gone.

'Did you see who took it?'

No-one had heard anything, but someone had come in at dawn and taken everything away.

Solomon was sitting on one of the wooden benches, looking at the drawings in his book of American flora and fauna. He had now copied almost all of them. Just then, Oswaldo appeared.

'*Hola, chico!* I've been looking for you!'

Solomon just smiled. He understood a bit of Spanish, but he found it hard to say anything.

'The doctor wants to speak to you. He asked me to come and

find you. He's waiting in the infirmary … You're not feeling sea-sick any more, eh?'

Solomon shook his head. He was tired, the night had been a short one. When he knocked on the infirmary door, the doctor opened it straight away, greeted him warmly and asked him to sit down in a chair. He perched on a stool.

'Solomon, I have to tell you that Habtamu has died. He had very advanced tuberculosis; there was nothing I could do … '

It wasn't the first time, nor would it be the last, that Solomon had been told that someone close to him was dead. He sat there, unmoving, looking at the doctor.

'Where is he?' he asked.

'Here, in the same bed we left him in,' he replied, pointing to the door at the back of the room, which was closed. 'We've burned the sheets, pillows and mattress and thrown the remains into the sea. A while ago, I asked for your cabin to be thoroughly disinfected. Tuberculosis spreads through the air, by coughing and sneezing … Your immune systems are very weak, and if you're infected with the bacteria you might easily develop the illness…,' the doctor went on explaining, using a mixture of Spanish and English to make himself understood.

Solomon remembered Habtamu's cough, how he was choking and spitting blood. For a moment he thought he might be sick.

'I wanted to let you know that tonight we will give him a burial.'

'A burial?' he asked, confused.

'Yes, a burial at sea. We can't keep the body on board until we arrive in Cuba … The sea is the world's largest cemetery. The captain has given me permission to invite you to the ceremony – you and your two friends. But on the condition that you don't tell a soul.'

Solomon listened to the doctor, unblinking, looking at the soft skin on his hands, his neat nails that were so different from those of the sailors on board.

'We'll come and fetch you from your cabin after dinner. Let your friends know, alright? And don't spread the news. I don't want to cause a panic. I'm relying on you.'

Behind the closed door lay that boy, so quiet and sick. Now he was dead. Perhaps they should have told the doctor sooner.

'Have other children died?' he ventured.

'Yes. Unfortunately, yes … '

Night had fallen and the *Africa–Cuba* was silent. A good while after they had returned from dinner in the dining room, there was a knock on their cabin door. It was the Amharic teacher. They followed him down the corridors and staircases to the poop deck, next to the Cuban flag fluttering in front of the boat's wake; there was nobody there because a chain blocked the way. The captain was dressed immaculately in his elegant uniform; he stood talking to the expedition leader and the other Ethiopian teachers. Nearly all of the crew were there. There were some sailors that Solomon had never seen before. They stood in small groups, talking in low voices and smoking. They turned round as they heard the three children approaching in the darkness. The whites of their eyes shone from afar like lanterns. Oswaldo shook Solomon's hand. To one side, on top of a wooden platform, lay the lifeless body of Habtamu covered in a white sheet.

'Come, we've been waiting for you,' said the captain. 'You can stand here in front. Come on everyone, we're going to start.'

The men gathered around the platform. Solomon couldn't take his eyes off the silhouette of the body that could be made out under the white sheet. Would it be shrouded in white clothing? Or naked perhaps? Would the sharks eat him? How long would it take for them to eat him? Would he be able to get to heaven from the sea?

'We are gathered here to say farewell to Habtamu Assefa, who died at the age of eleven at sea … ' the captain started speaking, holding his cap in his hand.

After his speech, one of the teachers read a passage from the Bible in Amharic and started to sing a prayer. All of the Ethiopians present joined in. Solomon, Siyoum and Werret did too. It had been many days since they had sung. Many days since they had prayed.

'Rest in peace. Amen,' finished the captain. Two sailors lifted the stretcher with Habtamu's body on it, tilting it so that the body slid downward and dropped into the water. A white shadow that sank into the depths of the Atlantic Ocean. A thud. And that was it.

One morning just like many others before it, seagulls started to appear and circle around the ship's chimney.

'Land ahoy!' shouted the sailors.

They hadn't yet had breakfast and some children were still sleeping. Cabin doors started flinging open. It was true. On the horizon, far in the distance, they could make out a thin, dark line: Cuba.

The hours that passed until they entered the port of Havana with the ship's siren blasting out were the longest of all. Almost all the children were up on deck. Clutching the railing, they looked intently at the coastline that was appearing before them, gradually becoming closer and clearer. They watched it all in silence, exhausted, some of them ill. The trade winds blew in the direction of the island that was waiting for them.

The children were told to line up on deck in their uniform, carrying their red suitcases. Then they filed down the gangplank in pairs.

'¡Hasta la vista, muchachos valientes!' cried Oswaldo and the other cooks who had climbed up onto one of the railings.

Solomon looked at Oswald and shouted goodbye. Oswaldo smiled and waved back.

'Can't you feel the ground moving?' Solomon asked Siyoum as they walked through the docks full of cranes.

'I was going to say the same thing. It seems like everything is moving, more than on the boat!'

Men sat on stone benches, fishing with rods. There were many small boats anchored in the bay of Havana. Clothes hung from the balconies of the ramshackle low houses, which sat in stark contrast to the taller, more modern blocks of flats behind them.

'Look how strange those cars are! Look at the colours of them!'

The line of children walked a very short distance. A few metres from where the *Africa–Cuba* lay anchored, on an esplanade lined with palm trees, they saw many coaches parked up. The expedition leader waited for them to arrive, holding a megaphone and stationed, as usual, on the highest point he could find: this time, a cart.

'You must get on the coaches as quickly as possible to continue the journey to our destination. There are not enough seats for everyone. Those who don't get a seat now will have to wait for more coaches to arrive. They won't be long … '

Solomon, Siyoum and Werret were among those who had to wait. As they sat on the ground, feeling like they were still on board the ship, they saw three ambulances pull up in front of the *Africa–Cuba* and watched the sailors carrying sick children off the ship. They watched as the children were taken into the ambulances which drove off with their sirens wailing.

They spent the rest of the journey sleeping. They were absolutely drained.

'Another port! They've brought us to the other side of the island!' said Siyoum, waking the others up.

'How do you know?'

'By the sun!'

'You're making it up!'

'Do you think we're there yet?' asked Werret, interrupting the discussion between Solomon and Siyoum.

They were at the port of Batabano, a small fishing village of unpainted wooden houses. They saw piles of fish drying all around. When they got out of the coach a man pointed them toward the boats anchored at the quayside. They were smaller than the *Africa–Cuba*.

'Another boat? Where are we going?' Solomon asked the Amharic teacher who had been in their coach for the journey from Havana.

'An island called Isla de la Juventud, also called Isla de Pinos.'

'And then we'll stay there?'

'Yes, that's where the schools are! Journey over!'

The survivors of the long journey from Ethiopia were reluctantly boarding the boats. They were boats without cabins.

'That must mean it won't be a long journey,' said Siyoum encouragingly.

'You think so?'

They were sitting on the floor of the deck, against the railing or walls, or inside in large rooms with benches. The glass in the windows was so filthy that they could hardly see out.

'I never thought that the first thing we would do when we reached land would be to drive even further and get straight back on a boat again,' said Solomon, standing holding the railing next to his friends.

'More sea … I can't take any more … '

Werret had been coughing for days now.

'We'll be there soon,' replied Solomon, trying to keep his spirits up.

They chatted in small subdued groups. They were too tired to complain. They just watched everything with their scared, dark eyes. They were all filthy, the girls' hair unwashed and matted.

The coast was very different to the other coastline they had seen up until then. It had palm trees leading down to the water's edge, beaches chock-full of people fishing between wooden boats, with nets and boxes full of lobsters or fish. It was a sea of blue and turquoise tones, quite similar to the Red Sea.

'Do you think people live on these islands?'

'I don't know,' said Solomon, looking at the small islands they were passing by, teeming with lush vegetation and tall palm trees. They had left the port of Batabano far behind them; so far behind that they could hardly see it any more.

'A lot of pirates and pirate ships used to hide out around here,' the teacher explained.

'When?'

'A long time ago … Over four hundred years ago. At the bottom of this sea there are many sunken ships. The frigate, the *Cuba*, for example … Behind each ship's name there is a battle, a pirate, a vengeance … The Caribbean Sea was the refuge of the most feared pirates … '

They could see more coastline on the horizon. The island was fairly small and round with mountains in the middle of it. From a distance it looked like a single mountain; a semicircle rising out of the sea.

Three hours after setting sail, they reached the port of Nueva Gerona. A band was waiting on the quayside to welcome them. Uniformed students started to play cheerful marches with trombones, trumpets and drums. The whole city including the mayor had turned out to watch the arrival of these children who had travelled such a long way. A huge crowd of people were waving enthusiastically from a bridge. The shouting and euphoric cheering contrasted starkly with the serious and sickly faces of the ship's passengers, who watched everything silently from the deck.

'*¡Bienvenidos a la Isla de la Juventud!*' shouted the mayor, beaming, with a red fabric sash slung across his chest, emphasising his sizeable paunch.

When they were told to disembark and get on yet more coaches that were waiting for them at the port, they couldn't believe it. Just like in Batabano, there were not enough coaches for all of the passengers. More than half of them had to wait, sitting on the ground. The same coaches would come back to pick them up after they had dropped the others off. It was a short wait as the school was just ten miles away.

'We're never going to get there,' Werret sighed.

Before leaving the city they drove up an avenue lined with palm trees, with a Colonial style church. The narrow highway passed through fields of orange and grapefruit trees, the warm afternoon sun bringing the colours to life like a painting. Along one side of the road ran a never-ending line of wooden telegraph poles carrying the telephone line. Occasionally, they overtook men cycling home from the fields, or a horse-drawn cart carrying people and packages. Everybody waved at them.

'This is the Karamara School, number 16,' said the driver.

Karamara was the name of an Ethiopian mountain located on

the outskirts of the city of Jijiga, where the Ethiopian and Cuban soldiers had defeated the Somalis a few months before. This was an Esbec school, or rural basic secondary school. A meal had been prepared for everyone.

'The tables are moving … And the benches! Can you feel it?' They clutched the table as if they were about to topple over.

'I feel sick,' said a girl, slumped over the table with her head on her arms.

After their dinner of beans, as they ate their oranges, the expedition leader and the Esbec director stood on some chairs and formally welcomed them through a megaphone.

'This building will house the six hundred youngest students, those who will study fourth, fifth and sixth grades.'

The Cuban said this in Spanish and the Ethiopian then translated it into Amharic.

'After dinner, the others will get back into the *guaguas* to go to the *Escuela Mengistu Haile Mariam*, number 43.'

'What are *guaguas*?' a boy asked in a small voice.

Esbec 43. This was to be Solomon's school. Fidel Castro's government had built two schools in the middle of this small, round island in southern Cuba, especially for the one thousand Ethiopian students. The speeches continued, explaining what kind of things they would study there and what was expected of them, but they were far too tired to take any of it in, even in Amharic.

There were two buildings: the two-storey building contained the classrooms and the other, with three floors, contained the dormitories. A corridor like a covered bridge joined the two buildings on the second floor. There were three dormitories for the girls and five for the boys.

'There's room for seventy boys in here! Go on, in you go and get your bunks,' said a teacher with a booming voice.

Solomon settled on a lower bunk. Siyoum climbed into the bunk above him, and Werret went to sleep next to him, also on the bottom bunk. They didn't even wash their hands or take off their clothes. They slept where they dropped, without saying a word. They needed to feel like they were on solid ground, that they had arrived. Solomon slept clutching his pillow, thinking about that island, which was moving as much as the ship did. His head was whirling with vivid images of their long journey.

The weather was hot and sultry. The classrooms had fans on the ceiling but at certain times of the day even the fans did not offer much relief. Solomon continued to prove himself an excellent student, just as he had been at school in Addis Ababa. He paid attention in class, studied in the evenings and did all the exercises they were set. During the first term they just took Spanish classes and worked in the citrus fields. They had uniforms for studying and clothes for the fields, with low gumboots like the ones they sometimes used in the fields in Ethiopia. They all had to do different work, depending on their age. Solomon was given a sickle to cut the grass that grew between the orange trees. There were long rows of orange trees, with hundreds of boys and girls cutting the grass and piling it up at the edges. When it was dry, they burned it.

A few days after they arrived, two doctors visited Esbec 43 to examine all the children and in particular to test them for tuberculosis. They lined up in the dining room to see the doctor one at a time and receive a small pinprick injection on their forearm.

'If your arm comes out in a bruise over the next few days

where the prick was, let your teachers know straight away,' they repeated to each child.

The journey had been a major upheaval for all of them and some had still not fully recovered. They had nightmares of ships sinking into the sea, of sharks leaping up on deck and attacking them. Most of them were homesick for their mothers and cried all through the night. Solomon couldn't shake off the image of Habtamu spitting blood; nor could he stop himself from wondering what kind of fish would have eaten him. He kept remembering Aster's final smile at the Jan Meda encampment when he had already boarded the coach; the songs that Maskarem used to sing; his father's last words before he went with the army to Somalia; the look on his mother's face before she died and the tattoo on her forehead. But he wasn't homesick. It was a much more powerful feeling than that. He wanted to learn as much as he could in that strange, faraway place; he wanted to be a good student, just as his parents had wanted him to be. The piece of sandalwood still smelled and if he folded a eucalyptus leaf in half, he could inhale its strong aroma. Sometimes he would sit on his bed with his eyes closed, remembering his world in the hills of Entoto; as if by following the traces of sandalwood he could return to it.

Werret's arm had come out in raised bump straight away. He was infected with tuberculosis. He had to take medicine and couldn't go out to work in the fields, along with many other children who were sick and extremely weak.

'We will make you better here, there's no need to worry,' the doctors said when they came to visit. 'We have a good climate and healing waters.'

In the rooms there were loudspeakers through which, at six

in the morning, they played music to wake the children up. At quarter to ten in the evening, they were told that they had fifteen minutes to turn out the lights.

'Hurry up! I'm going to turn the lights out!' said the boy who was in charge of their room.

The months passed and they got used to the routine of their new life. In the morning, one group assembled to the sound of Ethiopian music before going to class, while another group went to the fields to work. After lunch, they swapped over. Those who had worked in the fields lined up to go to class. The classrooms were always open for anyone who wanted to go there to study, write, or read.

'Tadele Alamnu, Solomon Teferra and Bisrat Meskel. Please go to collect your letters from the main corridor, in front of the dining room. I repeat: Tadele Alamnu, Solomon Teferra and Bisrat Meskel … '

The sound of the megaphone always immediately attracted the children's attention, in case it might be good news like this. Solomon left the book he was reading and ran downstairs to get the letter from Aster. It was so exciting to receive a letter with an Ethiopian stamp, to sniff the envelope and the paper, seeking out a familiar aroma. Aster told him all about her life in Addis Ababa; she had moved to the Shiro Meda neighbourhood to live with some people she knew. It wasn't safe to live alone in the Entoto hills. He replied to her letters immediately, on the day he received them, although he knew it would be a long time before he received a reply. He spent all of the monthly *pesos* they were given on stamps.

Solomon had been living on Isla de la Juventud for nearly two years when they finally persuaded him to leave his books for a few hours and go to the cinema.

'Come on Solomon, stop studying, you can practically see the steam coming out of your ears!' said Siyoum, who was part of the group of boys who were always messing about. Another group had arrived on the island with a thousand more Ethiopians of all ages, and it was a hive of activity. They went from Esbec 43 to the centre of Nueva Gerona in a *guagua* blaring out loud music. The Esbec had two small coaches that were always parked outside on the forecourt. Some weekends they took them to the beach or to Nueva Gerona for the afternoon.

'Where are we going?'

'To the Caribbean Cinema!'

Solomon didn't dare let on to the others, but he had never been to the cinema. This would be his first time. In Addis Ababa it was frowned upon to go to the cinema. His father always said that the cinema was just for rich people or layabouts. The film had a very strange title, *The 36th Chamber of Shaolin*. They told him it was a kung fu film; he had no idea what that was either. When the lights went out and the first images came up on the screen, Solomon couldn't believe what he saw. He was instantly engrossed in the story of San-Te, a Chinese student whose family had been murdered by the Manchus and who ended up living with monks at the temple of Shaolin, where they trained him in the art of kung fu in the temples' thirty-five chambers … Solomon felt as if he had to dodge the punches and kicks of the actors or else they would hurt him. He did not stop jumping around in his seat.

'Calm down, Solomon, it's just a film!' whispered Siyoum, grinning at him.

'Shut up!' said someone else.

When they left the cinema Solomon's head was so filled with the images and martial arts moves that he couldn't believe that none of it was real. This feeling lasted a long time and in the next few days he found it hard to concentrate in class and not think about kung fu. As much as he tried not to, he couldn't help thinking about all the unforeseen events that San-Te had to go through to overcome the trials set for him by the monks of Shaolin.

Life at the Esbec was hard. They were expected to work hard in class and in the fields. They were also responsible for their clothes, putting them into bags, taking them to the laundry, hanging them out, taking them in again ... The sixteen-, seventeen- and eighteen-year olds bullied the younger ones, making them take their laundry away, wash it and bring it back dry and neatly folded, with the threat of a good thrashing if they didn't. Gangs had formed among the oldest boys and there were frequent clashes. And sometimes, as revenge, the younger boys would grass them up. It was forbidden to smoke, but the older ones did anyway. Solomon wasn't involved with either the older or younger groups. He was always somewhere in the middle: this knack of being almost invisible was his saving grace. On Isla de la Juventud there were various Esbecs full of students of different origins. They had come from Angola, Namibia, Mozambique, Nicaragua ... The Esbec closest to his school was full of Mozambicans. The schools were only three miles apart and as Solomon liked to go walking and running, he went there vey frequently in the evenings when it was permitted. Sometimes he would go alone, sometimes with a group. There were always boys and girls strolling from one Esbec to the other. At night, the shadows of couples embracing at the sides of the road could be made out in the darkness. Ethiopian couples; teenage romances blossoming between the orange and grapefruit trees of the Caribbean.

'When you finish secondary school you will go and study in Havana,' the director of Esbec 43 told them. 'You still have almost four years to go, but it's best if you start thinking ahead.'

'I don't want to go anywhere else,' whispered the boy sitting next to Solomon.

'When the time comes,' continued the director, 'we'll give you the list of subjects you can study at university, and you must choose three or more that interest you, in order of preference. The ones who get the highest grades, and therefore the most points, will get their first choices.'

The Amharic teacher who used to read on board the *Africa–Cuba* always said to Solomon that, with his grades, he could do whatever he wanted. The same teacher also showed him how the school library worked and recommended the first novel he ever read in Spanish.

'Here you go, you'll like this,' he said suddenly one day, handing him a hardback book. 'I managed to read it in Spanish, so you can too! You know more than me now!'

'*Treasure Island* by Robert Louis Stevenson … Thank you. I like the title.'

Solomon spent hours and hours reading, sitting on the ground, leaning against the trunk of an orange tree. From the first chapter he was captivated by the adventures of Jim Hawkins searching for Captain Flint's treasure map on an island so round and similar to the one that he was living on. For several days, he looked forward to free time so he could immerse himself in reading. The main character of the novel was an orphan boy who had sailed to the Antilles, just like him. *Treasure Island* changed many things for Solomon, especially his relationship with the sea. Whenever he could, he would go to the beach and gaze out at the horizon, imagining the silhouette of the *Hispaniola*, the three-masted schooner on which Jim Hawkins sailed to the island. The uncomfortable sailboat the *Hispaniola* wasn't like the *Africa–Cuba*, but Solomon completely identified with the story.

Architecture. This was his first choice and the degree he started studying for in Havana. Over the years he had been accumulating a collection of notebooks packed with drawings of houses in Nueva Gerona or the villages on Isla de la Juventud; houses he remembered seeing in Ethiopia; and others he simply made up. When the time came, the decision was an easy one: he wanted to be an architect. Havana was a busy city with a lot going on, but he kept out of anything that wasn't related to his studies. He was still the reserved boy he had always been. He had been placed in the university residence; a small city within a city. He shared a room there with three other students: Siyoum, another Ethiopian called Girma, and António, who was Angolan. They were all studying different courses. They received seventy *pesos* and eight packs of cigarettes a month and they were allowed to watch television in the common room.

'How do you fancy earning a few more *pesos*?' Girma asked him.

Solomon was lying on his bed reading. He looked up at his roommate with a smile.

'What's this all about then? Yes, of course we'd all like to earn a few more *pesos*, but it depends how!'

'Hey, boys! The architect has shown some interest! Party time!'

Girma sat down on Solomon's bed and sparked up a cigarette, even though it was forbidden to smoke in the bedrooms.

'I'll explain ... It's the easiest, most fun job you'll ever be offered,' he said, exhaling smoke theatrically. 'Basically, lots of Cubans receive dollars from Miami. Illegal money, of course, dollars inside letters and packages sent by their families. And these Cubans can't spend their dollars or exchange them, because it's illegal. Only foreigners can buy things with dollars in Havana's *duty free shops* ... '

Solomon closed his book and sat leaning against the wall.

'If we go into the *duty free shop* in La Garadilla or the Siemens Club, for example, to buy some jeans, or a radio, or American shirts and T-shirts – you know the ones, with the shiny letters on the front – and we pay in dollars, nobody will say anything to us because we're Ethiopians ... You get me?'

'More or less, carry on explaining, I can't see the appeal of your business proposal yet ... '

'Uuufff!' said Antonio, 'you've lost a candidate already, Girma!'

'Let me finish! Look, Solomon: a Cuban gives us two hundred dollars to spend in a duty free shop and asks us to get him jeans, shirts and electronics. For each dollar we spend and deliver in the form of a purchase, he gives us a *peso*. One for one. What do you reckon? Easy, no? Then we divide it out between those who have taken part in the operation.'

'Sounds easy! But where do I come in?'

'It turns out that lately the police suspect that the Ethiopians are acting as *jinetes* – which is what they call the people who do this. And they're waiting for us at the doors of shops ... We have to make the team bigger, we need more allies with shopkeepers, someone else to be on the lookout so that the *fiana* don't show up … '

'The *fiana*?'

'The police! You need to get out more; you don't even know Cuban street slang!'

'And what happens if the police stop us?'

'Well it depends … The other day one came up to us and after he rummaged around in our shopping bag, he asked me, "What do you need twenty-pairs of Magnum jeans for?" And I told him that I was in charge of the campus and was buying clothes for all the students. In exchange for giving him three pairs of trousers, he let me go! It's so fun, it's like being an actor in a play!'

Solomon wasn't interested in being involved in the Havana black market but he started thinking about returning to Addis Ababa, about the few measly *pesos* he had to do the things he wanted to do. His roommates told him about their operations as if they were starring in an American action movie, like the ones they watched on TV on a Saturday night. They called their allies from a phone box in the street to see how things were looking, they divided the purchases out between all the bags and then they split in different directions …

'If you ever need me one day, I'm in,' said Solomon suddenly one morning, much to the astonishment of his friends.

The next operation involved spending one hundred dollars on girls' clothing and they decided that Solomon would go on his own, because none of the shopkeepers knew him. Solomon dressed very discreetly, in the clothes they were given at the Esbec – in a simple, Cuban style – not like Girma, Siyoum and António who dressed in designer jeans and brightly coloured

T-shirts with English slogans printed on them.

'You have to tell them that you're going back to Ethiopia and you want to take back a nice present for your sisters and cousins,' Siyoum explained with a chuckle.

Solomon went into the duty free shop in Old Havana. He was nervous. He went straight to the women's clothing section. He didn't know where to start.

'Can I help you?' asked a smiling saleswoman.

'Uh, yes I suppose so ... '

He managed to come out of the shop with T-shirts with silver lettering on them, some colourful patterned dresses and stylish sunglasses. His friends were waiting for him in an ice-cream parlour a little way down the street. In the narrow streets of Old Havana, no cars could get through, only carts and bicycles.

'Well done! The architect did it!'

Solomon collected the *pesos* he was owed, which amounted to much more than he could have saved in several months.

'Girma, I reckon the shop staff are more in cahoots with the police than with us,' said Siyoum one night, after having to hand over all of his purchases to some plainclothes policemen waiting at the door of the shop.

'How can they be on the *fiana*'s side? Didn't you see how Graciela was dancing with me the other night? It was just bad luck, that's all!'

But from then on, they were stopped every time at the shop exit and had all of their purchases taken away from them.

Solomon didn't understand why, but he decided not to be part of any more operations. One day they arrested Girma, Siyoum and António. They were later expelled from Cuba. Girma and Siyoum went back to Addis Ababa on a scheduled flight, which was paid for by the Ethiopian government.

Studying and taking advantage of all the facilities: that was all Solomon did. The top students in the final year of all degree courses started to receive offers to stay in Cuba to work or to continue with their studies and research, above all in the scientific disciplines. Some Ethiopian girls had fallen in love with Cubans and decided to stay. But Solomon knew that he wanted to go home. It was coming up for ten years since he embarked at the port of Assab and if he left it any longer before he returned, he would have spent more time on that Caribbean island than in his own country. He missed the smell of roasting coffee, the scent of freshly cut eucalyptus wood and burning sandalwood.

The charter flights of Ethiopian Airlines were full of that year's graduates. All of their suitcases, Solomon's and Werret's included, contained a framed degree certificate. They travelled from Havana to Berlin and from Berlin to Khartoum, where a sandstorm delayed them for almost a day. When they took off again they could see the majestic Nile below them, cutting through the Sudanese capital and all the bridges across it. When they landed in Addis Ababa it was raining.

PART TWO

LOS ANGELES, 2004

The Hotel Bel-Air was quiet. It seemed as if there was nobody around. But there was a lot of activity; soundless, efficient activity. There were many Hollywood actors and actresses who didn't have a house in the area, so they stayed at the hotel while filming or promoting their films, or held meetings with producers and directors there to finalize the details of new projects. Their PAs also stayed there and could be seen coming and going through the maze-like gardens of the hotel grounds, mobile phone in one hand and documents in the other. The hotel was made up of a number of low-rise buildings, one or two storeys high, spread out around a landscaped garden area filled with flowers, circular flowerbeds surrounding fountains, benches and drinking water fountains dotted here and there ... The reception was in one building, like a little house; the welcoming fireplace was always lit, regardless of the weather. The main dining room was in another building, which also had its own permanently lit fireplace. The gym, the meeting rooms ... It was like a traditional hotel in a an English style but divided into different parts. Its location was discreet and hidden away from the world. The entrance – at the end of a quiet road in the luxurious neighbourhood of Bel Air – was very unassuming, hardly noticeable in fact, except for the dark, elegant uniforms of the concierges standing outside. Blue Bel Air taxis, luxurious chauffeur-driven cars or limousines pulled up outside what looked like a wooded glade. People getting out of the cars disappeared through a covered footbridge, over a little river full of ducks and white swans, to who knows where. It was one of the most exclusive locations in Los Angeles.

Muna was alone by the pool. A waiter had placed a fresh mango juice on a low table next to her lounger, just as she had requested. Everything was perfect. The azure sky, the temperature of the water, the recently mowed lawns and the perfectly maintained flower beds blooming in a rainbow of colours, the tranquillity of the surroundings ... From the pool, Muna looked at the Californian palm trees, so similar yet so different to Indian palm trees. She had been staying at the Hotel Bel-Air for ten days now, promoting her latest film. She had a minor part. She was too old now to star in a commercial Hollywood film, but she was also too old to be the protagonist in any Bollywood film, to keep up with the demanding rhythms of the choreographers. Her body no longer had the same strength or flexibility as during her twenties or thirties. And without dancing, there was no film. Forty-three was old in the eyes of film producers, whether they were Indian or American. It was old in her eyes too; she felt the weight of a life lived to the full starting to catch up with her.

She had arrived in Hollywood too late. Now was the moment of Aishwarya Rai, Vimana Kadamba, Khushboo and Anita Madurai; and she was supportive of them. Muna had shot thirty-nine films. Many films; too many perhaps. As similar as they all were, thirty-nine films involved many different choreographies, many hours of rehearsals, a lot of physical training to be able to dance well, to be able to do all the moves with flexibility; movements that were sometimes like circus acrobatics. Dancing gracefully while miming and constantly smiling. On the other hand, a good playback also required many hours of rehearsal.

She had been one of the first Indian stars to make the leap to

America and although she had got there a bit too late, she was very excited about the experience. In India she was the most famous Bollywood actress, and Bollywood was all the rage. She could never have imagined that her films would be watched all over the world. Her fans came to her house every day in Juhu – one of Mumbai's residential areas, next to the beach – to try and catch a glimpse of her as she came in or out. Luckily, at her home she had people working for her who cared a great deal about her, and who were much more than just guards, gardeners or cooks; they were like her family. And they were all incredibly careful to protect her privacy. Some said that Muna Kulkarni had more fans than Amitabh Bachchan, the country's most famous actor, who despite being well over sixty years old, still stirred passions and was treated like a guru by many people. So much so that Bachchan opened his house to the public once a month so that anyone who wanted to – the old or young, blind or crippled, rich or poor – could visit him. They gathered there asking him for his blessing, touching his feet as a sign of adoration. Images of Muna and of Amitabh Bachchan could be found all over India's major cities. Their faces smiled down from billboards in the street, in car or insurance adverts … Muna was now reducing her presence on TV programmes and in magazines, but for many years she had no choice but to go from one to the other, from one interview to the next. As a result, she was recognized by everyone wherever she went. On the internet there were more than 15,000 websites dedicated to her and her films. They were all created by her fans, apart from one, the 'official web page' which was created by her American agent, Charlie. Muna Kulkarni was more than a big film star. She was a legend; she was the ultimate success story of a woman who had gone from having nothing to having everything. And a person who hadn't forgotten where she came from, despite reaching the top.

'You have an urgent fax, Mrs Kulkarni,' she heard someone saying to her.

'Thanks, leave it on the table, I'm getting out of the water now.'

She slid out of the pool gracefully and looked at the fax out of the corner of her eye to see who it was from. Smiling, she dried herself with a white towel, sat down on her sun lounger, drank half of the mango juice in one gulp and settled down to read the fax.

Hi Mum!

How are you? I didn't send you an email because I know you never check them; you're useless with computers! And this fax will reach you wherever you are, in record time.

I've passed all my exams!! I thought you would want to know. Now we've got two weeks of holiday and I'm already all booked up with tennis matches and the school cricket championship. I'll be at home nearly every day this holiday, I already can't wait to be in my own bedroom … and that way, Aditi will have some work to do. She says she's bored when I'm not there and she doesn't have me to cook for! Dad is busy as usual, but he finds time to play golf with Paul and Rajvinder and the rest of the gang and I don't think he's missing you too badly. I hope you're getting on okay in Los Angeles and that the film is a success! Next time, I'll go with you, okay? Call me when you get a moment, I can never work out the time difference and I don't want to wake you up in the middle of the night! Lots of love…Come home soon!

Arun

She gazed at the hibiscus bushes surrounding the pool, their vibrant red flowers bursting open. The fax lay there in her hand. She knew that the moment had come to deal with her more distant past. She couldn't, and should not, put it off any longer. The opportunity she had always wanted had now arisen; the perfect moment.

Kevin was waiting for her outside in the black car, the Lincoln Town that would take her anywhere she wanted to go in LA. As usual, the car was spotless and shiny – as if it was brand new every day – and its leather interior was also black and gleaming. Kevin had been her chauffeur ever since her first trip to Los Angeles. He was wearing a uniform of an immaculate white shirt and pinstriped tie.

'Where are we going, Mrs Kulkarni?'

'To William Morris,' replied Muna as she got into the back seat, shutting the car door determinedly.

'Would you like to listen to some music?'

'Yes, can you put that Jagjit Singh album on please?'

'Coming right up, Mrs Kulkarni.'

As they listened to the voice of Jagjit Singh and the smooth rhythm of the Indian percussion – the indescribable sound of the *tabla* – Kevin drove down through Bel Air, along the gentle curves that wound round in front of huge white mansions with spectacular gardens belonging to world-famous singers, actors, actresses and film directors, until they reached Beverley Hills. Muna had always been impressed that her agency had a street named after it. Charlie Shawn had been her agent for many years, since long before she shot her first film outside India. Charlie wasn't yet forty but he had worked at William Morris for nearly twenty years. He had started in the agency as an intern, in the office of one of the most important agents. He was used to dealing with the most highly paid actors and actresses; big name stars like Catherine Zeta-Jones or Russell Crowe didn't impress him much because he was the one who had seen them rise, step by step, from absolute anonymity to world fame. When he became an agent and was allowed to build up his own client portfolio, Charlie was convinced that the future of cinema lay outside the United States and that he should represent talents from other continents and cultures. He was the company's most eccentric agent but he bought in the biggest profits, so he was allowed to do as he wished and choose clients according to his own criteria. He was a big fan of Bollywood cinema and so one day he turned up in Mumbai, all set to convince Muna Kulkarni and a couple of other popular actors in India to let him represent them in Los Angeles.

They passed the hotel where *Pretty Woman* was supposedly filmed and Kevin immediately turned right onto William Morris Road. Muna had to make herself known to the receptionists on the way in. She was never sure if they really didn't recognize her or if that distant attitude was part of the job description of those boys and girls – with their tiny headpieces and wireless microphones – who were responsible for greeting visitors and working the switchboard which looked like something out of a sci-fi film. There were more than fifty agents working in that building for all kinds of artists. A few minutes later, Charlie came hurrying out of one of the lifts toward where she was standing in the middle of the hallway.

'Muna! What a surprise! Well, don't you look fabulous! Always so elegant! You look gorgeous in that *salwar kameez*, darling! And you keep turning up unannounced ... '

'You know that I'm not used to this thing of making an appointment, when I'm staying so nearby, Charlie! Can you spare me a minute in your office or can I kidnap you and let's get out of here? I can't wait for you to find time to come to my hotel and I only have a few days left in Los Angeles … '

'I was just finishing off a meeting with someone who I'd love to introduce you to … In fact, I don't understand how you two haven't met! Let's go up right now and then we'll go and grab a drink, the three of us, what do you say?'

Charlie always talked flat-out and made decisions so quickly that it was impossible to turn him down.

'I'm absolutely snowed under with work, Muna, you can't imagine how much I've got on, but never mind! I'm off on vacation next week and you know how it is – all those urgent issues and problems always surface at once!'

Charlie's tiny office was almost directly opposite the lift door on the second floor. All of the offices in that building were small, although the people working in them had major responsibilities and earned huge profits. Sitting on a small dark green upholstered sofa was a younger woman, dressed in eye-catching ripped jeans and a classic white shirt with the sleeves rolled up to the elbow.

'This is Nighat Nawaz.'

Nighat had already stood up when she saw them come in, and held out her hand to Muna.

'It's an honour to meet you, Mrs Kulkarni.'

'Muna, please call me Muna. Are you Indian?'

'Yes, I'm from Delhi, but I live in Mumbai.'

'And she's one of the best photography directors there is! If not yet, then she will be! When they told me you were here, and Nighat told me you hadn't met, I just couldn't believe it!'

The three of them walked up Rodeo Drive, lingering in front of some of the shop windows to look at the displays of the most famous brands, criticising the models and most of all the prices. Muna had remained loyal to Indian style and her country's designers, who made clothes exclusively for her, and which she quickly transformed into the latest trend. They arrived at Charlie's favourite cafe in Beverley Hills, a neighbourhood that seemed more like the set of an advertisement than a place where anyone lived or worked. Nothing was, or seemed, real. They managed to find a seat in a secluded area and the waiter immediately came over to take their order.

'Have you come to see me for any particular reason, Muna?'

'Yes, actually, but it has nothing to do with work or films. It's to do with my past. I thought that you might be able to help me, seeing as you're the most efficient and persevering person I know. Much more than my husband, which goes without saying!'

'If you need to talk about personal matters, I can leave you two to it … '

'No, please stay! Charlie has known me for years and knows a lot about me. But there is one thing he doesn't know, and I don't mind telling you as well! I don't think I've ever spoken to you about my sister Sita … '

'I didn't know you had a sister.'

'Well, I do have one … I was five when she was born and eight when the nuns took her away from my village, down a long dusty road. From that day on, I never forgot her. And now I need to know what happened to her; if she is alive or dead. If she's alive I need to know how her life turned out … And if it turned out badly, I want to help her. I looked after her from the day she was born and I would have gone on looking after her if they hadn't taken her away … '

'Are you saying that you want to look for a sister that you haven't seen for more than thirty years and that you don't know where she ended up after they took her away? What if she's changed her name? What if she doesn't appear in any census records, like so many thousands of Indians?'

'I need to find out what happened to her.'

The waitress arrived with three vanilla ice creams and three coffees. Judging by the expression on her face, she recognized Muna (and Charlie, who was a regular customer), but she didn't say or do anything, just like the receptionists at William Morris.

'But, Muna, that's so hard to do! There are a billion people living in India! And why do you want to find her now, exactly?'

'Because now I can. Now is the time to do it. Now I've got it all! Between Irshad and you, you've helped my career reach the top, I've got more money than I need, and if I keep on working it's only for the love of working; I have a fantastic family, a son that's now older and is growing up happy and responsible … And I don't want to wait any longer.'

'And why didn't you do it before? Why have you waited so long?'

'I don't know, Charlie … I've always wanted to try but something would get in the way. Or I'd start filming, or I got scared of not being able to deal with what might have happened to Sita. It's a long story.'

'And what does Irshad have to say about it? Your husband has lots of contacts in India and could easily help you.'

'Irshad thinks that the past should be left behind and that this is the only way we can move forward as a person. I've talked to him a lot about it and he thinks that it would be a mistake to go over painful old ground. Irshad helped me to believe in myself, to change my life forever, to learn to be free ... It wasn't easy. For many years I didn't listen to him. However much he listened to my memories and consoled me, he always insisted that I should look toward the future. And I know that he won't want to help me find my sister!'

'I'd like to help you,' said Nighat suddenly.

'Seriously?'

'Yes. I get back to Mumbai a few days after you. I have the time; they still haven't given me the dates of the new shoot I'm going to be working on. Plus, I'm sure it will kick off late as usual. I don't have a partner or any children. In Mumbai I hardly have any family; they all live between New Delhi and Lahore ... '

'You see! A modern Indian woman! Single at thirty-eight years old, does whatever she wants, travels from one place to another, has all the lovers she wants ... '

'Charlie!'

'Sorry, sorry!' said Charlie with an amused look, emptying two whole sachets of sugar into his coffee.

Muna looked out of the window. The streets of Beverley Hills were deserted, noiseless, clean. Suddenly she was reminded of images of the streets of Bombay, of *her* Bombay before it was called Mumbai; streets overflowing with smells and colours and animals wandering about all over the place; the noisy, dirty streets full of cows and goats. Always such an explosion of life ...

'If Sita were alive, she would be about your age,' said Muna.

'Do you know where to start looking?'

'I don't have many leads, but I do remember the names of the villages and some people's names ... And obviously I'll pay all the necessary costs.'

'Don't worry about that. I have a 4x4 and can go anywhere I want.'

Muna clasped both of her hands and smiled warmly at her.

'Thank you so much! You can't imagine how long I've waited for this ... '

'It wasn't the right time to do it until now, was it? You said so yourself ... '

Three days after the conversation with Nighat and Charlie in the cafe in Beverley Hills, Muna arrived back at her home in Juhu just as dusk was falling. Irshad and her son Arun had come to fetch her from the airport, as they always did. Irshad had always been waiting for her at the arrivals gate without fail, ever since her first trip. She didn't have any upcoming trips planned for several months. She liked getting home and going for a stroll in the garden before she unpacked, even before she got changed. There, you could breathe in the salty smell of the sea like in no other place. Irshad and Arun sat on the porch, laughing amongst themselves. Everything was ready and waiting for them to sit down to dinner; to tell each other their news. She knew that her husband was watching her, spellbound. Sometimes she got the feeling that they had only just met; it was a lovely feeling. Wearing the same clothes she had worn for the long journey, Muna crossed the green expanse filled with colourful flowers, toward the cottage at the end of the garden, to say hello to Kiran's family and let them know in person that she was back.

'*Namaste*, Mrs Kulkarni!' they greeted her with their hands together in front of their chests.

'*Namaste*,' she replied with the same ceremonious but warm gesture.

Kiran was one of the first children that – several years ago now – she had rescued from one of the illegal sewing workshops.

She had managed to get her out of that inhumane place at the age of thirteen, after the girl had been raped when she was still only a child, and with her eyesight destroyed from embroidering and sewing for five years practically in the dark. Five years shut away, enslaved, embroidering for more than fourteen hours every day of the week, without ever going out of that dark, dismal warehouse in subhuman conditions. Muna had reunited her with her family who lived in a small village in Madhya Pradesh, where they had been deceived by false promises of Kiran receiving an education in the city. She had ended up employing her parents, her older brother and the girl herself as guards, gardeners, cooks, laundrymen ... They each had the security of a decent salary, healthcare and the garden cottage for life. They were a happy family and the best employees she could ask for.

Muna was a founding partner of the Stop Children's Slavery Foundation, the organisation that her best friend had created to help eradicate child slavery. Indira Raghavan was her oldest friend and would always be her best. Muna was so proud of Indira, who deep down, was like a sister to her. One of India's most courageous lawyers, she defended the rights of women and those most in need. She knew she could count on her if, in the end, she didn't manage to find Sita. But she didn't want to bother her with this; it wasn't as important as all the things that Indira was dealing with and which meant so much to so many millions of the country's children.

Nighat and Muna met several times to talk, drink tea and pore over the map of Maharashtra laid out on the table in front of them, in Muna's Juhu beachside house which combined modern, Western style with more traditional Indian decor. Since they met in Los Angeles they had spent many hours talking, mostly about Muna's memories, but also about other things. And they were always left with the feeling that they never had enough time to talk; that there were still questions left unanswered. There were even more things about Muna that Nighat didn't know. She was a very reserved woman. She preferred listening and observing to talking. She was strong, very strong; Nighat was sure of that. She admired her greatly and had a lot of respect for her. In her work, Nighat was used to being surrounded by famous people; actors and actresses who appeared in all the magazines and all the TV programmes. But it was one thing working with them and quite another to go to their house to watch films or look through old photo albums. Muna Kulkarni was nothing like the Bollywood stars who had become famous overnight and could be seen at all the parties with the wealthiest fashion models and pet miniature dogs in their handbags. Muna had everything; she was extremely rich, but she didn't seem it.

It had been almost two months since the film that Nighat was supposed to be working on should have started shooting, but for various reasons it kept getting delayed. The production company kept telling her it would begin the following week. The shooting schedule was ready, they would start on Monday. But that Monday always turned out to be the Monday of the following week. The world of cinema was like that – erratic and unpredictable – but that was what she had chosen. She had managed to become what she wanted to be: a director of photography. In India, as in many other countries, there were hardly any women in this role; it was usually men. Nighat relished being in the middle of a street closed off to traffic by the police, with huge cranes holding powerful spotlights, directing the lighting, giving instructions to the cameraman sitting on a crane that moved along a rail and to another one filming with a camera on his shoulder, supported by two others. She liked being right there in the thick of it in her work outfit – scruffy jeans and a blue T-shirt – watching the four hundred extras in their make-up and costumes, ready to receive their orders for their positions. When she had to think on her feet, with the pressure of the shoot and the lack of time weighing on her, she would put one hand on her waist and pull her hair back with the other; or she stood with her hand resting on her head, as if supporting it while she dealt with the last minute problems that always arose. She would scan the scene with her eyes, as if it were already filmed. She preferred shooting outdoors than on a film set, but in the Andheri area there were some fantastic film studios and the hours she spent inside them, in a fantasy world, were just as exhilarating. She watched the images being shot by the various cameramen as they appeared on the screens. She took the scenes again and again; now from one angle, now from another. The directors usually stayed sitting in front of the screens while she was the one standing up, giving orders to the cameramen, lighting departments and make-up artists, discussing all sorts of technical problems, so that everything was running as it should be. She never stopped. Everyone respected her and she had gained as much authority as if she were the director.

In the Andheri neighbourhood, not far from some of the Bollywood studios where she worked, was the Saint Catherine's Home. She had gone there to see her cousin Vandana with the list that Muna had given her of surnames and villages in Maharashtra. Vandana was a volunteer at the centre for orphaned boys and girls. Her husband earned enough money that she had never needed to get a job and since her two children had gone off to study in the United States she spent all the hours she could helping out at the orphanage. Vandana was one of many high-class women who dedicated their free time to helping the country's poorest and neediest people, building the foundations from which they could promote educational projects for children and adults living in the slums of Mumbai, which were increasing in number. Nighat had never been inside an orphanage before and this first visit made a lasting impression on her. In fact she had never actually been in direct contact with so many orphan children; children so helpless and alone in the world. She was used to the poverty that she saw in the streets; it had always formed part of the landscape without affecting her too much but it had never been part of her life. Vandana told her that in India there were tens of millions of children who grew up and were educated in those institutions; those were the lucky ones. A great deal of effort went into finding Indian families who wanted to and could afford to adopt a child, in particular those older than five or six. The children who suffered most were those of a certain age – of seven, eight, nine or ten years old – whose parents had died and no-one else in the family could look after them, that is, if there was anyone left in the family who was vaguely healthy enough to.

Vandana was fifty-three years old and her husband was several years older. Although she would have liked to, at her age, her husband didn't approve of the idea of becoming parents again to a boy or girl with an unknown past, now that they already had children who were finishing their university degrees.

'Sita, you say? But Nighat, there must have been so many Sitas in all the orphanages! You said she remembers a nun dressed in white? In that case, it's possible that they were Catholic nuns who took the girl away, but who knows where to and which nuns they were. You're talking about thirty years ago.'

'Look, I've marked all the villages on this map of Maharashtra,' said Nighat, unfurling the map she was carrying in her bag. 'Can you help me look for Catholic convents and orphanages close to these villages? You must have some sort of list, don't you?'

'Wouldn't it be easier to go to the villages first and talk to the people? Perhaps there's someone left who remembers something ... I mean it's been thirty years, but many of these villages are the same and the same families are still living there.'

'Perhaps, yes, I'll do both. But do you have a list of the convents and orphanages?'

'Yes, I've got the list, wait a moment and I'll get it for you. Since when were you interested in anything apart from cinema, anyway?'

Vandana left the office and Nighat carried on looking at the photos and a large notice board that was hanging on the wall. There were photos of boys and girls of all ages dressed in brightly coloured Western clothing, smiling and healthy looking, their black hair glossy. Vandana had told her that all the children in those photos had left the centre and been adopted by European and American families, some by Indian families. It was a nice touch that they went on sending news and photos of the children, although it only happened occasionally; not all of the families did it. Every letter that they received was like hearing news from several children at a time. Most of the children they had heard nothing from, and never would. However, sometimes the children returned to visit the Saint Catherine's Home from Belgium, England, Holland, Sweden ... Either with their adoptive parents, alone or as a couple. There were also those who returned to spend a few weeks of their holidays helping out there, with whatever it might be: organising games and songs; helping to wash the orphans' hair with Permethrin cream to kill off an outbreak of head lice; or feeding the youngest children.

'Here you go, here's the list,' said Vandana, coming back into the office. 'The nuns who went to Shaha, Patri and the villages in that area during the sixties and seventies must have been from Nasik or Puna. There was a parish in Sinnar, but it no longer appears on the list ... Puna is too far away for them to have gone very often, so I'm pretty certain they were from Nasik. At that time, the most active nuns were the Missionaries of Mary, a French organisation that still has some centres in India. I'd pay them a visit.'

So off she went, in her 4x4 and with a digital camera. She never went anywhere without a camera in her bag. Nasik was a small holy city. Everything there revolved around the river Godavari. Women did their washing in the *ghats* at all hours of the day. They laid out their colourful *saris* flat on the ground. Rectangles of orange, fuchsia, red, turquoise ... There were large posters up recalling the celebration of Kumba Melah that had taken place almost a year ago. It was one of the largest pilgrimages in the world, which was celebrated periodically in different Indian cities. Once every three years it took place in Nasik and the nearby city of Trimbak.

Finding the centre belonging to the nuns was easy. It was a convent where only nine nuns of different nationalities lived, looking after more than eighty orphan girls in a modern building, set back from a garden full of roses in bloom. Two nuns greeted her warmly, looking at her curiously as she drove through the garden and parked up next to a swing. They offered her an orange soda and they sat around a table in the living room of the small convent to discuss exactly what it was she wanted. The room was very bare, with just a few items of furniture and a TV as the only luxury; the only sign of modernity. Gradually, other nuns joined the conversation; attracted by the novelty of the guest, they appeared silently, dressed in white habits with grey aprons fastened behind their backs to keep themselves clean. One of the most elderly women – with white hair and a wrinkled face – remembered Sita because she was one of the first girls that they took in when only the main building existed, the one they were in now. She only vaguely remembered her as it was many years ago and she said she sometimes confused one girl's story with another. All of the stories were unique but they all merged into one. Girls found at dawn at the entrance to the garden near the iron gates with a brief note, sometimes little more than a name scribbled on a piece of paper. Or left without a name or a note; just a starving baby almost dead from dehydration. Older children also arrived with some distant relative who could no longer look after them, or with the police, because they had been found wandering the streets … Nighat had always turned a blind eye to the reality of her country. She had lived in her easy bubble. She came from a good, educated family. She had ignored a reality that most foreigners seemed more aware of than Indians themselves; obsessed as they were with wealth, with making India one of the most powerful countries in terms of the film and technology industries, with having a satellite dish on every roof, with studying at the best universities in the world. There were many Indias within India. At least two: India and Bharatvarsh, the Hindi name of the country. India was the name given to the country by the British colonizers. It came from the word Hindustan, the name of the country in Urdu. She didn't know, or want to know, the reality of Bharatvarsh, which half the world already seemed to know and which she found hard to contemplate.

'You might find the information you're looking for in this notebook,' said one of the nuns, coming back after leaving the room briefly. She handed her a long, narrow notebook with a black cover. Nighat thumbed through the notebook and immediately saw a list of arrivals and departures of girls, written in impeccable handwriting in blue ink. It began in 1969 and finished in 1976, because that is when the book ran out of pages.

'Thank you so much! I don't want to put you out … would you let me look at this book here for a while?'

The nuns didn't mind her staying there in the least; quite the opposite in fact. They watched Nighat's every movement as if she were a major attraction.

'The water's back on!' cried a young nun that Nighat hadn't seen yet. 'At last all the buckets are filling up!' she added excitedly, drying her hands on her grey apron and leaving the way she came in.

'We have a lot of problems with the running water,' explained one of the women. 'It goes off first thing in the morning and we never know when it's coming back on. We leave a load of buckets out ready, under each tap. We need the water mainly for the toilets. There are a lot of girls … '

'It happens in Mumbai too,' said Nighat, holding the notebook and flipping slowly through the pages. 'According to our calculations, Sita was taken to Shaha in 1971 or 1972, so from those dates she must have arrived here … '

She looked for the page on which 1971 started. It only contained five names. Sita was one of them.

The nuns left the notebook with her for a while so she could photocopy the pages she needed at a local shop nearby, which had three computers connected to the internet, phone booths and a photocopier. After spending a night alone in the Taj hotel on the outskirts of Nasik, Nighat returned to Mumbai and went to see Muna straight away to tell her everything. The next steps were fairly simple: visiting the nuns in the Mumbai convent, going through the discoloured pages of another register from the seventies, speaking to some nuns, then to more nuns who remembered the very Sita who had ended up going by herself to Barcelona when she was six or seven years old and who, at the age of twenty, had visited them with her adoptive parents.

'You're sure that Sita is my sister, right?' asked Muna, setting down the tray with the steaming teapot and two cups on the coffee table.

'I'm very sure! Why aren't you sure?'

'I don't know. It's a weird feeling. It has all been too quick and easy, after thinking about it for so many years. What if we have nothing in common? We've lived such different lives that it'll be impossible to connect! And she was so little that I'm sure she won't remember anything about it … '

'Everyone lives different lives. My sister and I both stayed in India and we have nothing in common! She asked our parents to find her a husband, like our family has done for generations and generations. I was so angry when I found out! So much studying, so much travelling around the world only to end up asking our parents to find her a husband. After the wedding, I wanted to go to Europe for a long time and I grew very distant from her; she had let me down … '

'So they found her a husband?'

'They sure did. You can't imagine how happy my mother was that my sister asked her. It kept her busy for an entire year! She spent hours in front of the computer, browsing website after website. All the *matchmakers.com* sites you can imagine. Websites overflowing with photos of Indian boys from good families that worked so hard to be rich that they couldn't find time to meet their ideal woman, and were putting themselves on the internet to get somewhere with it. Most of them lived in New Delhi, Mumbai and Bangalore. But there were also some from England or the States who were looking for Indian women who hadn't lost their roots, even commenting that they didn't mind about caste!'

'So, who was the husband they found for her then?'

'The weirdest thing – the thing that always surprised me – is that he really is the ideal husband! They have three children, a fantastic house in New Delhi, they never talk about anything, they're modern, they both work … But I would never do it. Getting married to a man you've known for two weeks after only meeting him because your parents think he's a good match for you? Absolute madness, I tell you!'

'Lots of people think that nobody knows you better than your parents. I guess I'll never know because mine died when I was very young. For many people, a marriage between two people is also a marriage between two families … '

'Don't tell me you think it's a good idea?'

'I don't know, but I do get it. Luckily I was able to choose. Women who can't choose are always told that you marry first and then the love grows … '

'The formula seems to have worked for my mother and sister … or that's what they say anyway. But I wouldn't risk trying it.'

Muna poured the tea out into the two glasses.

'Have you been to Barcelona?'

'Yes but only for four days. During the years I lived in London studying film and photography, I took the opportunity to visit all the European cities I could. I looked for the cheapest flights I could find on the internet and would spend long weekends in Rome, Paris, Amsterdam, Stockholm, Prague ... And Barcelona too. March 2002 I think it was ... '

'People say it's like Mumbai.'

'Mumbai? Not at all! It's like a big city by the sea, perfect, clean, organized, the streets are set out in a grid formation. Everyone looks happy; there are all kinds of shops, the Gaudi architecture ... People complain about the noise, pollution and dirtiness of some neighbourhoods; if they came to live here, they'd just die!'

They had arranged to meet and go for a walk on Juhu beach. Every evening at sundown it filled up with couples, children flying brightly coloured kites, fishermen mending their nets, people strolling along, sandals in hand, paddling in the water, hawkers selling peanuts and ice creams ... They ended the day watching *Monsoon Wedding* together at Muna's house. As the lively music played and the credits rolled up the screen, Muna sat unmoving, sprawled on the sofa with her shoes off as if the film hadn't finished yet. As she watched the long list of names of actors, actresses, sound technicians and so many other people that had worked on the project, she found it hard to understand how that story had managed to achieve such international success; but she was happy about it. It was one of her favourite films of recent times; she would've loved to have worked on it. She would love to work on any of Mira Nair's films. Bollywood was starting to fade into her past. She didn't know if she would carry on in that world much longer. Increasingly she wanted to do different things.

'Every time I watch this film I miss Delhi!' said Nighat, after a large yawn. She was sitting on the floor on a heap of cushions, leaning against the sofa where Muna was sitting, with her legs crossed, emphasising the slits and holes in her designer jeans. 'Here in Mumbai, I miss how open and extrovert the Punjabis are!'

'Are they really so much like that?'

'Yes, haven't you heard that the Punjabis are like the Italians of India? Oh yeah, and the Hindi in this film is so real, it's so packed with Urdu words, or perhaps the other way round. At the end of the day, it's the same language but they cut it in half when they divided the country in 1947 ... '

'Are all your family from the Punjab?'

'Yes, but very few of them stayed in India after the partition. Most of my uncles, aunts and cousins, both on my father's and mother's side, live in Pakistan. And even now, over fifty years later, there are still unresolved family wounds and traumas.'

Muna switched off the DVD player and the television and went to the kitchen to fetch two glasses of water. She turned on the living room lamps at the same time; darkness had crept up on them. They were alone in the house. She liked Nighat's company and would always be grateful to her for helping to find out what happened to her little sister. She felt completely different, altered somehow. It was impossible for her to go on living as if nothing had happened. Her sister was alive: she was thirty-eight, she was a doctor and she lived in Barcelona.

It was unbelievable. What would she say to her when she saw her? What do you say to a sister that you haven't seen for more than thirty years? What do you say to a sister that doesn't speak your language and lives on the other side of the world? How could it have been so easy to find her?

The two of them had been sitting in silence for a while. Muna had brought in a bowl of pistachios and a jug of lemon juice with sugar and they finished it all off, listening to a Norah Jones album that Nighat had given her. They found it funny that this singer, who was a global success story, was Ravi Shankar's daughter.

'I'd better go, it's getting late.'

'Thanks so much for everything!'

Nighat had parked her jeep at the entrance to the garden and Muna walked her to it. The night was calm and still; you could hear the sound of the sea.

'Irshad really wants to meet you. I'll call you soon to invite you to dinner!'

'I'd love to meet your husband. See you soon!'

Nighat's 4x4 disappeared into the darkness behind the iron gate that one of the guards had come out to open. Muna stayed in the garden, breathing in the intense perfumed aroma of the jasmine flowers that trailed up the walls of the house, as she strolled slowly around the pond teeming with goldfish, listening to the soothing babbling of the fountain. The magnolias were already in bloom.

Nighat was delighted to be in such a classy house in Juhu, sitting at such a beautifully laid table with candles and plates made from English porcelain. She found it strange that, seeing as there was a cook and a pair of serving girls in the house, the hostess kept popping up to fetch something from the kitchen or even serve the others. She found it even more unusual that her husband and son also kept getting up to take an empty tray to the kitchen, fetch another bottle of wine or fill the water jug, as if this were completely normal, and not even complaining about the inattentive service. She would never have imagined that in the house of a wealthy family belonging to one of the most famous actresses in India and a powerful Bollywood producer, the servants would do practically nothing. At her parents' home in New Delhi – and they were not half as rich or famous – nobody ever got up from the table and it was the servants who ran around, at the sound of the little bell that her mother rang constantly to ask for this or that.

'Do you remember Olivia Cooper?' Muna asked Irshad.

'Olivia Cooper … the American multi-millionairess who has more money than she knows what to do with?'

'That's the one! Well she wants to make a big donation to our foundation! I explained to her that we had bought a house to convert into a children's home for girls and she wants to help out … '

'That's fantastic!' said Irshad, smiling and reaching for his wife's hand over the table, to give her a kiss.

Irshad was an extremely attractive man. Tall, with an olive complexion, grey hair and dark, piercing eyes that glittered when he looked at Muna.

'They're so annoying! They're always like this, like in one of those soppy romance films!' Arun said to Nighat, who was sitting next to him.

'How many years have you been married?'

'Soon it will be twenty-five … ' replied Muna, her eyes lighting up as she turned to Irshad and smiled.

'You see? They're so gross! Twenty-five years together and they're still like this … '

'How did you two meet?'

'Oh no! You really don't know? Don't tell me that I have to listen to the legendary family story for the millionth time!'

Arun was a lively teenager, aware of his good looks and very at ease with himself.

'Why don't you tell it, if you know it so well?' said Irshad.

'Yes, you tell it!'

'Uugghhh … I told you, Nighat, they're so annoying. Okay, okay, go on then … Ladies and gentlemen, the legend of Godavari! The river that is as sacred as the Ganges! The story will begin, but if I get it wrong, you correct me, okay? Sometimes they act like I was actually there.'

So Arun began telling the story of his parents while Kiran cleared the plates from the table with a smile so wide it skewed her glasses – she also knew the story by heart – and brought in the desserts, the tea service and a pot of steaming tea trailing the scent of cardamom and other spices. Arun told how Muna was working in the house of the Raghavan family when she was still just a child, as a servant – if not a slave, as she didn't get paid a single *rupee* and worked from sunup to sundown. She slept on the floor of the kitchen and spent hours scrubbing, sorting lentils, peeling potatoes, sweeping and ironing, in the house of a couple with five children, plus a grandmother and guests every two or three days. Meanwhile, Irshad was studying at King's College in Cambridge where he had become best friends with Sanjay, the eldest son of the Raghavan family. Although they studied different degrees, they were inseparable. Irshad had heard a lot about Muna: it was because of her that Sanjay's relationship with his father had become very strained and Sanjay had decided to stay and work in England. This had enraged his father. He had sent his son to study in Cambridge so that he could return to India with the best possible qualifications and take up a position of responsibility and reach the top of his profession. The situation worsened when he married Emily, who was English, born and bred. Mrs Raghavan was distraught when he very resolutely told her that she wouldn't have an Indian daughter-in-law, disciplined and well-educated in a Brahman family, with whom she could go to buy embroidered silk *saris* and share confidences; but instead, a foreign daughter-in-law with different customs altogether.

The first time Irshad came face to face with Muna was when he was twenty-seven and she was sixteen. Irshad had already returned from Cambridge and, unlike Sanjay, felt that the only place in the world for him was in India. He had returned to Mumbai after experiencing a thousand love stories with English women with golden hair and skin covered in freckles, after spending endless hours punting down the canals of Cambridge in his King's College uniform ... One day, he went to dinner at the Raghavans during one of Sanjay's rare visits to Mumbai, and he was absolutely hypnotized by Muna's beauty as she served them at the table. Muna spoke very little; her voice was so quiet she could barely be heard. But Irshad could tell she had a lot to say. From that day on, Irshad found all kinds of excuses to visit the Raghavan household: borrowing a book from Sanjay's library, making an enquiry to Mr Raghavan – who had many contacts in the various ministries and a great deal of information about the most important companies in the city – or even asking to borrow a Keralan recipe from Chamki, supposedly for his mother ... Indira, alert and observant as ever, knew that something odd was going on. Irshad was visiting their house so often when Sanjay wasn't in. And as nice as he was to her, he didn't look at her in the same way he looked at Muna. She could clearly see that. Irshad worked in an advertising production company and eventually he found the perfect excuse to get close to Muna: they needed a model for an advert for a shopping centre that was becoming quite fashionable. And she was the girl he wanted for it. It wasn't easy to persuade Mr and Mrs Raghavan.

In the end they accepted because the photo session would take place in their own garden and because Muna would get paid for the work, something that helped to ease Mr Raghavan's conscience over exploiting minors. Irshad descended on the house one day with a whole team of assistants: a hairdresser, makeup artist, lighting technician ... The stylist brought a suitcase full of clothes and jewellery with her. Indira and Muna were as excited about it as Chamki and Mrs Raghavan, who scurried up and down with trays of *samosas* and glasses of tea with milk, and water for everyone. Even the gardeners watched on with interest, as they worked more slowly than usual between the rosebushes, carrying their pruning shears and brass watering cans.

'See the way Irshad looks at you ... You'll see I'm not making it up!' Indira said to her friend, giggling.

After trying on many items, Muna came out of the house in the perfect outfit. And when Irshad focused his camera lens on her, he realized that he never wanted to let her out of his sight; that he needed to see her every day; that he wanted to make her happy. Sanjay had told him the whole story: the story of an orphan girl enslaved in an illegal carpet factory, of her attempts to learn to read, write and do maths when she was already eleven years old ... Yet now it turned out that Muna was a natural at posing for the camera; she knew how to follow the photographer's directions and express what needed to be expressed. She knew how to look, how to be. Her beauty paralysed him. The photos were a great success and the clients were so happy with the results and the choice of Muna as the model that they asked her to do the first televised advert for the shopping centre, which would be opening branches in all of India's major cities. Irshad would direct the advert and it would be filmed during the daytime in the streets and the port of Mumbai, around The Gateway of India; from early in the morning until dusk. Mr Raghavan once more had to allow Muna to leave her household chores to go and do modelling. Once again he asked Chamki for her opinion and as always, she supported Muna. There was less work to do in the house now than before. Sanjay was in England and Bani had married the judge's son. The others, Parvati, Indira and little Rajiv didn't make as much of a mess as they used to, now they were a bit bigger.

'It's a wonderful opportunity, Mr Raghavan! A TV advert, imagine what a great opportunity that will be! Our Muna! I can manage perfectly well on my own, and if not, I'll find someone to help me, I promise.'

Indira had exams on those two days so she couldn't take them off and needed all the hours she could get for studying, so Irshad alone was responsible for looking after Muna; collecting her in a car from the house in the morning and dropping her off at night, after a day's filming. Muna noticed that Indira was right. Irshad looked at her in a special way. He really looked at her. When he wasn't directing the filming, giving instructions to people here and there, he was a young, timid-looking man. At least, he was when he was around her. But even so, he always managed to find some excuse to go and drink a mango juice or a tea near to where they were brushing her long, black hair or touching up her makeup. He pretended he wasn't watching, but he was taking in every last detail. He found it incredible to think of where this girl had come from when he saw her performing like an actress who had been trained in a top theatre school. He liked hearing her speak, when she finally gained the confidence to do so. Muna observed a lot before she said anything. But when she overcame her shyness and the shame of not having any education – apart from what the Raghavans had managed to give her – she talked nonstop.

The advert was a success. Muna filled the screen with her smiling face, the wind ruffled her sari on the deck of a ferry, with the Gateway of India monument and the majestic Taj Mahal Hotel in the background like a film set. This was the first scene of the advert which they filmed on the second day. Muna had never been on any kind of boat until then. She told Irshad this on the way to Elephanta Island. They were going to film a few shots there and, in particular, some shots on the way back to the city so that they could get the best light. The journey lasted around an hour and Irshad finally got the chance to sit up on deck alone with her. He didn't know what to say. He asked her the first thing that came into his head.

'Did you know that Bombay's name came from the Portuguese?'

Muna shook her head.

'They called it Bom Bahia, or Bombaim, which means "good bay". In Bom Bahia, everyone was welcome, provided it was to do business.'

Irshad told her everything he knew about the city's history and then carried on talking about Elephanta Island, where it got its name, about the four temples carved into the rock, about how he went there on a trip with his grandparents when he was little, like so many families in Mumbai still do on holidays … Irshad spoke incessantly, looking at her the entire time as if looking for some kind of treasure hidden in the depths of her dark eyes. When he occasionally turned his head to look at the landscape and grumble about the sweltering heat and how his trousers were sticking to the wooden seat, Muna looked at his profile, his hair which was longer than most Indian men normally wore it, his perfectly manicured nails … And her heart started beating faster.

'I'd like Elephanta Island to be further away. I'd like to stay here, on the deck of this ferry, with you, for hours and hours,' Irshad ventured, finally.

Muna remained still, gazing out at the coastline of the approaching island.

'Seeing as we don't have time to visit the temples, would you like to bring me another day? I'm sure you can make up a good excuse so that Mr Raghavan will let me go out!'

And they looked at each other, laughing, both of them now hypnotized by one another, until one of the team came to find them because they had reached their destination.

Muna was paid the usual fees for work as a model in a major advert like that, which was much more money than she had ever seen before in her life. She kept it in a biscuit tin, in a secret place in the kitchen suggested by Chamki. On Indira's insistence, the Raghavans bought a TV set so they could watch the advert for the shopping centre.

Nothing would ever be the same for Muna after filming that advert, nor could the Raghavans treat her the same as before. Indira insisted that she studied something, so she could spend the money she had earned on a course in something interesting. Indira was always well-informed about what was happening in the world and she wanted her friend to be too. One day she showed her a clipping from an English newspaper explaining that the only way to succeed in life was through education. 'The more education and knowledge you have, the more freedom you have,' she read out loud.

'And we have to be free, Muna, you see? Free women. That's what Sanjay always says in his letters. Don't waste time; learn as much as you can ... In Europe the women are free, educated and independent.'

Once she had permission from the Raghavans, Muna enrolled in an English literature course and another theatre course, in a private school in the centre of Mumbai not far from Victoria Gardens. That was when Mrs Raghavan and Chamki decided that Muna could sleep in Indira's room, which had two beds in it. For a long time now, the two of them had been talking late into the night and fell asleep wherever they ended up, usually on the floor. Muna would go on working in the house as well as studying elsewhere. Such modernity was all too much for the mindset of someone like Mr Raghavan: a servant sharing a room with his daughter, going to school to study ... He had never seen anything like this in any other family! In the end, however, he had to accept that he no longer had the authority he once had, in that matriarchal household, and that the times were finally and permanently changing.

Irshad became a partner of the advertising production company, which gradually moved away from advertising and into the realm of fiction, until finally they were just making films. A year passed: a year of ferry trips around the harbour, long conversations and frequent trips to the cinema. One day, at the kitchen door that opened out onto the garden of the Raghavans' house, as Irshad was about to leave, the two of them found themselves standing immobile, staring into each others' eyes until, as if in slow motion, they moved toward each other and shared their first kiss. Afterwards, Irshad asked her if she would marry him.

Muna was nineteen years old when she became Mrs Kulkarni, of her own free will and fully aware of what she was doing. It was her first significant act as a free woman. Just before they got married, Irshad went with her to register in the census. Until that moment, Muna didn't feature in any official records. She simply didn't exist.

Arun finished telling the story of his parents, who had been listening to him, holding hands. There were no cakes or fruit left on the table and all the candles had burned down. In one corner of the room, Kiran had lit some sandalwood incense. The fragrance filled the room.

'So? Did you like it?' Arun asked Nighat, who had been following the story attentively.

'A lot!'

'And now you see how they're still so soppy with each other … Is that normal to you?'

'I think it's lovely … It's really great!'

'And you know the rest, right? Dad produced his first film and obviously Mum was the leading actress, on the back of which she became the biggest film star in the country. All the directors wanted to work with her and she shot one film after another. She even went on filming when I was born!'

Irshad poured a glass of water with a smile.

'Do you know what I remember most about that time, just before I married Irshad?' mused Muna. 'Above all, I remember how I felt when I came home from school on the bus. I don't know how I did it, but I almost always managed to get a window seat, however full the bus was. As I watched everything going on in the streets, the usual traffic chaos, I thought about everything I had experienced as if it was a film, not as if it was real. Shaha, Kolpewadi, the carpet factory, the years serving in the Raghavans' house … And I was happy because I had learned so much, and was realising that the better I behaved, the more they appreciated me and the more I learned … My whole life until then was behind me. I was leaving everything behind me, except the memory of Sita; that was still very much in my mind. I remembered her every day.'

BARCELONA, 2004

Sita turned off the television. She couldn't watch any more. She had watched all the news bulletins on all the channels, one after the other. She had spent three hours sitting on the sofa, surrounded by coloured cushions, gripping the remote control in her hand. It was now evening and she hadn't even eaten yet. She had watched all the news bulletins on all the channels, but all they showed were the same scenes everywhere. She knew them off by heart now. She felt like she was going crazy. Pulling on a woollen jumper, she stepped out onto the balcony. She found it hard to draw breath and she stayed out there a while, quietly, looking at the buildings opposite, the different windows through which she could see various scenes: a couple sitting on a sofa watching TV; an old woman knitting as she sat in an armchair, the area around her brightly lit, with the television on too; a man smoking peacefully, leaning against his balcony railing (more and more people seemed to be smoking out on their balconies, even though the weather was getting colder) … At this time of night, the city was gradually going to bed, the noises faded and you could just hear the faint far-off sound of the cars and buses, a rubbish truck, a dog barking. Her neighbourhood was full of working people and, during the week, it seemed as if everyone followed the same schedule. Many people had left the city for the Christmas holidays and everything was less hectic. There were more darkened windows than normal. She took a deep breath. She was feeling too many emotions at once. Above all, an overwhelming sense of anger and powerlessness. Zombie-like, she went back inside her apartment.

She was hungry but she didn't feel like eating anything more than a yoghurt. Tsunami was a word that made her feel sick. It was only four days since she had returned from India, where she had spent a whole month working as a voluntary paediatrician in a hospital a couple of miles south of Chennai, the city formerly known as Madras. Then she had escaped for a few days to Karaikal and Pondicherry with Mark. She had wanted to stay there. In India, with Mark, working as a volunteer. But she had come home. It was the second time she had travelled to India and the second time she had confirmed that Barcelona was her home. At the Primary Care Centre where she worked they needed her too, and she couldn't take any more days off as holiday. She had also wanted to come back to spend Christmas day and Saint Stephens day with her parents. That time had always been magical for her, and even at thirty-eight, there was nothing she looked forward to more than being with them, and her whole family, cousins, aunts and uncles, every 25th and 26th December.

Mark's mobile was turned off and his voicemail was now not accepting any more messages. She wanted to believe that no mobile phones were working on the coasts of the Indian Ocean. She had called all the phone numbers that she had. Nobody was answering any of them. The feeling of desperation was impossible to define. She had images etched in her mind of the tsunami suddenly sweeping away houses, people, trees and everything in its path. A tingle ran down her spine, making her shudder.

She looked for all the information she could find on the internet. The coastline of the state of Tamil Nadu had been seriously affected by the shockwave from the strong earthquake that had hit northern Sumatra and crossed the Indian Ocean, destroying thousands of hectares of the coastline of many Asian countries and killing many thousands of people. They were saying that more than five thousand people had died in Tamil Nadu alone. The districts of Pondicherry and Karaikal were on the list. Mark was there, but on the first lists of the identified dead, there was no Mark Howard. They had said goodbye in Pondicherry and he was planning to go further south, back to Karaikal to explore the fishing villages and even try to go fishing with them, to go to Nagapattinam and find out how the nurseries of shrimps and lobsters worked, before returning to London. Now all of those nurseries had disappeared, as well as many of their owners and workers, along with the fishermen and boats of many families. And Mark was there. The emergency phone numbers that had been posted on the Tamil Nadu government website were always busy, or sometimes not working at all. There was no way of getting through to anybody at any of the help or information centres that had been set up in each district.

The letter was on the desk, next to the computer, just as she had left it the morning she received it. On top of it was the bison bone fossil that Mark had given her. A representative of some Indian actress wanted to meet her in Barcelona regarding an extremely important matter. She had proposed a series of dates from January onwards, to meet at Hotel Omm, where she would be staying. Muna Kulkarni was a name that meant nothing to her. She had typed it into Google and a never-ending list of websites came up, all about her. If she felt up to it, the next day after work she would go to an Indian video shop that she had seen on a street in Raval (she couldn't remember now if it was Carrer Hospital, or Sant Pau or even del Carme) and she would ask if they had any of her films to rent.

'Any news?' Judith asked her as soon as she saw her walking down the corridor toward her office, wearing her white coat.

'No, I haven't heard anything from him … '

Judith shook her head and said nothing. They had worked together for five years. They got on very well and had become great friends, even though they lived very different lives now. Judith's was slow-paced and predictable, with a husband and a three-year old son. Her husband was her first love, from her youth, and they knew that they would be together forever. She loved paediatrics but she worked the exact amount of hours she needed to, so that she could spend the maximum amount of time with her family. Before her son was born, Judith and Sita used to go the cinema together at least once a week. They used to go clothes shopping together. Now they hardly saw each other outside of work. Their consulting rooms were next door to each other, shared with other paediatricians depending on days and shifts.

Preoccupied, Sita sat still, staring out at the inner court-yard she could see out of her window. The large palm tree in the middle, the facade of the house opposite … The idea that something had happened to Mark terrified her. Now she realized that he was the closest thing to the perfect partner she had always dreamed of. She hadn't had much luck with men. She had accumulated a large collection of disappointments in her life. She had always ended up falling for men who didn't understand her or who she didn't understand, or those who had way too much emotional baggage from their past: an ex-wife who was constantly involved in their life; or a difficult teenager who made him feel guilty any time he wasn't paying them attention; or two rude, badly behaved young daughters, that, along with the invisible presence of their mother, the ex-wife, were doubly unbearable … Why do some people find it so easy having a partner, and others find it so difficult, if not impossible?

They had met on an intensive tropical medicine course in London. It tickled her when she remembered her first impression of him: what an enormous Englishman! Mark was incredibly tall and broad, with fair skin and brown hair which emphasized his greyish-blue eyes; eyes the colour of a frozen Nordic fjord. He had a very kind face and the nicest smile she had ever seen. When he held her, she felt suddenly saved; protected from anything. She was hypnotized by his boundless energy, his curiosity and his sense of humour. His commitment to helping people in need fascinated her. Sita would always wonder if Mark had been attracted to her for her, or for her life story.

'Are you really Indian? You're joking, right?'

These were the first words Mark said to her during a break, as they drank coffee with their other colleagues. How many times had she had to answer the same incredulous question? If she didn't tell people she was from India, Sita could pass for Mediterranean. She had quite dark skin, but she could have passed for Catalan, Andalusian, Greek, Corsican, Italian, Lebanese or Berber. Her hair was also dark but not especially so, and her eyes were so brown they were almost black, the kind of eyes that are a passport to anonymity; you could be from anywhere with those eyes. She wasn't tall, or short, nor excessively thin or fat. If she didn't tell people, then nothing about her would suggest that Sita had been born in a small village in Maharashtra, that she had spend the first years of her childhood in an orphanage in Mumbai and that she had arrived in Barcelona at the age of seven. So sometimes she just said nothing. She liked playing the game of posing as just another person from Barcelona. Which is actually how she felt. Where was she from, if not Barcelona? She had enrolled in that particular course because Judith had firmly insisted that one of them should go; they should be informed on the topic. For Judith it was hard to take two weeks off and she didn't fancy being away from her little son for such a long time. Although she would have liked to go, her English wasn't very good and English was essential for doing the course. As well as being grateful to her father for passing on his passion for public health care, his commitment to treating all patients with equal dedication and professionalism, Sita would always be grateful to him for his insistence that she learnt perfect English; all the classes he had paid for, the trips to Europe and the United States during her teenage years which had allowed her to practice. They even had a Canadian university student to stay with them for a year, on the condition that she only spoke English to them. That was a defining year for Sita because although the girl was a lot older than her, they ended up becoming good friends and spent many hours talking. These days she had more and more patients from other continents; the children of immigrants with illnesses that had never been seen before in Barcelona, or that had been seen many decades ago by other doctors. There were also more adopted patients, children from Africa, Asia and Central America. More paediatricians with knowledge of tropical medicine were needed. So that is why, as the course was completely subsidized and she didn't have to pay a penny for it, Sita signed up for the two-week intensive course at the London School of Tropical Medicine. It was in the Bloomsbury area, two streets away from the British Museum and Russell Square, the perfect place to sit on a bench among the enormous plane trees and watch the squirrels clambering up the vast tree trunks. Although it was cold, it was always nice to spend a while outside, reading. There were seventy paediatricians on the course from more than fifty countries, mostly in Europe, but also from the United States and Japan. Sita's way of talking and moving, and her clothes, tone of voice and accent when she spoke English all pointed toward Sita being an authentic Mediterranean woman.

'So, you're Indian ... Did you know that the course director is Indian?' Mark asked her during another of their breaks. 'He was my lecturer at university. Doctor Raghavan is brilliant, the best. He's the reason I made my first trip to India. I even went to his house in Mumbai. He wanted me to meet his parents and his family. Lovely people. And they had an excellent cook, although she was a very old woman, she gave me a lesson in cooking southern Indian food. If you want, we'll find him and I'll introduce you.'

After several idyllic weekends spent between London and Barcelona, they knew that they wanted to spend more time together, longer than just a weekend at a time. Sita's holidays were coming up, which she usually took when none of her colleagues wanted to. They all had children apart from her and they all tried to go on holiday when their children were on holiday too. She could go from the end of November until the end of December. Once, when they were talking on the phone, Mark suggested that both of them should go to work as voluntary paediatricians in a hospital in Tamil Nadu, in southern India. An Indian friend with whom he had studied at university worked there and had told him that they would be more than welcome and could stay at his house. They needed doctors all the time, particularly in isolated rural villages. Mark took an unpaid week off from the hospital in London where he worked, so he could make the most of Sita's month of holiday.

'India? But why can't we go somewhere else?'

'It's the most special place in the world; the most extreme. You either love it or you totally reject it. And it's your country!'

'No, it's not now! I don't feel like I'm from there. I already explained to you that when I went there I hated it … so much dirt, so much misery, so much noise … I know I saw some beautiful things too, but I don't know … Let me think about it, okay? I'll call you tomorrow!'

'Alright, call me tomorrow … But Sita, I would really love to go to India with you!'

Working for free for people who couldn't afford a doctor, let alone the services of paediatricians like her and Mark, seemed like the least she could do to give something back to her country. Mark was right. India, whether she liked it or not, was her country; the country that had given her life. Although it would only be a few days, a few hours spent curing the poorest children in India, – children just like she had been once – it seemed like a good idea to her.

She was twenty years old the first time she had gone back to India since she was adopted. She went with her parents, who had always told her that when she was older the three of them would go together to the country where she was born, since they had never been. When she was twenty, the day came to return to Mumbai, to land in the same airport she had left from as a little girl. The journey from the airport to the city made a huge impression on her. Millions of people lived along the sides of the road, with plastic for roofs, cardboard for walls and huge rats leisurely scampering between the flimsy shacks. The day had come for Sita to walk back through the iron gates of the Missionaries of Mary orphanage in Mumbai. It was less emotional than she thought it would be. Perhaps this was because her parents had helped her not to erase her memories, and she had kept them clearly in her mind for the thirteen years since she had left Mumbai. From the first day she arrived in Barcelona, her parents went on sending drawings and photos of Sita to Sister Valentina. She, in turn, had found time to send Ramón and Irene what they had insisted on: a photo of the orphanage and some of the nuns that had known Sita. She had always sent a Christmas card every year, like clockwork until she died, which was two years before Sita's return to India. They received a letter from Sister Juliette with the news and a commemorative card of the day of her death. They didn't go into detail about how she died; just that it was through illness. Sister Juliette became the new director of the orphanage.

They spent the whole week in Mumbai, staying in a small hotel in Colaba, an area on the city's southern peninsula. They could walk along the sea front promenade to reach the Gateway of India, opposite the Taj Mahal hotel. At dusk, the enormous triumphal arch – a colonial monument, but inspired by Muslim architecture of several centuries earlier – was all lit up. The lights reflected in the water of the port, like something out of a film set. The gateway was built to celebrate the visit of King George V from England. British troops had marched through it before setting sail and leaving India for good in 1947. The facade of Victoria Terminus which was more like a gothic church than a train station; the hawkers selling fruit, newspapers and hot snacks on every street; the colourful flower stalls at the temple entrances; the mingled smell of incense and burning oil; the bicycles, *rickshaws* and taxis with their horns beeping all day and night; the dogs scavenging around huge mounds of rubbish; an elephant with a boy sitting on top of it, mutely plodding along the street carrying its 400 kilo load, overtaking bicycles and pedestrians; the street tailors with their mobile sewing machines; the *sadhus* dressed in orange … Sita had the feeling that nothing had changed, particularly whenever they caught a taxi. Sitting in the backseat, she looked at everything inside the car in detail … The jasmine flowers hanging from the rear view mirror, the picture of *Sai Baba* … On every journey, memories of her excursions with Sister Valentina came flooding back to her like stills from a film. All of the taxi drivers reminded her of Layam.

They visited the orphanage. Sister Juliette spent a lot of time with them; the whole day in fact. Sita went up the spiral staircase with her parents, feeling choked up. She showed them the room where she slept on the floor with all of the other children under the ceiling fans. They ate together, going over the events of the recent years and sharing stories. Sister Juliette told them how, during the monsoons, the upstairs floor had flooded. The ceiling caved in from so many poorly repaired leaks over the years. Sister Valentina's office suffered the worst damage; all of her papers, books and documents that she kept – the orphanage's memories – were destroyed.

'I think that the flood is what made her ill,' Sister Juliette went on in English with a marked French accent, as they had tea and biscuits on the veranda at the back of the convent.

'So I guess there are no documents related to Sita's story,' said Ramón, pipe in hand.

'No, I'm sorry. They even had to throw away the photo albums; they were too badly damaged.'

They sat in silence for a while. They could hear the sound of a raven cawing in the garden.

'It's strange,' said Sister Juliette, 'in this country there are monuments over three thousand years old that are still in one piece, and then there are buildings built only thirty years ago, or less, that can fall down at any moment; always surrounded by scaffolding.'

After travelling several thousand miles on a train that looked like it was made of tin, packed to the rafters with people and packages, they covered thousands more miles in a rented white Ambassador with a driver who was an expert in Indian roads, with all the cows and the deep potholes that could bring traffic to a standstill at any moment. They went from Agra (to see the Taj Mahal) to Varanasi, from Jaipur to Udaipur, Jodhpur, Pushkar and other cities that all blurred into one for Sita.

Sister Juliette had a surprise waiting for them on the veranda. They were returning to Mumbai, where they would catch a flight back to Barcelona, but before they did, they had stopped at the orphanage to say goodbye. A young woman dressed in a shiny turquoise blue *sari*, with her hair in a long plait down to her waist, was sitting at the table which was empty apart from a vase containing a bunch of flowers from the garden. When she saw Sita, her parents and Sister Juliette drawing near, the girl sat up timidly. Yes, it was her. Sita recognized her immediately.

'Sundari?'

Unsure of how to greet her, Sundari stood up and smiled. She had the same face as in the photograph Sister Valentina had sent many years ago, but she had grown older. With her elegant sari and jewellery (bracelets, earrings, nose stud and gold necklaces), she looked womanly compared to Sita, who looked like a typical twenty-year old European tourist. Sita had completely forgotten Marathi. It had been erased from her memory. And Sundari only spoke about four words of English. But Sister Juliette acted as the interpreter, helped by Sister Urvashi – who was very elderly now, and quite blind – and a pair of nuns that Sita didn't know. Sundari had become what most Indian women become: a full-time wife and mother. Sister Valentina had found her the best husband she could, and she had married at the age of eighteen. She had a one-year old son, whose birth had been celebrated for several days by her husband's whole family. Sita listened to her whole story and felt very distant. She had just finished her first year of Medicine, which she had devoted herself to, body and soul, after repeating a year at school and having studied incredibly hard in order to get in to university. She lived comfortably with her parents, who also helped her with her studies and homework. When it started getting late, Sundari told them that she had better get home. Her mother-in-law had been left looking after her son. This time, Sundari didn't hold back from giving Sita a big hug and looked firmly at her, before reaching out and gently tracing the small scar on Sita's face with the tip of her finger. She didn't say anything.

Sita still hadn't heard anything from Mark and she didn't know what to do. She had no more numbers left to call. If he was alive, then she found it strange that he hadn't called to let her know. She chose not to watch any of the news on TV. She bought two or three newspapers a day, but she didn't know which was worse: seeing the images or reading the news coming in from Southeast Asia, in all its horrific detail. She searched desperately for one paragraph that might mention southern India. All of the media attention was focused on Thailand and Indonesia, but what had happened in India? What had happened in Tamil Nadu, apart from the few pieces of information from the internet that she already knew by heart? She imagined those white sandy beaches, deserted in the golden late afternoon. That long strip of fine, white sand and the sea, stretching away to infinity, just for the two of them. At low tide, Mark would start walking along the beach looking for sea treasures while she, sitting looking out at the landscape, watched how passionately he collected shells and coral. Mark told her about his father's great adventure and his first childhood memories. When he was little they had lived for several years in Ethiopia; years that had left a permanent imprint on his life. His father was a paleoanthropologist and had been part of a team excavating and researching in the east of the country when Donald Johansen discovered the remains of the oldest hominid skeleton ever found.

'It was a female *Australopithecus afarensis* that died between the age of twenty-five and thirty years and was barely over a metre tall. I remember the day my father told me, like it was yesterday. It was shortly after the discovery. It was the 30th November 1974; that was the day that ruined everything.'

'Do you think you would have gone on living in Ethiopia if they hadn't found it?'

'That's the question my father always asked himself. I don't know ... He always says he is a Texan with Norwegian and Irish roots, but an Ethiopian at heart.'

When Mark reminisced about his childhood in Addis Ababa and the story of his father, his face changed. It was the only time that he seemed vulnerable and revealed his sensitive side to her.

'It was obvious that the remains had been discovered thanks to the work of my father's team, but Donald Johanson took all the credit without recognising the work of any of the other paleoanthropologists. My father has never got over it or forgiven him for it.'

'Why did they call her Lucy?'

'When they found the skeleton, a Beatles song was playing

on the radio that they always listened to at the excavation site. "Lucy in the sky with diamonds" … ' sang Mark, his head swaying. 'So that's why they decided to name those fossilized bones, which are more than thirty thousand years old, Lucy. But the Ethiopians now call her Denekenesh, which means "you're wonderful" in Amharic.'

They walked along the sea shore for hours and hours, holding hands, the water up to their ankles. Sometimes they came across a sacred cow also strolling along the beach, minding its own business, stopping to gaze out to sea just like they were.

'Sometimes I ask myself why I didn't follow in my father's footsteps … I suppose I went my own way, to be different to him … '

'And because you enjoyed Medicine?'

'Yes, I enjoyed it. But now I think perhaps I made a mistake not carrying on all the work he did, by not being filled with his passion for Ethiopia … He never got over the fact that they threw him out of the country he was so fascinated by. He has published very interesting books on the expeditions he took part in, and he still does writing and research on the consequences of competition between different paleoanthropology teams around the world, on the "bones business", as he calls it … '

'The bones business … '

'It's a business just like any other. An open war between teams. There are some Ethiopian paleoanthropologists who still can't understand why they threw my father out of the country after all his research and discoveries.'

They were staying in a small hotel on the outskirts of Pondicherry, run by a woman who was a descendent of the French people who colonized that area. From their room, which had a balcony with two rocking chairs, they could look out over the sea.

Now, at night, she found it hard to sleep. She dreamed about that calm sea suddenly rushing in through the window, dragging away the bed and everything else … She woke up bewildered. She spent the day in a daze, anxious about the nightmares.

She spent New Year's Eve at her parents' house. They ate a lovely meal together and saw in the New Year with the tradition of the lucky grapes at midnight. It was just what she needed. Afterwards, her parents went to a party at the house of some friends, and as much as they tried to persuade her to go – it would be a fun party, with people of all ages, a lot of music and dancing – what she really wanted to do was stay in and watch an old film out of the cupboard. *Marnie* was one of her mother's favourites. They had it recorded off the television, full of adverts from fifteen years ago in the breaks, which they sometimes hadn't managed to cut out. Sita preferred staying in her parents' cosy flat, with Tippi Hedren and Hitchcock. She didn't feel like doing anything else.

She had just seen to her last patient of the day – a case of tonsillitis so typical of the winter months – and as she took off her white coat and turned off the computer in her consulting room she thought that she might take a walk around Raval and try to find one of those Indian actress's films. For days now she had been hauling herself from her apartment to the consulting room at the clinic in Carrer del Rosselló, and back to her apartment again, occasionally stopping at the supermarket or the Chinese restaurant on the corner. The restaurant owner – a small, curly haired Chinese lady who, every time she saw her, told her how she had regained her Shanghai habit of cycling around the city

– let her have a takeaway egg fried rice and chicken with vegetables, even though it wasn't technically a takeaway restaurant. She barely ate half of it.

The cold January weather chilled her face. She parked her scooter in Carrer de Pelai, just off La Rambla, took off her helmet and walked to the La Central bookshop. She liked going in through the main entrance in Carrer Elisabets. It was her personal haven, quite unrelated to the fact that the bookshop was actually inside an 11th century church. She walked among the bookshelves, gazing idly at the books on display. Looking without seeing; seeing the titles of the books without reading them. Out of habit she drifted toward the cafeteria at the end of the bookshop. A coffee would do her good. She didn't feel well. Constant worry makes anyone feel unwell. She felt too lazy to go and look for a film starring that Indian actress from the letter she still hadn't replied to yet. At any other time, she would have found it fun and interesting and would have sent an email back straight away. But now she didn't find it amusing at all. Now the only idea going round her head was catching the first plane out to India. She had even checked how much money she had in her current account. Not a lot. But she had nobody depending on her and she didn't care. She had no debts, she had paid off the apartment and she was a civil servant. She forced herself to leave the library through the entrance on Carrer Elisabets, and walked down the backstreets in the direction of Carrer Sant Pau where she had been told there was a video shop where they had loads of films; one that shared its premises with a call shop. She hadn't been down to Raval for many weeks and it took her a while to find the place. In the streets there were mostly tourists, who looked more lost than her, with their maps out. In a small park next to Carrer del Carme

238

some children who looked Filipino were playing ping-pong at a table under a tree. It must have been difficult to see the ball as it was now quite dark and they were playing just by the light of the streetlamps. She passed a makeshift second-hand market. It was mostly shoes, sunglasses, radios and alarm clocks. It looked like a market in the Sahara or south Sahara; an African market in a little corner of Barcelona. The sellers, who were all men, were gathering in their goods which were laid out neatly on pieces of fabric. After asking in a supermarket selling African, Asian and Caribbean produce and a hairdressing salon called New Fashion, with signs in Urdu and Arabic, full of men with eyes the colour of dark caramel, she found the place she was looking for. It was more of a call shop than a video shop. When she went in, all the men inside fell silent and looked at her. She was the only woman in there, apart from the ones in the photographs hanging on the walls. The men were all of an indeterminate age, although they were certainly older than they looked. They sat side by side on a row of plastic chairs as if they were waiting for something. Behind the counter was a younger man dressed in Western clothing: jeans and a navy high neck sweater. The upper part of the counter was glass, behind which were some neatly arranged film posters. To the left was a wall with shelves full of films, videos and DVDs, and next to that, some cupboards with glass doors containing CDs of Indian music, like the music playing in the background. Further back there was another small counter similar to an old doctor's reception. Behind it sat a man with very dark skin; he was sitting underneath four clocks with large numbers on the faces, showing different times with a sign under each: Lahore, Quito, Bogota, Santo Domingo. A collection of sheets of paper pinned up on the wall showed the rates and times for calling

Ecuador, Pakistan, Colombia, Romania, Morocco, Dominican republic, Senegal, Argentina...

'Do you have any films with an actress called Muna Kulkarni?' she asked the boy, who was looking at her from behind the counter in the video shop section.

'Do we have any? We've got them all!' he replied with a smile, in correct Spanish, but with a heavy accent. This raised some smiles among the social gathering of men sitting in the shop. A young African man came out of one of the phone booths at the back of the shop. He pulled his wallet out of this pocket to pay for his phone call and then went over to greet the men sitting at the entrance.

'If you had to pick one Muna Kulkarni film, which would you choose?'

He turned toward the shelves on the wall and without hesitating, picked one out.

'This one. It's about a man who falls in love with a woman ... It's hard to explain. But it's really good.'

'What language is it in?'

'Hindi with English subtitles. Five Euros.'

'When do I have to return it?'

'Return it? We only sell films here. Five Euros per film. Nine Euros if you buy three.'

'Are they pirate copies?'

'No way! We only sell originals here. Look, Muna Kulkarni is this one,' said the boy, pointing to one of the women in the photos on the cover. 'And that's her too,' he said, pointing to one of the photos hanging on the wall.

Sita looked closely at the photos of the actress. A very beautiful woman, with black hair sometimes tied back, sometimes very long and straight. She had a very special look about her.

'I'll take it.'

'You only want one? We've got them all!'

'One's enough for the moment, thanks.'

'Wait, have you seen this one?' asked the boy, holding out another DVD.

'*Mughal–e–Azam, The biggest Indian film ever,*' Sita read out loud.

'It's the greatest Indian film, a classic, like *Gone with the Wind!* I think it was in black and white before and they've made it colour, but I'm not sure.'

'You reckon I have to watch it?'

'It's the most important film we have in the shop! And it's five Euros too … '

'I don't know … '

While Sita read the text on the sleeve, the boy got another one out from under the counter.

'And *Lagaan*?'

'What-what?'

'*Lagaan!* In 2002 it was nominated for the best foreign language film at the Oscars. But it didn't win.'

Sita stared at it without saying a word. Her face was tired and despondent. She felt dizzy all of a sudden.

'But if you don't want to buy it now you can come back another day. We always have these ones in stock! Hey, are you feeling okay?'

When she opened her eyes again, Sita was lying on the floor in the middle of the call shop-video shop and seven men with very dark brown eyes were looking at her gravely. The boy with the films was kneeling next to her, fanning her with a newspaper, with a can of Coca-Cola in his other hand.

'Hey, are you alright? Can you hear me?'

Sita nodded.

'What happened?'

'Nothing, you fell over, you were out for a while. I don't know how you say it … '

'I fainted … '

'You what?'

'Nothing … Thanks, I'll have a sip of Coke,' she said, doing her best to sit up on the floor and drink from the cold can of drink, that one of them had run next door to fetch from the bar. She realized that four of the men, the oldest ones – with their wrinkled dark skin and dressed in light-coloured *kurtas* that poked out under their wool jumpers and anoraks – were still sitting on the white plastic chairs by the entrance to the shop, next to the cupboards with glass doors containing the CDs. They all looked at her with the face of someone watching a film they didn't understand.

'I'm so sorry.'

'Don't worry. At least they'll have something interesting to talk about when they get home! Apart from going to the mosque every day and coming to spend a while here, they don't do much else! Can you get up?'

'Yes, I'm fine, it's okay now. I'm just feeling weak.'

One of the men pulled a chair over and Sita sat down to finish drinking her Coke. She had keeled over with her bag slung over her shoulder, the way she wore it on her scooter. The Indian music was still playing, just as it was when she had come into the shop and she suddenly she found it strange to think she was in Barcelona. She felt as if she was far away.

'Where are you from?'

'We're all from Pakistan, in the Punjab, near Lahore. Do you know where that is?'

'Yes, of course I know where it is!'

'It's not that obvious! There are loads of people in Barcelona who have no idea where Lahore is!'

'Have you lived in Barcelona long?'

'I've lived here nearly five years.' He pointed toward the owner of the call shop who had enclosed himself back behind the white Formica counter. 'He arrived here first, about eleven years ago now, in 1993, along with his cousin who owns the *halal* butchers in plaza Sant Agustí, just behind here.'

Sita drank the last sip of Coke, put the two films in her bag, pulled out a ten Euro note to pay for the DVDs, picked up her helmet and said goodbye to everyone.

'My name's Hassan. If you need any more films, you know where we are!'

Brahma, Vishnu and Shiva are the three main gods of Hinduism, and together they are called Omm. Omm is the sound of universal power, of divine power. Maybe that is why she wanted to meet in Hotel Omm? Or perhaps it was because it was the most fashionable hotel of the moment, the coolest and most stylishly designed hotel? Sita hadn't been there for a drink yet; it seemed as if she was the only person in Barcelona who hadn't. Sita didn't feel 'cool' and she didn't really like the 'chill out' music in bars; she still loved listening to old Leonard Cohen songs. In any case, she was very out of touch with the design that seemed to be all the rage. She didn't like going out for drinks at night; she felt out of place. She would much rather sit quietly in the light of day, next to the window in any little bar Martinez or bar Montseny, in a hidden corner of Barcelona … One of those bars that was all too quickly becoming a rarity. Homely places, with an old mirrored Cacaolat advert on the wall and the same tables and chairs that the owners bought when they opened

243

the bar thirty years ago. She had re-read the letter again and was sitting at her computer, not sure how to reply. "A matter of the utmost importance relating to the Indian actress Muna Kulkarni", Nighat Nawaz had written.

She sent a short email back and received a reply almost immediately, just as she was about to turn off the computer. Some people seemed to be permanently glued to their emails. As she surely knew, Muna Kulkarni was a very important actress and wanted to do things properly. She couldn't make any assurances before they met each other in person, but she could tell her in advance that they had sufficient evidence to prove that the two women were biologically related.

Sita decided she couldn't deal with this on her own and called her parents that very minute.

Two weeks after the tsunami tragedy, Mark finally called Sita to tell her that he was alright but he had decided to stay in India to help as much as he could. There were many wounded people to deal with, bodies to identify, bodies to photograph before they were cremated because they couldn't wait any longer, photos to develop and organize so that families could at least identify their loved ones, even if it was just from a tiny printed image … He had to help and console many people who had lost everything and were traumatized. He felt he couldn't leave just like that, even though it wasn't one of the places in Asia that had seen the most people wounded, dead or missing. He wasn't the only foreigner in Pondicherry or Karaikal who had stayed as a volunteer despite not being part of any of the displaced NGOs out there. He would stay indefinitely, even though it meant losing his job.

'But, he's alive, you must be happy!' said Judith for the millionth time.

'Yes, yes, I'm glad ... But I had imagined something different ... I don't know, it seems incredible that after all we shared together he could go for so many days without letting me know he was alright, without thinking that I might be suffering ... '

'But I've already explained it to you! The experience of surviving a tsunami and seeing so much destruction around him affected him a lot; he must have spent whole days and nights helping to rescue people from the rubble, treating the wounded without thinking about anything else! Knowing him like you say you know him, doesn't staying there seem like the normal thing for him to do?

'I suppose it is what I'd expect of him. But don't you see? All the men I meet always have other priorities than me ... I thought Mark would be different ... But he finds himself in the middle of a natural disaster and for him, the priority is staying there instead of coming to find me, to celebrate the fact that nothing bad happened to him ... '

'Surely you would have done the same as him, Sita!'

'I don't think so. But never mind. It's my own fault. I didn't know how to hold onto him; I don't know what to do to make men want to stay with me.'

'Stop saying it's your fault, come on Sita!'

Sita and Judith were in one of the offices at the clinic, the walls covered with children's drawings and photos of their little patients. Judith was sitting on her chair with Sita across the desk from her, as if she were a mother being told her child's symptoms. But this time, her friend didn't know what else to say to her.

It was Thursday night and everyone was supposed to be working the next day, but in that area of the city there were a lot of people going in and out of bars and clubs. Sita parked her scooter in Carrer de Muntaner, a few metres from the entrance to the bar called Underground. It was the first time she had been there. She didn't even know it existed until she had read about it in a newspaper article. On the last Thursday of every month they played music from Bollywood films and people danced wildly to the beat until the early hours of the morning. Still wearing her gloves, she stood at the door looking at the dance floor and the sort of people going in. It looked like a good crowd. It was nothing like the atmosphere she was used to at the few nightclubs she had been to. There were young people, or perhaps not quite so young, dancing and laughing nonstop, lifting their arms up toward the coloured spotlights that lit them up, moving like the dancers she had seen in Indian films … Their happiness was infectious. They were people her age. Most of them were over thirty, perhaps even pushing forty years old. Were they young people? In a 21st century Western city, youth was eternal. In your twenties, thirties, forties, fifties, sixties, seventies … Everyone could be young and live a young person's life. Some women were wearing round, red stick-on bindis on their foreheads and lots of coloured glass bracelets on their wrists.

'Hi! DJ Kabir is the best, isn't he?'

It took her a while to recognize that charming smile, showing brilliant white teeth against his dark skin.

'Don't you remember me? My name's Hassan: Indian films for all your needs!'

'Oh hi! How are you?'

'How are you, more like? Are you better now? Round our way people are still talking about your fall! How do you call it, what happened to you?'

'Fainting … '

'That's it! Faint! I'll have to remember that one!'

The music was very loud and they had to shout to make themselves heard. Sita still had her jacket on, with the gloves stuffed into the pocket.

'Are you coming or going?' Hassan asked her.

'Well I'm not actually sure. I suppose I was arriving! It's the first time I've been here; I just wanted to see what it was like … '

'What *what* was like?'

'Bollywood music … '

'Well now you see! You just have to get out on the dance floor and let the rhythm carry you away!'

'Hmm … I think I'll just watch for a bit first. I'm not exactly the world's greatest dancer!'

'But this music is just for dancing on your own; you just have to feel the rhythm and let yourself go. Anyone can do it! Everybody just dances however they want to!'

'Okay, okay … But I think I'll just watch first.'

'Would you like a drink? I'll get you one! A Coke in case you … faint?'

Before Sita could answer, Hassan was already at the bar ordering drinks. If Underground had one thing going for it, it was a good atmosphere. Everyone seemed happy and keen to have a good time.

'Here you go! A Coke, just in case, and another for me in case we need reinforcements! Does that happen to you often?'

Hassan and Sita sat down with their glasses at the furthest table away from the dance floor, the colourful flashing lights and the tireless dancers.

'What's your name then?'

'Sita.'

247

'Sita? How come you're called Sita?'

'I was born in India and I lived there until my parents adopted me … I came to Barcelona when I was seven. And I can assure you that I am completely from here now. They don't come more Catalan than me!'

She told her story casually and Hassan listened to her without asking any questions. It was perhaps the first time that anyone had believed her straight away and accepted her story as the most natural thing in the world.

'I have cousins in Mumbai, in the Madanpura area. Half a century after the partition there are more Muslims in India than in Pakistan!'

'Did you come here to dance on your own?'

'No, I came with a friend … You see the one dancing like a total weirdo? The one who looks like he's unscrewing light bulbs in all directions?'

Sita looked at him and laughed like she hadn't laughed for days.

'What about you? Why are you living in Barcelona?'

'Because I had no future in Lahore; I didn't know what more I could do to move forward … My best friend Khalid – the one dancing like a maniac on the dance floor – and other friends told me about Barcelona … Khalid's older brother is the one who runs the call shop where I work. He opened it by pooling his savings with three other friends from Lahore, although at first he also had to go door to door selling gas bottles! He had to give that up as he had a bad back though … '

'That must be really hard work … '

'Especially if you've never done manual labour before. We're city people! Khalid and I had the idea of devoting part of the call shop to selling videos of Indian films … They let us try it out and now we aren't doing too badly. I don't know if it's just luck or if there's an increasing interest in Indian cinema, but all kinds of people are coming in to buy films!'

Khalid waved enthusiastically from the dance floor, surrounded by girls throwing their arms up toward the lights.

'Did you get used to the city quite quickly?'

'Oh, no ... Your way of life is as strange to us Pakistanis as a game of cricket is to you. In the beginning I didn't understand anything. Not just because of the language – or the two languages you speak here – but also the freedom that there is to walk about the streets, the respect that the police have for the people, not like in my country ... I was also struck by how bosses here work just as hard as their employees; and how people marry for love ... '

'Or we try to at least!'

'And the first time I went to Barceloneta beach. I was so shocked! All those half-naked bodies lying on the sand ... If my mother had seen it, she would have died of shock immediately!'

Hassan started laughing again. It was impossible not to join in with his hearty laughter.

'The truth is, what impressed me most about your way of life is the freedom you have. It's not easy learning to live with so much freedom all of a sudden!'

'I'd never really thought about it. In fact I probably thought it would be harder for you to adapt to the strict rules here ... '

'You're saying that because of what happened the other day in Raval? The problem is that the Pakistanis and lots of people who come to the area from other countries, we aren't used to living in apartments. We live in houses. And by the time we realize that noise annoys the neighbours, that the walls are very thin, we've already got complaints. The same goes for the Senegalese and the Dominicans, who need to learn to turn their music down! And children who come from the Philippines, Morocco or Pakistan aren't used to being cooped up all day long. They have always played out in the street and they can't do that here because of all the cars … Adapting is hard. We have very different customs and nobody is there to greet us at the airport with an instruction manual!'

'And you don't want to go back to Pakistan?'

'Not for the moment, no. Here I have a better life, although it's not the paradise that lots of people expect when they step off the plane. Here, there's the possibility of a future. I have lots of plans! I love cinema; it's my favourite thing after cricket! I want to own the best Asian video shop in Barcelona! A video shop where we also have film screenings and people come to watch them in nice, comfortable surroundings.'

DJ Kabir was driving the crowd on the dance floor wild every time he put on a new song. An explosion of joy. With his arms lifted up high and still dancing and smiling, Khalid gestured to his friend to come and dance. But Hassan gestured back, signalling that he would come and dance later on.

'Hey, what do you know about Muna Kulkarni?'

'Ah! You like the films then? I told you so!'

'Yes, but what do you know about her as a person?'

'As a person? What, do you think I know her or something? I haven't got a clue! I only know her films and that's about it. Why do you ask?'

'No, no reason … '

'Now I don't believe you! What do you want to know about Kulkarni? Are you a journalist?'

'No, I'm a paediatrician.'

'But you like cinema.'

'Yes, I like to go to the cinema when I can, on my own if possible.'

'Look how strange you lot are! What's the obsession with doing everything on your own? It's easier … It's more practical … I just don't get it … Everyone living in their own little world, thinking about themselves and no-one else … There are people in my building who don't care about meeting or even knowing the names of the other neighbours! Is that normal to you?' Hassan was shouting more than necessary despite the volume of the music in the bar. He was gesticulating in an animated way.

'Do you want to know a secret?'

Hassan finished his Coke in one gulp, nodding.

'Tomorrow I've arranged with Muna Kulkarni's representative to come and meet me.'

'What? Why?'

'They want to meet me!' said Sita, excitedly.

'But why, if you're a paediatrician?'

'When I've spoken to her I'll explain it to you, but there's a possibility that we might be related.'

Hassan was left speechless, his eyes shining. Sita didn't know him at all but she felt as if she had met the conspiratorial brother she had never known; she didn't care that she barely knew anything about this young Pakistani man who was trying to seem Western and succeeding.

'What?! Is it some kind of a prank?'

'No, I don't think so. I'll let you know. It's late and tomorrow I have to get up early, don't you?'

'Yes you will have to let me know! Tomorrow is Friday, my day off. The day I go to the mosque; as you know, we're Muslims. And then I have a training cricket match because on Saturday we're playing a match for real at the Sant Adrià del Besòs stadium ... '

'Cricket in Barcelona? Now that's funny! Where do you train?'

'In the Tres Xemeneies park, in Poble Sec ... '

'I don't know where that is ... '

'But what city do you live in? Hey, I'll give you my number and when you've spoken to Muna Kulkarni's representative, you call me and tell me everything! Promise?'

'Alright, I will.'

Hassan wrote his number down on an Underground drinks mat.

'I've never seen a cricket match.'

'You can't dance, you've never seen a cricket match ... are you sure you're really Indian?' said Hassan, shaking his head and laughing. 'Sometimes we play on a site that's under construction behind the Rambla del Raval, with a tennis ball covered in Duct tape. But for playing in good conditions, the best grounds are the Sant Adrià. There we use a proper leather ball, a fast one!'

'Perhaps you could call me one day and take me to see you play?'

'But first I'll wait to hear from you about what happened with Muna Kulkarni, okay? Don't forget!'

Sita went home on her scooter, feeling the cold air on her face, her head full of the joyful rhythms of Bollywood music.

At seven in the evening that Friday, practically all of the warm-coloured sofas in the entrance of the hotel Omm were taken. Under the huge ball-shaped lamps hanging from the ceiling, Sita could hear the buzz of many different languages being spoken. She glanced around the contemporary design space, without anyone noticing her, and instead decided to head toward the red counter at reception.

'Nighat Nawaz? One moment please,' said one of the boys in black uniform, picking up the phone.

She looked at the metallic cuboid sculpture opposite the glass door that automatically slid open and closed every time anyone went in or out. She wondered what those cubes were even made of.

'Sita? I'm Nighat Nawaz,' she said, shaking her hand as she came out of the lift, guided by the boy from reception. 'Let's find somewhere to sit; it seems pretty rammed in here but I can usually find a spot!'

ADDIS ABABA, 2005

It was raining and the street was on a hill. With one hand in his jacket pocket and the other holding his open umbrella, Solomon walked as slowly as he could, dodging puddles and moving back whenever a car went past so he didn't get splashed. There were some children playing barefoot in the mud and puddles of water in front of a small stand selling onions and potatoes. It belonged to two women who were sitting on the ground on a sheet of plastic, sheltering from the rain under a huge brightly coloured umbrella. Algeria Street. He found it hard to get used to the new street names, especially when it came to remembering them. They had only existed for a short time and nobody said them or used them; they only read them. Everyone still described places as being "on the street opposite the cathedral", "three streets after Meskal square", or "next to the Ethiopian Airlines sign". At the top of the steeply sloping street, he could see a row of umbrellas next to some green painted iron fencing and a sign indicating that it was prohibited to take photos. A queue of people were waiting to go inside and sort out their documents at the US Embassy; the queue was very long, as it had been every day for a while now. Most of the people in the queue were men, but there were also some women; young women in particular.

A fine, persistent rain was falling. Since he had sold his car, anything he had to do in the city became an excursion. He liked walking; he had always walked a lot since he was a boy. He only hailed a taxi or got on one of the collective minibus taxis when he was running late. His life would soon be changing and he already didn't care about anything. He hoped it would change again; he needed the definitive change, the final change. The horns of cars, scooters and lorries mingled with the monotonous drone of a sermon coming from a nearby church. He couldn't imagine living in a city where you didn't hear the sermons of the Orthodox chaplains at all hours. Nobody understood them because they gave the sermons in *ge'ez*, the traditional Ethiopian language which disappeared as the spoken language in the 12th century and was now only used in church. When he reached the queue for the US Embassy, everyone began to close their umbrellas as it seemed that the rain might finally be letting up for a while. He closed his too and went on striding up the street. There were a lot of armed men, both at the end of the street and in watch towers. He looked at the faces of the waiting people, imagining the reasons each of them might have for wanting to leave Ethiopia. Or rather, for wanting to go to the United States, one of the countries with the biggest Ethiopian population in the world. As he walked he wondered what would happen if everyone left. He had to stay, had to do something to help his country move forward, so that they could achieve true democracy one day; so that there was water and food for all; so that Ethiopians could exceed an average life expectancy of forty-six years of age … Yeshi had barely reached this average. He had to force himself to keep on walking whenever he remembered that he was a widower; that Yeshi had died and that he was more alone in the world than he had ever been. Angrily clutching his closed umbrella, he carried on walking up the street. He had now passed the length of the queue for the American embassy and the building surrounded by security measures. He was thirty-eight years old and he was a widower and an orphan. How could he be more alone? His sisters lived far away. Maskarem had only been back once, for two weeks, to show her English husband Ethiopia; he preferred to be an expert on Africa without leaving his suburban semi-detached house in England. Aster had married a professor she had met in the library after Solomon went to Cuba. She had gone to live in Awasa, a university city to the south of Addis Ababa. She had two children, like Maskarem. If only he and Yeshi had managed to have children. But they couldn't because of her illness. In Ethiopia they were in need of doctors, resources, hospitals. What would happen if all the good medical professionals ended up leaving the country? Nothing very different to what was already happening. People were getting ill and dying, one after the other, without being diagnosed, without receiving any help. He had done the right thing by going to say goodbye to Sintayehu's family. His father had also died in the Somalia war. By walking around the city he could drop in on everyone he knew when he passed their houses, to let them know he was leaving. He could see the gate from the distance. He had left the steep hills behind him and he was now walking down a street that used to be tarmacked, as he approached the two guards outside the Spanish Embassy. Only one in ten streets plus the large avenues in Addis Ababa were tarmacked, and many of them that were tarmacked no longer looked like it. There was nobody at the entrance apart from the two guards in beige uniforms. The peace and quiet there contrasted starkly with the daily queues outside the American Embassy. The guards already knew him from the three times he had visited before. With a bit of luck this would be the last time. He showed them the documentation he had with him and they opened the gate to let him onto the gravel path leading into a large, well-kept garden surrounded by a small wood of tall eucalyptus trees. That garden seemed like a different world. The various green tones of the plants, the red-dish coloured shrubs along the edges of the path, the perfectly mowed lawn, the willow trees, palm trees and silence. There you could hear the birds singing. To the right of the path there were five blue taxis parked up next to the other cars belonging to the embassy employees. The taxi drivers were a little further away, talking and smoking together. It was strange that there were so many taxis there; the other times he had come to the embassy there hadn't been any. The red and yellow flag had been drenched by the rain, hoisted up a flag post in the garden where it could be seen by all, next to the bronze sculpture of the bust of a contemporary king, in the middle of a flowerbed. It amused him to think that there were still kings and queens. In Ethiopia, one of the oldest monarchies in the world, the kings and emperors were part of the past. He went up the steps of the veranda and, before he went in, he noticed a boy that reminded him of himself as a boy. He was leaning against the railing of the veranda, looking at the garden and singing quietly to himself but loud enough for Solomon to hear that it was a song about wolves. The boy saw him and stopped singing. He was very well dressed, in bright colours with white sports shoes that looked brand new. He had the same troubled expression that Solomon must have had, however well dressed he was and how ever well his life was apparently going. Solomon wore his hair quite long with big, ringlet-like curls. This boy, however, had his hair almost shaved and there were some patches that were bald.

'Hi,' he said to him, unable to avoid that dark gaze. The boy didn't reply.

'What's your name?'

The boy remained silent, not moving. Solomon realized that his face wasn't happy or peaceful.

'Biruk,' he replied in a tiny voice, once Solomon had already started making his way toward the door.

'What are you doing here? Don't you go to school?'

Biruk had a plastic figurine of a character from a sci-fi film in his hands and he started fiddling with it, showing him how it fired its weapon, without answering.

'All the best,' said Solomon, gently stroking the boy's head before he went into the reception.

The room was busier than he had ever seen it. He noticed that most of the women and some of the men had babies in their arms or in prams next to them. A little girl who had clearly just learned to walk was tottering around the table, giggling. The dark skin of the children contrasted with the pale, pink skin of the adults who were sitting waiting, taking up all the available chairs. Some were dressed in safari gear, in shorts and boots with cameras round their necks, as if a descendant of Haile Selassie's lions might suddenly come running out of one of the offices at any moment and need to be immortalized in a photograph. There were a least six small children there and two adults for each child.

'My name's Solomon Teferra; I've come to collect my passport and visa,' he said in perfect Spanish with a Cuban accent.

'Yes, it's almost ready, but we need a signature. You'll have to wait until we've finished with all these people, they all have to travel tomorrow,' explained the woman behind the counter.

'I'll wait as long as I need to. I'd like to leave here with my passport in my pocket.'

When he turned round he realized that all the people in the room had been listening. One of the babies started crying and everyone started talking amongst themselves once more. He went outside and found that the mournful-looking boy was still there, playing with his plastic figurine, singing the same song in a quiet little voice. The sun had come out slightly and the rain-drenched garden glistened in the sunlight. Now he understood what that boy was doing there and why he wasn't at school. He knew that every day, many orphan children were being adopted and leaving the country with their new parents from all over the world, but he had never seen it firsthand. He had talked about it with Yeshi once. Since they couldn't have children and there were so many orphan children in Ethiopia, perhaps they could try and adopt one, like some other people they knew. But when Yeshi became ill they didn't talk about it anymore and it remained yet another of the many projects they never got to do together.

One of the men who had been waiting in the room came out onto the veranda. He was tall and lanky, and was dressed appropriately for being in an embassy in a capital city doing paperwork, not as if he were scaling a four-thousand-metre high mountain. Did the *farangis* who dressed in boots and shorts in Addis Ababa also dress like that in their own cities?

'Hi,' he greeted him in Spanish, looking like he wanted to chat. 'You're travelling to Spain, aren't you?'

'Yes, to Barcelona.'

'We're from Barcelona! Have you been there before?'

'No, I've only been to Cuba.'

'Before we came here we didn't know there were so many Ethiopian people that speak Spanish! I supposed you went to Cuba to study as well.'

'Yes, I did secondary school on Isla de la Juventud and then I studied Architecture in Havana. But now my Spanish is a bit rusty. I came back in 1988 – many years ago!'

The boy was watching them from one end of the veranda.

'Biruk, *vine!* Come here!' he said to him in Catalan, gesturing with his hand. 'My wife and I have just adopted him; we've only known each other for eight days ... Please can you tell him in Amharic not to be afraid?'

'Afraid? What's he afraid of?'

'Of everything; he's very insecure and scared ... Put yourself in his shoes ... '

'Do you know his history?'

'No. We only have a few lines of a report ... '

'He'll tell you it.'

'We hope he will talk one day ... But for the moment, if you could just tell him not to be afraid ... '

The boy approached the two men timidly. Solomon crouched down to his level and stuck his hand out, as if he were shaking hands with an adult.

'*Salam*, Biruk. My name's Solomon and I'm going to Barcelona too.'

Biruk looked at the floor, following the traditional educational rules of not looking strangers in the face.

'You're going to Barcelona with new parents, you're pretty lucky!'

The boy looked up shyly, looking at him without saying anything, his sad, dark eyes open wide. Now that Solomon was close to the boy, he could see how thin he was and that the large bald patches on his head had been caused by ringworm.

'If you manage to get him to talk ... We're worried about him, he hasn't said a word for eight days now; it's like he's in a state of shock ... We've been to one of the best paediatricians in Addis and they told us to give him time and show him a lot of affection whatever he does, but we're worried. They told us that when they came out of the orphanage the children were very happy, but this isn't the case … Perhaps they told us that so as not to worry us unnecessarily, so that we didn't pull out.'

'It can't have been easy for him,' said Solomon. 'I think I'd be in shock too.'

'Shall I leave you two alone and you try talking to him?'

'Alright, I'll do what I can.'

Solomon sat down on the bottom step, facing out toward the garden. He took a packet of Nyala cigarettes out of his jacket pocket and lit one. From there he could see the taxi drivers still chatting and smoking cigarettes. A bird landed on the white globe of a garden street lamp. In the streets there were no street lamps like that. When it got dark, people could hardly go anywhere because they couldn't see anything. He tried to remember how he felt when his mother died, when Maska-rem went to London; and when his father went off to war with Somalia to cook for the soldiers; and when the coach taking them to the port of Assab pulled away and Aster was left alone, waving goodbye to him … And he started telling Biruk, as if it were a story. The story of a boy who lived in the Entoto hills and was afraid of hyenas, a child who had to say goodbye forever to his parents and leave everyone he loved behind and go on a long journey on a boat to another part of the world, where he had to learn a strange language so he could study and be the top of his class, just like he had promised his mother … A boy who grew up, married the happiest woman he had ever met and then lost her a few months ago to illness … Biruk was gradually moving closer to Solomon, until he was sitting close to the steps, listening intently to every detail of the story. By the end of it, he was sitting next to him, on the same step.

'And because you're alone, is that why you're going to Barcelona?' asked Biruk in a quiet voice.

'Yes … '

'Me too … '

Solomon and the boy found themselves hugging, sitting on the step on the veranda of the embassy, holding each other as if they were two castaways in the middle of the ocean. Solomon started to cry uncontrollably, and Biruk went on hugging him. He had never seen a man cry before. He had thought that men didn't know how to cry.

'You know what, Biruk? The feeling of being absolutely alone in the world can only be shared with those who have experienced it too; I understand you.'

Then Biruk, in his barely audible little voice, started telling him his story: the story of a boy of seven or eight from the mountains of Debre Tabor who had been through so much since he became an orphan, without any grandparents or close relatives. After a nomadic childhood, he found himself totally alone in the city of Gondar. First he was taken in by the Missionaries of Charity when the police found him living alone on the streets and then the nuns took him by car on a long journey, to the centre in Addis Ababa where they looked after sick and dying people and where they also took in healthy boys and girls who could be adopted. Without him asking for it and without being able to prevent it, he now found himself very far from home, far from the birthplace of the Blue Nile, and although he didn't want to, he had to go even further, with those *farangis* who had come to find him, with their brightly coloured clothes that he was embarrassed to wear and toys that he didn't understand or enjoy playing with.

After a while, Biruk's new father came out with a woman who had a kind face. She was carrying a small digital camera and, before she said anything, Solomon said that yes, she could film it. The woman came up to the boy and stroked his cheek.

'We'd like to film Biruk talking in Amharic, or you talking to him if you don't mind … In case he loses his language … We're sorry we haven't learned more than just a few phrases, and the numbers from one to ten … '

Solomon offered to act as the interpreter and explained to Biruk everything that the couple were saying to him: where they were going to the next day in the plane, how they would live, why they were waiting there at the embassy, what his passport was for, why they had to go to visit Doctor Markos that afternoon … The two of them looked confident, but they must have been as scared as Biruk. He gave them a card with his phone numbers on it and insisted that they call him as soon as they arrived in Barcelona.

'I'll come to see you when you arrive in Barcelona, I promise. Don't be scared, Biruk, it seems like they really want to be your parents and I'm sure that it'll be much better living with them than alone on the streets of Gondar … '

One of the men who was dressed in safari clothes with a camera hanging round his neck had come out to smoke a cigarette and behind him came a woman with a brown-skinned baby in her arms.

'What that boy needs is to get out of this miserable country as soon as he can and never come back! The sooner he forgets everything, the better. Luckily our Paula is little and hasn't lived here long! That way she won't remember a thing!'

Solomon looked at them, not knowing what to say. He said nothing. Biruk's new parents didn't say anything either. They looked embarrassed.

He entered Yohannis' office after knocking on the door with two sharp raps. Yohannis was talking on the phone and sitting in front of his computer. When he saw Solomon he gestured for him to wait a moment. He had maps all around him, unfolded on his large desk, pinned up on the wall … There were also many books on Japanese architecture piled up or lying open among the maps. The room was big but homely, with a wooden floor, walls painted the colour of ochre and matching chrome lamps on all the desks. From the fourth floor window was a view of Churchill Avenue, the same view that Solomon had contemplated during the last few years, but from the next door office. To one side, at the highest end of the landscape, were the city hall and the obelisk in front of it. On the other side, the train station and the bronze Lion of Judah sculpture could be seen through the trees and cars. He watched the people crossing the street wherever they pleased, without taking any notice of traffic lights – if they were even working, that is – and the blue and white minibuses swerving to avoid them with a beep of their horns. Two men were tying some wooden boxes onto the roof-rack of a car parked on one side of the street. On the roof of one building there were satellite dishes; they were springing up everywhere lately. That view reminded him of Yeshi. His regret over working instead of spending every hour of the day with her, the long phone conversations with the doctor, looking out of the window … He vividly remembered those days of going back and forth from the hospital to the laboratories, taking test tubes of Yeshi's blood for analysis and so many trips from their home to the hospital to take her clean clothes and food, or deciding with Yeshi's brothers who would take the food and who would take the clothes … The logistics of hospitals, where there were practically no other services offered apart from that of the doctor, were very complicated.

Yohannis Kebede was one of Ethiopia's most famous architects and the person that Solomon owed the most to, professionally. Working for him and with him had been a great challenge and a unique experience. Yohannis had spent all of his younger years between Sweden and Denmark, thanks to a scholarship from the Swedish government. Part of his studies were spent in Uppsala and the other in Copenhagen. It was the end of the seventies and an inconceivable feeling of freedom was forming at the time in Ethiopia. He had lived the most time in Denmark, working for the architects Friis and Moltke who, according to Yohannis, had permanently influenced his style. Before returning to Ethiopia he spent some years in Kenya as a professor of architecture at the University of Nairobi. If Solomon was going to Barcelona now, it was only because he was following the advice of Yohannis who he admired and listened to like a father or older brother. In the office there was a new picture hanging on the wall behind the desk. Yohannis collected contemporary Ethiopian art. The entire Kebede studio was a fusion of Scandinavian style and Ethiopian modernity and was without a doubt one of the best places to work as an architect.

'Solomon! So great to see you!' said Yohannis, hanging up the phone and coming over to shake his hand enthusiastically, gripping his arm at the elbow with the other hand.

'I've come to say goodbye; I'm off in three days.'

'Three days ... Shall we have lunch together?'

'I'd love to.'

'Well then, let's go right now!'

Yohannis scooped up his jacket from the back of a chair and they left the office. In the corridor they bumped into two young architects – recent graduates – who had worked on a project with Solomon. They both shook his hand vigorously and wished him a safe trip.

'Let's walk down. I could do with the exercise, I've been sitting down all day,' said Yohannis.

'How are the Japanese gardens going?'

'We're waiting for them to authorize the work to start! The project is finished and approved – I'm very happy with it.'

They walked a few metres down Churchill Avenue in the direction of the station, listening to the shouts of the public minibus drivers announcing the route and letting people know they were about to leave. A long line of blue minibuses were parked outside the open side entrance; some already had passengers inside, waiting for more people to get on so that they could set off. In this area of offices, banks and businesses, there were many men wearing ties and women in suit jackets and high-heels. There were also a lot of newspaper hawkers and men waiting for someone to finish reading one, so that they could ask for it and sit down to read it themselves.

'Shall we walk to Lalibela?'

'Sounds good to me.'

Lalibela was an institution in Addis Ababa, and one of Yohannis' favourite restaurants. It was supposed to be *art deco* but it was not; and it had a section on the menu of 'Italian cuisine' which was also anything but. It was an endearing place. They turned onto Stadium Avenue. The pavement was so full of stalls selling bananas and oranges, watches and shoes, clothes and travel bags that people had to walk in the street and the cars had to toot their horns to let people know they were passing. When they went into the restaurant they went straight upstairs to the second floor which was a bit quieter. It was early and there were lots of empty tables. A cheerful woman who knew them well brought over a brass jug of water, a bowl and a towel so that they could wash their hands. She promptly served them a tray of *injera* with *doro wat, misr wat, shiro wat, goment,* hard-boiled egg, chicken with gravy, lentil and chickpea purees, spinach … They had the works.

'Eat up; you'll miss it when you leave! In Barcelona I don't think they eat much *injera*, apparently; there's only about seven Ethiopians that live there,' said Yohannis, taking a large piece of *injera* with *shiro wat* with his fingers and putting it in his mouth in one swift movement.

Solomon and Yohannis ate and chatted as they had so many times, at that very table next to the window. Through it they could see the stadium and the towering Nani Building, a modern light green glass skyscraper that had been recently opened and was a new addition to the Addis skyline.

'Have you got everything ready and organized?'

'I supposed so. My suitcase is packed, I've got my visa and my packets of Nyala … They've found me an apartment in the centre and I can walk to work … '

'How are you?'

'Not great, to be honest,' sighed Solomon, leaning back in his chair. 'It's not easy starting over again. I can't be bothered. I miss Yeshi so much. I don't think I would have accepted a job like this if Yeshi was still alive. I feel like a traitor, leaving … '

'Don't say that.'

'I should stay here and work; there's so much to do!'

'You've already done so much for the development of our country! And you're leaving so that you can keep contributing to improving Ethiopia, aren't you?'

'I don't know. I suppose so.'

'Of course you are! If we want to improve the infrastructure and town planning we need to form partnerships with foreign companies. It's the only way to get funding from the World Bank and African development Bank ... There had to be some point to you going to Cuba and learning Spanish! And anyway, you're only going for a little while; anyone would think you're leaving forever!'

They finished nearly all the *injera;* the waitress took the tray away and came back with two glasses of hot tea smelling of cardamom.

'It will do you good to get a bit of distance and work in an international architects firm. Right now, Barcelona is the perfect city for an architect like you. By the way, the other day I met a Spanish specialist from the Spanish Agency for International Development Cooperation who spoke English. He spoke about you and knew who you were. It seems like they're taking your project seriously and are already deciding which projects to start working on at the new cooperation office. We need to make the most of people like you, who've got a foot in the door in Spain!'

'I've committed to a year. If I don't like it there, I'll come back sooner.'

Solomon slowly sipped his still steaming tea.

'You'll always have a job at the firm here, you know that,' replied Yohannis. 'In the Kazanchis area there is a real construction boom going on. There'll be a lot of work for all the city's architects for years to come. Oh, and when you come back, with a bit of luck, all the streets in Addis will have names! Those Germans from the Centrum für Internationale – or whatever it's called – have promised to have fifty names sorted by the end of the year, all with their corresponding inauguration ceremonies! We always complain about being a country that functions on the basis of aid from wealthy countries but I don't know what we'd do without them. There's more help on offer than we need!'

'Are the Germans also taking care of numbering the streets?

'Yes! Every house will be numbered in an ordered, logical way. In a city of more than four million people, it's about time, even if it's the *farangis* who do it. When you come back, the streets will have numbers and names, and you'll be able to receive your mail directly to your house without having to go to the post office.'

'You don't believe that, do you?' said Solomon with a wry smile. 'It will be decades before we have a functioning postal service and before we know the names of the streets they're giving us ... Addis is still a very young city; it can't all move so fast!'

He put down his tea and lit a cigarette. Solomon looked at his friend, taking in the dazzling white teeth that dominated his facial features.

'I've been doing some clearing out at home; I've thrown away a lot of old papers and things I don't need. A few days ago I gave all of Yeshi's clothes to her sister and some neighbours ... I don't have anything left of her. I don't know if that's the right thing to do,' he said, exhaling smoke.

'Yes, of course it is. You have to do what you feel is right.'

'And guess what I found in my pile of papers? A cutting from *Granma*, the Cuban newspaper, with an article saying that in 1982 they towed the *Africa-Cuba* to the port of Barcelona to be scrapped!'

'Are you serious?'

'Totally! The story of the boat that took me to Cuba ended in Barcelona. Perhaps mine will begin there. Isn't that the weirdest coincidence?'

They were at a party held by Yoseph, a mutual friend. Yeshi was dancing relentlessly to any music that played. She was the happiest girl there; she danced to the rhythm like no one else. With her hands on her hips, she shimmied her shoulders back and forth, laughing. She laughed a lot. They were dancing the first time they met. Yoseph was opening his architects firm, at a house with a little front garden and a covered terrace at the back. The music was playing inside and out, and the house and garden were full of friends and colleagues, drinking, smoking, talking and eating. That day Solomon and Yeshi hardly spoke about anything; hardly told each other anything about themselves. They simply danced for hours and hours. As if they were the only people in the room. Dancing without touching; they danced opposite each other, to the music of Aster Aweke, Teddy and Gigi. Dancing and looking at each other, in a courtship ritual that was almost animalistic. Yeshi's hair was long, tied back in a thick, wavy ponytail that also danced in time to the music.

'They told me you never danced!'

'I know they think I'm oh-so serious, but I'm Ethiopian, of course I can dance!'

After that they went out for coffee several times, on the roof of the British Council, which Yoseph had converted into the best cafe in Addis Ababa. It had an inviting wooden structure and a large mural of an artist who was soon to become well-known outside their circle of friends, who had made this their favourite meeting place. The view of the city from that rooftop was spectacular at any time of the day. They spent many hours together, sitting at a table away from the bar, watching the city from the top of that urban lighthouse, telling one another stories of their lives since childhood. Solomon wasn't all that young anymore and he felt that this woman who was almost ten years his junior was the very one he had been searching for. One clear day, as they sat looking at the distant hills surrounding the sprawling city that spread out before them in all directions, he managed to tell her that he wanted to spend the rest of his life with her; that her happiness was something he needed, every day. Yeshi laughed and said yes. What they didn't know at that moment was that their life together would only last five years. Five short years. Until Yeshi's illness soundlessly appeared, invincible, and it was too late.

Yeshi worked in an antiques shop in the Piazza area. It was a shop that sold all kinds of religious antiques: silver crosses big and small, and 14th and 15th century bibles with parchment pages and leather covers. Some of the crosses were not that old, but they looked it. And many of the bibles were not more than fifty years old, but they sold them as if they were four hundred years old. She was mainly responsible for dealing with customers. Most of them were foreigners looking for merchandise for their shops in Paris, New York and London. Some were even looking for pieces for collectors and museums. She loved her job. She liked dealing with people from Europe and North America and always shared her daily anecdotes with Solomon. Very occasionally she had to go and visit antiques dealers; they were usually quiet, strange types who seemed like they wanted to sell the whole country to the *farangis*.

Solomon crossed Revolution Square and walked to the neighbourhood of Arat Kilo, where almost all his friends lived and where he would like to live one day if he found the right house. He and Yeshi had gone to live far out of the centre. He passed the former Emperor's palace and continued walking up various streets until he reached the main road leading up to the

Entoto hills, just like when he was a boy. He was tempted to go to the House of Lions, a kind of run-down zoo with some lions in cages that were supposedly the descendents of the lions of Haile Selassie. That place reminded him of his father. Going there made him feel closer to him. But in the end he carried on going, until he reached the Shiro Meda minibus station, to head up to Entoto. On both sides of the street there was a market with all kinds of stalls, in particular selling clothes and *netelas*. The Entoto road was full of bulls going down, loaded up with fresh grass and women going up, carrying baskets of corn on their heads, herds of goats and little girls carrying bundles of firewood on their backs. There were also athletes who trained here, running up and down the Entoto hills, athletes following in the footsteps of Haile Gebrselassie and his Olympic medals. Their brightly coloured kit in synthetic fabrics and their modern running shoes contrasted with the clothes of the people using the same road simply to go about their daily business. The minibus dropped him in front of the entrance to the Entoto Mariam church. The grounds were still surrounded by eucalyptus trees, and sick and dying people. He had heard that they now evicted them from the grounds at night and closed them off. He didn't even want to imagine where these people went; where they spent the night. He went up the steps and walked around the building, looking at all the details of the facade, the images of the Virgin that had been put up on the windows and walls. Images printed on cardboard or paper, some covered in plastic, all of them brought there by unknown people. Hymns sounded out over the loudspeakers. A woman was kneeling in front of a wall, motionless. Another was kissing the wall, touching it with her hands and then touching her belly, repeating the action over and over again. She moved her hands from the wall to her stomach with intense, dramatic gestures. Solomon's eyes filled with tears. How many times had he seen Yeshi do the same gestures in front of those very walls. And before, many years before, his mother had too. The belief was that the sacred walls of the temples had healing powers. God, if he wanted, could also make bodies healthy, not just souls. That is why sick people stayed huddled there for hours. To try and be cured or to die as close to God as possible.

Solomon had bought some sticks of sandalwood incense and he lit them when he was inside the church. The smell of sandalwood drifted upwards, mingling with the scent of the eucalyptus groves.

'I've been imagining this moment for years, but never like this ... Now everything just seems so normal ... Being here, talking to you, making plans to visit the city as if it were nothing,' said Muna in English.

The two of them were alone in a room that had modernist architecture, full of columns and decor that was hard to define. The sofas were asymmetrical shapes, in velvet the colour of pomegranate. The waitress had just brought over two pots of tea and some biscuits that they hadn't ordered.

'What did you imagine?'

'I don't know exactly. I suppose I imagined a scene from a film: dramatic, with lots of crying ... '

'I'm glad you didn't want our first meeting to be in the airport ... '

Sita poured the tea out into two cups and hesitated as she tried to choose from all the different types of sugar on offer. She opted for a sugar lump the colour of amber glass, like the kind you find on the beach. She felt uncomfortable. The woman sitting opposite her had been thinking about this scene for many years. Although it wasn't as she imagined it, she had at least been thinking about it. But for Sita it was all so unexpected, so sudden, so strange. She didn't know what to feel.

'Why did nobody tell me I had a family? Why didn't they even tell me which village the nuns from Nasik took me from?'

'I suppose because they thought it was the best thing for you. You were so little, they must have thought there was no point telling you about what you had left behind. Do you really not remember anything?'

Sita shook her head and looked out of the huge windows. She could see the little gardens at the end of Passeig de Gràcia and a woman feeding stale bread to the doves, as she sat on a bench next to the fountain.

'I don't remember anything. Everything you've told me in recent emails and everything you've written to me is totally new to me.'

'Writing to you all these months has really helped me to put my memories in order. I never heard anything more about Nadira and Pratap, I don't even know if they're still alive ... I suppose not ... Or perhaps they are. I never knew what happened to Raj either. He would be about your age now. Nadira loved both of you the same; I remember it like it was yesterday.'

'It's strange to think that I survived thanks to my sister; to our sister. I still don't understand why the nuns didn't tell me anything about my childhood ... '

'I'm sorry for suddenly turning up in your life like this. I guess it must be weird for you.'

Muna looked at Sita, trying to find a trace of that little girl she had loved so much. But thirty years on, it was hard to see it.

'Why did you want Nighat to come to Barcelona?'

'I wanted to be sure that it was you; I was scared of making a mistake, or that you might ... I don't know ... That you might ask me for money and I wouldn't know how to react ... Explaining it like that, it sounds ridiculous, I'm sorry.'

'I do find it hard to understand, yes. We've lived such different lives! Mine is much simpler ... Sorry, but I'm going through a difficult time. I'm all over the place.'

They both drank their tea in silence.

'I'll come and pick you up in the morning then … '

'Do your parents really want to meet me?'

'They can't wait. In fact they wanted to come with me today, but I asked them to wait. Tomorrow we'll go to their house for lunch. Is that alright?'

'Perfect! With the time difference I won't know who I am soon … I've been awake for so many hours! I'm going to go to bed right now.'

When Sita left the Hotel Casa Fuster it was already dark. It wasn't very late but the days were short during the winter. If she hadn't had her scooter parked up outside, she would have gladly walked home. She didn't know anyone who had gone through something like this; she would have liked to have been slightly more prepared, stronger. She was certainly not the only person to have a sister suddenly appear, from the other side of the world. Or from another world, more like. The feeling of having an Indian sister who could afford six nights in a five-star luxury hotel was strange. A sister who spent more in one night than many Indians earned in a whole year.

At reception they told her that Muna was waiting for her in her room. She went up in the lift. The modern building was beautiful; Muna's was the most luxurious hotel room she had ever seen. Muna was dressed in completely Western clothes: jeans and an ecru jumper that set off her dark skin and long, straight hair.

'Good morning! Did you sleep well?'

'In a hotel like this it's impossible not to, right? I feel like a new person!'

'Have you had breakfast?'

'Yes, thanks. Here, I've brought you some presents from India … '

Muna went to the desk next to the window and took out a wrapped package. Next to it were four more.

'Here, sit down, I hope you like it.'

Sita started to unwrap the package and out slid a black velvet box. When she opened it she couldn't believe her eyes.

'Muna, this is too much for me … '

'It's just a traditional necklace and some matching earrings.'

'But are they gold?'

'Yes, of course. I really wanted to bring you some traditional jewellery from Maharashtra. In India, we love to wear jewellery whenever we can. Here, open this other package.'

Inside the wrapping, Sita found a turquoise silk sari with silver embroidered edging on one side. It was so neatly folded that she didn't dare to unfold it.

'That's for when you come to Mumbai! You have to always keep it with this piece of sandalwood inside.'

'Thank you … You didn't have to bring me anything. Honestly, it's too much.'

They caught a taxi at the hotel entrance and went up Gran de Gràcia toward Park Güell. Sita had decided to show Muna *her* Barcelona. The school she went to when she was little, where her mother worked, was just opposite the main entrance to Park Güell and as they didn't have a playground then, every morning and afternoon the children used to cross the little Carrer d'Olot in pairs, holding hands and go up the steps to the large square to play. She had come to know some of the Gaudí mosaics by heart and along with the other children in her class, she had invented secret maps and pathways hidden between the pieces of coloured tiles.

'Shall we sit for a while?' asked Sita. 'I haven't been here for ages. This square is one of my favourite places.'

There were not many people sitting on the curved mosaic benches, just a few Japanese tourists taking endless photos and some elderly people reading their newspapers in the sunshine.

'I really like it here. I like the fact I can be anonymous!'

'I suppose in India you must get recognized all over the place, wherever you go ... '

'Yes. Actors and actresses have to play an important role for people; we need to be attentive to them. We can't disappoint them ... '

'Some famous actresses here complain if anyone says anything to them in the street!'

'I know, in America it's the same, and I don't get it. We are who we are thanks to the audience! In India it's very different. There, people don't just watch a film, they live it. People laugh, cry, dance, sing ... '

'They sing and dance in the cinema?'

'You'd better believe it! I won't ever forget the first time I went to the cinema. Such an explosion of life ... it had such an enormous impact on me.'

After strolling through Park Güell they spent a while looking at Sita's school from the outside, then they made their way down to Travessera de Dalt through steeply sloping streets.

'I used to come down here with my school friends. Look! There's the bakery where we used to buy our afternoon snack.'

They took a taxi to Sita's parents' house, right at the top of Carrer de Cartagena. From the small terrace of the penthouse apartment where they lived, the same apartment where Sita had lived until she finished her studies, there was a spectacular view out over the whole city, from Montgat to the mountain of Montjuïc, with the recently completed Torre Agbar by Jean Nouvel, the eternally unfinished Gaudí's Sagrada Familia and the intense blue of the sea in the distance. Sita's parents were retired but they were still incredibly active. They did all kinds of activities and had always carried on with their weekly English classes so they didn't lose the language that had taken them so long to learn. They had made a delicious rice casserole and afterwards they had dessert, accompanied by a long session of looking at slides and perfectly organized photo albums.

'This is the first photo we saw of Sita,' said Irene, taking the framed black and white photograph down off a shelf.

'I really admire you for what you did ... '

Muna looked at the photos with great interest. She was clearly moved.

'It's amazing to think of everything that happened to us before we met. I'm sorry I didn't try to find you sooner, Sita ... '

Sita had taken a few days off to spend some time with Muna. It was the least she could do. Her parents offered to show Muna around if Sita had to work, but in the end she preferred to spend the entire time with her. Her parents also went with them to many of the places.

'I need to ask you a favour,' Sita said to Muna. 'I'd like to introduce you to a very special friend of mine. I've only known him a little while, but I like him a lot.'

They showed up unannounced at the call shop-video shop on Carrer de Sant Pau. As usual, there were a few Pakistani men sitting on the plastic chairs by the door, chatting amongst themselves. All of the phone booths at the back appeared to be occupied.

'Hi, Hassan!'

'Hi, Sita! I haven't seen you for days! Do you have the morning off?'

'Yes and I've brought you a surprise ... I'd like to introduce you to my sister Muna ... '

Muna took off her sunglasses and held out her hand.

'Muna? Muna Kulkarni?'

'I've also bought a can of Coke with me in case you faint,' said Sita, laughing.

Hassan rushed out from behind the counter and shook her hand. Half of the men in the shop gathered round, incredulous. One man ran out of the shop and came back a few seconds later with two women dressed in *salwar kameez* and an Indian man who worked in the shop next door. They were all regular customers at the video shop.

'Muna Kulkarni! *Namaste!*' cried the women, grabbing her hand and smiling.

More and more people were coming in. They all either came up to Muna to shake her hand, or just stood in front of her, not saying anything but looking at her, especially the men. Smiling and unable to move. The shop was buzzing with excitement.

'Hey, we're going to be smothered! Can't you tell them to move back a bit?' said Sita to Hassan, amused by the people's reaction.

The shop continued to fill up until no more people could fit inside. Outside, a crowd of Indians and Pakistanis looked through the glass. That stretch of Carrer Sant Pau, near La Rambla, was completely full of people. Some men were talking on their phones, gesticulating, mentioning Muna's name. When people walking past saw the euphoric crowd they asked who was inside and if they had time, they hung around, full of curiosity.

'Can we take a photo of you?' asked Hassan.

'I'm fine with that … '

Muna said it wasn't a problem, and suddenly the flashes of digital and disposable cameras were going off like fireworks.

'But, what have you done? Told the whole of the Raval?'

'I supposed that word got around … She's a big star, I told you!'

The photo session went on a long time. Muna and Hassan, with all the video shop regulars. Then with the grocery shop keepers and their husbands. Then with the street barbers, the employees of the *halal* butchers in plaza de Sant Agustí, which they closed, pulling down the blinds and leaving the lights inside on because nobody wanted to stay behind and work. Muna was incredibly patient. Sita could tell that she was used to crowds of fans and that kind of veneration.

The next day, Hassan obtained permission from the city council to screen one of Muna's films in the square by the MACBA, and to organize a small fiesta in the neighbourhood. Among its other uses, the Barcelona Museum of Contemporary Art had become a popular meeting place for Pakistanis. It wasn't hard to convince the two representatives of the Distrito del Ciutat Vella who they had to speak to, because they were customers of the video shop and they already knew each other. They understood immediately that the neighbourhood couldn't be indifferent to a visit from Muna Kulkarni. They wanted to meet her as well.

It was a chilly Friday evening, just before it got dark. The city council had installed a huge screen covering the Chillida mural, a projector and rows of wooden folding chairs, as well as ensuring the security and surveillance of the fiesta. It was up to Hassan to organize the rest. The Indian women in the neighbourhood were in charge of food and those who ran local shops would supply the drinks. There was no alcohol. Hassan's friend Khalid prepared a selection of music and brought his stereo down to the square. There would be no party without dancing to Bollywood songs. His music system would be enough, since they were not allowed to make too much noise.

Sita and Muna discretely arrived at the MACBA square once the film had already started, just as they had arranged with Hassan. The imposing white Richard Meier building was lit up with the colourful reflections of the film being projected onto it. There wasn't a single empty seat in the square; it was full of people wrapped up warm. A few young boys were crossing the square, bringing chairs from their houses. Sita's parents didn't want to miss the show either.

'There's almost as many people here as when we celebrated the independence of Pakistan in the Rambla del Raval!' Hassan whispered to Sita, before showing Muna to the front.

Muna was wearing a very elegant red *sari*, her hair was done up with some very realistic fake jasmine flowers. After Hassan welcomed the crowd with a few words which were met with applause, Muna took the microphone and spoke to the people in Hindi.

'She's saying that it is very moving to see how much her films mean to so many people who are so far from their home country, and that she's very glad to be here,' said Hassan, translating into Spanish.

The cheering and applause rang out around the square, full of colourful *salwar kameez* and *saris*, teenagers with baseball caps and skateboards and children running around, not quite sure which of the many festivals it was they were celebrating this time.

'My wife makes the best *pappadams*; here, try one!'

'*Pappadams*?' offered another woman, holding out a tray full of the delicious lentil flour pancakes, freshly fried at home.

Two women with *bindis* on their foreheads approached Muna with a jug of mango juice and filled her glass.

'The mangos we get here aren't like the ones back home, but it's all there is!'

Muna talked to everyone, thanking them all for their kindness and affection. The councillor for the Ciutat Vella wanted to have his picture taken with her. The camera flashes were never-ending. Some people were also taking videos. Khalid got his stereo up and running and was, of course, the first to start dancing in the middle of the square. In a few seconds there were more people dancing than there were eating or sitting on the stone bench in front of the museum. People of all ages moved to the lively rhythms of the songs, each dancing in their own way; nobody was too shy to dance.

'Hey! Today you're going to dance; you can't get out of it this time!' Hassan said to Sita, lifting up his arms and laughing.

The days flew by. Sita wanted to go with Muna to the airport, so the two of them took a taxi, which was plunged into the dense afternoon traffic on Carrer de Balmes. Sita would then catch the bus back to the city centre.

'I feel like I need this trip back to Mumbai on my own to sort my head out … Thanks for such a fantastic few days,' said Muna. 'What would have happened if we had both stayed in Shaha, if we had gone on living with Nadira and Pratap?'

'Seeing as I don't remember them, I can't really answer that question.'

'I don't want to lose you again, Sita! We won't lose each other again will we?'

Sita went back to her daily routine, which felt the same, apart from the fact that she now had a sister called Muna. Her work at the Medical Centre kept her busy and she worked all the hours she could. She didn't mind filling in for Judith when her son was ill and neither her mother or mother-in-law could look after him. The centre was overflowing with patients but they managed not to keep anyone waiting. Since she had been working there, she had noticed how there were more and more children, either from outside the city or who had been born there. The Centre was always a hive of activity, with patients from all walks of life.

A team of Ethiopian and North American paleoanthropologists carrying out excavations in eastern Ethiopia have discovered hominid remains that appear to be older than the famous Lucy who is calculated to be 3.2 million years old. The discovery of twelve fossil species of an estimated age of 3.8 to 4 million years will be important to understanding the early phases of human evolution before Lucy...

She was about to close the newspaper and pay for her coffee when she noticed the article. She had been putting the memory of Mark and her anger at his sudden disappearance behind her, but that piece of news suddenly transported her straight back to the beaches of Pondicherry and their long walks on the sea shore, holding hands, collecting red coral and oddly shaped shells, sharing their life stories with one another. Forgetting

Mark wouldn't be easy; but she had to do it.

When Hassan called to ask if she wanted to go to Underground that Thursday, she said 'yes' without a second thought.

'I thought you would say no! What a nice surprise!'

'Well, here I am.'

They sat at a table with their drinks. It was early and there were not many people on the dance floor yet. Hassan had come by himself; without his friends.

'I still can't believe what happened ... Some mornings I wake up and think I dreamed it all! What a treat! They won't forget about that in Raval in a hurry ... ' said Hassan, smiling. 'Did you know that the shopkeepers have put up the photos they took in their shop windows?'

'No way.'

'It's true! And on the mirrors in the hairdressers too! So that the customers can see her while they're getting their hair cut!'

The two of them started laughing. Hassan was always in a good mood but this evening his happiness was contagious.

'You have to come and have a walk round the neighbourhood,' said Hassan, patting her shoulder gently. It was the first time he had dared to touch her.

'Have you put a photo up in the video shop too?'

'Not a photo, no; we've made a poster of Muna and me together and put it up on the glass door! And underneath there's a blown-up photocopy of an article that came out in *El Mirador de los Inmigrantes* with photos of the party.'

'In where?'

'*El Mirador de los Inmigrantes* is a weekly magazine run by one of my Pakistani neighbours. "*Bollywood star comes to town!*" That's the title!'

'I'll come soon. I have to see all this!'

285

'Tomorrow?'

'Soon, but I don't know if it'll be that soon.'

She loved Hassan's friendliness and the fact that everything seemed so much fun when she was with him.

'So … Let's dance!'

'Now?' But the Indian music hasn't even started yet … This one sounds a bit slow.'

'Exactly.'

Sita found herself dancing with her arms around Hassan's neck and his arms around her waist. They were the same height, making it impossible for their cheeks not to touch. The DJ, who was preparing the show, punched the air euphorically with his fist in Hassan's direction. However much they might have been from the same city, from Lahore or Mumbai, from Delhi or Karachi, they were separated by many miles, by many things. Hassan was wearing cologne. It was an old-fashioned scent that reminded Sita of her grandfather. A smell that reminded her of her first years in Barcelona. When she stayed over at the house of her mother's parents, it was the scent of her grandfather after he had shaved, when he came out of the little bathroom in their apartment on Carrer Anglesola. The street might have disappeared to make way for the L'Illa Diagonal shopping centre; but the scent had not. The song finished and without saying anything, they went back to their table. Immediately afterwards, the DJ pumped up the volume of the music with a Bollywood song. The dance floor filled with people enjoying themselves and dancing energetically.

'I've never seen you so quiet before.'

'That's not funny,' said Hassan seriously.

'I'm not joking! I just said that I'd never seen you go so long without saying anything.'

Hassan stared at her.

'It's just that I can't find the right way to say how I feel.'

There was a lot of traffic; even on a scooter it was slow-going. Sita made the journey from her house to La Rambla as if she was in a bubble; all her feelings trapped inside her helmet. Isolated from the world. Hassan had risen very early and left without saying very much; without even having a cup of coffee. They had spent the night together – a passionate but strange night; tender and awkward for both of them. Perhaps it had been his first time. Sita hadn't dared to ask him anything about his love life but he seemed nervous and inexperienced. Fortunately she had the day off that day. She parked her scooter and went into the video shop on Carrer Sant Pau. It was empty. Hassan wasn't behind the counter and there were no men sitting in their usual seats.

'Hi, can I help you?' the owner of the call shop asked from behind the counter.

'I'm looking for Hassan; his phone's off.'

'He must be at the mosque, the one just there, on the first floor of the building where Mohamed's grocery shop is. You know the one, right?'

'Yes, thanks. If I can't find him, can you tell him I stopped by and ask him to call me?'

She saw the poster with the photo of Muna and Hassan stuck up on the door and smiled. When she arrived in front of the building, the street was full of Pakistani and North African men coming out of the mosque. There were also some women covered with white veils. It was impossible to imagine herself wearing one of those veils. Or in a world that seemed so masculine. Hassan had told her that in Barcelona not many Pakistani women were seen on the streets, because for every ten men that had left their country to try their luck in Barcelona, there was only one woman. Hassan saw her first, on the pavement opposite, holding the helmet that she had forgotten to leave with her scooter. He approached her shyly; he seemed like a different Hassan altogether.

'Let's go and have a drink by the sea,' Sita said firmly.

They walked down La Rambla among a stream of tourists. There was no such thing as 'off season' in Barcelona. There were tourists there all year round, taking photos with the mime artists and living statues. At the end of La Rambla before they crossed over Paseo de Colón to the wooden footbridge, they could smell the strong sea breeze and hear a boat's foghorn as it set sail.

'It's not going to work, Hassan. I think it's best if we're just friends, like we have been … Don't you think?'

Hassan watched the seagulls wheeling in the sky above some fishing boats, opposite the terrace where they had found a free table.

'Don't you think?' repeated Sita.

'Yes, I suppose so. It would be too complicated.'

'I don't think there's any point in us trying. We wouldn't be happy. I couldn't be part of your world … '

'How do you know that?'

'Because I just couldn't. I know.'

Sita couldn't bring herself to tell him that she wasn't in love with him.

'You were educated in a society that divides men and women. In your school they taught you the Koran … '

'And you spent years in a convent full of Catholic nuns, just with girls. It's the same thing!'

'It's not the same. And I was very little. I've been here since the age of seven!'

'The Koran always gets the blame! Careful what you say, Sita or you'll make me angry!'

Hassan was more serious and tense than ever before. The sentence hung over them like a threat and Sita didn't know how to tell him that it had nothing to do with religion – or maybe it did – but she didn't know how to finish what she had started saying to him. It didn't matter. She hadn't needed to spend the night with him; but it had happened.

'I think I'd better go; I don't want to order anything,' said Hassan. 'If you ever need me you know where I am. But I don't think you ever will. Bye Sita.'

Sita just sat there, unable to find the right words, watching him walk away across the wooden bridge over the water toward the city. To one side was the Sailing Club; on the other was a boat that would soon set sail to the Islands, loaded up with passengers and cars.

She asked the waiter for a sparkling water and sat there for a long while, idly watching the comings and goings in the port and the seagulls flying over head. A girl was rowing energetically in a long, narrow boat. Sita watched her until she rowed out of sight. Once again she heard the foghorn of the boat leaving.

The next patient that afternoon was new. Sita opened the door to her consulting room and called his name.

'Biruk Álvarez!'

A woman stood up hurriedly and came toward her, leaving a man and a child behind her. They were finishing off a jigsaw puzzle. They both had curly hair, dark skin and fine features.

They had a striking look about them.

'They're just coming, they've just got four pieces left … ' apologized the woman, taking a seat across the desk from Sita.

'Biruk is from Ethiopia. He's only been here three weeks and we've brought him for his first check-up and to start his programme of vaccinations, mainly because the school asked us to … Essentially he hasn't had any vaccinations, although we don't know for sure.'

'How old is he?'

'We don't know that either and neither does he; he's never had any idea of his age. We're also waiting for the results of his blood test … The test for tuberculosis was negative.'

Biruk appeared at the door followed by Solomon with the completed puzzle balancing on a notebook, as if he were carrying a tray full of delicate crystal glasses.

'Here he is! This is Biruk! Look, Biruk, this is your doctor!'

Sita stood up and held out her hand toward him. Biruk smiled.

'You've won him over. He can't stand being kissed all the time!'

Biruk smiled again as if he understood.

'Hi, my name's Solomon,' said the man as he came into the room, holding out his hand to Sita.

'Nice to meet you.'

'We don't know what we would do without Solomon. He's a friend from Ethiopia – he speaks Spanish very well and he's come along as our interpreter. Biruk has found it so hard to get used to us, coping with leaving his environment and what he knew, discovering that here we speak two languages … Luckily we've had Solomon here almost right from the start to help him; he's explained everything that's going on and what he has to do!'

Sita weighed and measured Biruk, checked his hearing, looked into his eyes, examined the nails of his two big toes that were deformed – as if a rock had fallen on them – and the bald spots left by ringworm. The scabs were still visible. When the nurse came in to give him the first two injections – one in each arm – it was Solomon who sat next to Biruk to tell him not to be afraid, that it would just be two small pricks. He held his hand tightly as they counted to ten out loud together, slowly, to see what number they reached by the time the injection was over.

'*Ant, hulet, sost, arat, amest* … '

Solomon was also getting used to his new city. He had started working and realized that Barcelona wasn't as far away from Addis Ababa as he thought it would be. He could speak on the phone to Yohannis and his contacts for the project he was working on. He received and sent so many emails every day that he stayed connected to everything he had left behind. When he was out of the office he spent time walking from one neighbourhood to another, discovering squares and streets, all the buildings he wanted to see, which he had written down in a little notebook … It wasn't hard to get used to walking down well-tarmacked, flat roads, without puddles, without herds of goats making everything filthy, without the thick black fumes emitted by lorries and cars with broken engines. He discovered the metro and found the network of underground trains absolutely fascinating. Sometimes he would catch the metro and travel to a station with an interesting name. From there he would walk back, getting lost and walking in circles, engrossed in everything he was seeing, without a map or compass. If he could, he did it without asking anyone; acting as if he knew exactly where he was and didn't need any directions to find his destination. People seemed friendly and easygoing. He had heard that people in Europe kept to themselves; that they were unfriendly, cold and arrogant. But he didn't find that to be the case at all. At least in the part of Europe where he had ended up. In the shops in the Llibertat market where he went to buy his food, they thought he was Cuban because of his accent. When he told them he was not, they always struck up a conversation about something or other. They were curious to know who he was and to know more about Ethiopia. What he liked most was going to the beach and listening to the sound of waves breaking on the sand. He sat down near the water's edge, closed his eyes and let the smell of the sea carry him back to his teenage years in Cuba, to the hours spent reading the adventures of Jim Hawkins on Treasure Island.

He often went to eat dinner at Biruk's house. They had become like his family in Barcelona. It was Biruk who had asked him to visit. They would do jigsaw puzzle after jigsaw puzzle, chatting in Amharic. Biruk had been given many puzzles as presents and they spent hours on the floor of his bedroom, hunting for pieces and sharing stories. The boy had more objects in his room than Yeshi and Solomon had owned in their whole house; even though Yeshi had acquired some really beautiful things from the shop.

One afternoon in May, Sita left the Medical Centre after work; she had already decided to go to the cinema to see the new Wim Wenders film. She had suggested to Judith that they go together but, as usual, her friend had said that she had to go home to do bath time and dinner with her son and wait for her husband to come home so that they could eat together. So Sita went on her scooter up Carrer del Rosselló, toward the neighbourhood of Gràcia. She had time to grab a coffee before she went in to the Verdi cinema. They always showed good films there. Although for years it had been her favourite thing to do, since Sita had met Muna, going to the cinema was a different experience for her. She had watched all of Muna's films at home – Muna had sent them to her from Mumbai.

As the lights went up and the credits hadn't yet finished, she stayed sitting there, like nearly all the people in the room. As the names rolled up the screen, a Leonard Cohen song was playing that she knew because a friend had burned her a CD of his music. The song was about letters that are sent and read much later on, and it made her think of the tsunami that had whisked Mark away out of her life. She always sat quite near the front and she was unaware of how many people were in the cinema. There were only three people in front of her. They were not getting up or speaking to each other either. She put her jacket on and as she stood up, she saw him. He was in the middle of the cinema, alone. Sita couldn't help going over to him.

'Hello, doctor!' said Solomon in his Cuban accent, still sitting down.

'Hi, how's Biruk getting on?'

'Quite well … He's going to school now, but he doesn't like it at all. He spends the whole day silent, just listening … Out of school he is much more open now, but in class he seems to be mute … '

'He'll get over it. I did the same when I arrived here at his age … '

'When you arrived from where?'

They left the cinema together, talking about themselves and what they did. Without either of them realising, they found

293

themselves sitting opposite each other at a table at Café Salambó, one of the few places where Sita liked to go and where she felt at ease, particularly after she had been to the Verdi to see a film. You could always get something to eat, the music was discreet and the huge cylindrical paper lampshades hanging from the ceiling created a cosy atmosphere. The tables around them – lined up against the wall – filled up and emptied again as the two of them went on talking.

'If we put your life story and mine together, along with my sister's, there's enough material there to make a film out of it!'

'Unfortunately there are too many stories like ours in the world. And it seems impossible to imagine they exist when you're somewhere like this!'

The waitress appeared with two individual clear glass teapots. The tea leaves were still seeping into the boiling water, turning it golden brown. Solomon wasn't sure how to work a modern teapot like that, so Sita poured the tea for both of them.

'It's funny when you think how many things have to happen in order for two people to meet,' said Sita.

Solomon held his teacup in both hands, his elbows on the table.

'I watched a film on DVD recently, where Sean Penn says that. It really stayed with me … '

'Who?'

'Sean Penn.'

'Should I know who that is?'

Seeing Solomon's face, Sita was overcome with a desire to laugh.

'No, I don't suppose you should!' she replied, laughing.

Solomon laughed too. He hadn't laughed for a long time and his laugh sounded strange to him.

'You feel at home here though, don't you?' Sita asked, her laughter suddenly cut short. She couldn't help herself from looking him straight in the eye.

'Life is good in Barcelona, but everything is so different to my city … At work there are architects from all over and the project is interesting, but I don't think that I'm adapting and I'm still wishing away the months … I'd have to find a very good reason to change my mind and not go back to Addis Ababa before the year is out.'

Sita listened to him intently. And she watched him. His elegant gestures, his shy look, the unique tone of his skin … He had a different, particular beauty to all the other men she had met.

'If you asked me why I still live in Barcelona and not somewhere else, I wouldn't know how to answer. This is where I went to school, where I have my roots and my culture. But … '

'I don't know if I'll get used to all this; I find it hard to understand the things I'm seeing,' said Solomon, from deep within him, before Sita could finish talking. He clutched his tea cup as he said it, like he was clinging to a buoy in the middle of an ocean of unknown feelings.

'What are you talking about in particular?'

'Everything. Your way of life, the convenience of everything, the prices! Take the cinema, for example! I always catch myself converting the price in Euros to *birrs* … And it's so many *birrs* that on more than one occasion I've been tempted not to buy the ticket! Not to mention other things!'

'I suppose it's best not to think about it too much. This world is so strange and imbalanced that it's best not to ponder it too much … Is there Ethiopian cinema?' Sita decided to change the subject.

'There's more and more of it. But most of it is produced out-side of Ethiopia. You could say that Ethiopian cinema is made by Ethiopians living in America! *Journey to Lasta*, *Thirteen Months of Sunshine* … I guess you haven't heard of them.'

'Well, no.'

'I actually wasn't that interested in cinema and I went very rarely in Addis, just to see the new films that everyone was talk-ing about. But here I've found it a good way to pass the time alone. And I watch very original films. Like the one we've just seen, for example!'

Solomon was the youngest widower that Sita had ever met; and definitely the most handsome. It was such an interesting com-bination that she couldn't help thinking about him. She pinned the piece of paper with his phone number up on the notice board next to her phone and every time she walked past it she thought about calling him, but didn't. Neither of their hearts seemed ready or willing to open themselves up to new emo-tions. Solomon had told her that in Addis Ababa people didn't call to arrange to meet up and see each other. They simply met; they bumped into each other in the street and decided to have lunch or dinner with a friend or their neighbours' whole family. Or they would turn up unannounced at their friends or rela-tives' house, because people are welcome any time and can join in with whatever is happening. The only place where they might bump into each other was the Verdi. He had told her he lived close by and went there often; at least twice a week.

It was almost a month before she bumped into him on the stairs in the cinema. He was coming out of one of the screens on the floor above and she was going up for the next showing.

'Hi! I thought you would call me!'

'So did I!' laughed Sita, standing a few steps below him, frozen halfway up the stairs. Solomon looked even more attractive than she remembered.

'What are you going to see?'

'Nothing, I don't think. Want to know the truth? I came here just to see you.'

PART THREE

From: sita.riba@yahoo.com
Sent: Wednesday, July 12, 2006 11:48
To: j.torres@hotmail.com
Subject: News from Addis Ababa!

Dear Judith,

Finally I've managed to find a quiet moment to sit down and write to you. I'm sorry for only sending you group emails or one–liners but it's because we haven't got the internet connection up and running at home yet (if we ever get it to work at all!) and it's hard to find time to go and write to you from an Internet cafe. I'm writing to you from Solomon's office, using his computer while he's out visiting sites all afternoon.

I would never have imagined that I would end up living in Ethiopia, and even less that this country would be the place that would make sense of my life ... But it is! I've been living here for several months now and I don't know how long I'll stay for. Sometimes I think this is where I'll live forever. Other times I'm not so sure. What I do know is that, I'm sorry to say, I don't miss you! I think about you a lot, about everyone I've left behind in Barcelona. My parents, family, you ... But I prefer living here, knowing that you exist. Here, everything I do every day, as little as it might be, is important and meaningful. And I am madly in love with Solomon. No man has ever made me feel the way I feel when I'm with him. You see! In the end it took a widowed, Ethiopian architect to drag me out of my pit of melancholy. And he … Well he says he still can't believe what's happening. Despite so many differences we're very similar and everything's very easy between us. As you grow up, I guess you know straight away when things are for real.

Ethiopian society – at least in the city – is more modern than I expected. Nobody cares that we're living together without being married. Life in Addis is much slower than life in Barcelona. Here it's impossible to do half the things you can do in one day in Barcelona. Getting around is slow work, any process is slow, personal relationships are slow … And this pace is exactly what I needed! Muna showing up in my life after Mark's disappearance, meeting Solomon … I need this more leisurely pace of life so I can get to grips with all my emotions.

Our future as a couple is not all that clear. We would both like to have a family but recent events are still too raw. Solomon suffered a massive blow when his wife died. On the other hand, if we wait any longer, I'll be too old. I'm pushing forty. I've never been sure about my exact age but I'm sure I must be a couple of years older than it says in my passport. Adopting a boy or girl from Ethiopia is something we often talk about. In some ways, for me it would be a way to complete the circle, giving a child the same opportunity to have a family that I was given by Sister Valentina and my parents. I respect them, it can't be as easy as it seems, or as easy as my parents made it seem. Here in Addis I think about them a lot, about what they did for me, in the orphanage … The streets are full of boys and girls who do what they can to get by, selling packets of tissues or sweets. I often watch them, particularly when I am sitting in the car in a traffic jam. I always have small change on me to buy something and sometimes I take bananas and oranges to hand out.

I'm still working in the hospital and I also help out at Dr. Markos' private clinic. Working in the hospital is really hard. Everyone tells me that I work in one of the best hospitals in the country, but that doesn't mean a thing ... Let me just say that the families of in–patients have to bring them food from home, change their clothes, take their blood and urine samples to the laboratories of private clinics and then come back with results ... They have to do pretty much everything. And that's if the relations actually have the money to look after their ill family members. The whole healthcare system is like stepping back in time. Solomon had already told me what he went through when Yeshi was admitted, but now I've seen it with my own eyes. Every day I see poverty, but I also see the will to overcome it and the enormous solidarity of so many people. The best X–ray equipment, for example, has been donated by hospitals in the most incredible places. Surprisingly, it's a country with very little corruption. The international aid that arrives, whether in the form of money or actual equipment, doesn't get lost along the way and is actually visible.

Most of the children that we visit at Dr Markos' clinic are children who will be adopted or who could be if they aren't HIV-positive or have serious illnesses; if we can try and improve their health. When children are adopted by Spanish families, I become the interpreting paediatrician. Sometimes it's been hard for me to watch children leaving with certain adoptive parents ... There are some that come to the consulting room as if they're assessing the quality of something they're about to buy, asking if that mark or blemish is a manufacturing defect; obsessive about it. I understand that they're scared of adopting a sick child, but they already know that's one of the risks they're taking! No-one can guarantee that your biological child won't be born with a problem either. I know you'll think that what I'm saying is a bit harsh but lately I've found it so sad watching children leaving the country. I don't want to think about how many go off every day in various directions … To France, America, Sweden … The healthiest ones go because nobody wants to adopt the sick ones, of course … A few days ago I dreamed that Ethiopia was left without any children, without a future, that all the ones that were left died, that there weren't enough doctors to cure them and the healthy ones were taken away. All the planes at Bole airport were full of boys and girls leaving … I woke up so confused, covered in sweat; and that anxious feeling stayed with me. I know they're orphans and that foreigners adopt them because the Ethiopians who could do it, don't. I know that there aren't enough decent orphanages for them to grow up in their own country in a more or less safe environment, that there are no institutions with the resources to ensure that illness doesn't spread from one to the other, so that they can study … But there are almost five million orphans in Ethiopia and only a few thousand are adopted by foreigners every year. That's a drop in the ocean. Ethiopia will not end up a childless country without a future, even though I dreamed it.

Last week I went to visit the centre of the Missionaries of Charity. What an amazing place! It's so hard to describe

… Opposite the area where they treat sick and dying men and women there is another iron door painted turquoise blue, with a sign saying that it's a shelter for children. Sick or healthy; small or big. When I went, there were many sick children, mostly blind and with mental disabilities. There were about forty children who were quite healthy and waiting to be adopted. They were slightly older, perhaps between four and ten years old. There wasn't a single baby there. As soon as one arrives, it immediately gets snapped up for adoption. I offered my services as a volunteer paediatrician and I go there whenever I can. There's so much work to be done.

Addis Ababa is not a very touristy city and has no major attractions; quite the opposite in fact. That's why I like it and I feel at home in the chaos of the traffic, the cars and motorbikes beeping their horns, the herds of goats and carts pulled by mules and horses along the edge of the roads, the holes that fill up with water when it rains: it's the contrast between modern and traditional life that I like … The political situation has become a bit more stable, although the opposition is imprisoned and sometimes people get arrested just for the sake of it, just to intimidate them. It's a very young, very fragile democracy (if you can call it democracy). The relationship with neighbouring countries isn't very clear either, either with Eritrea or Somalia. There are constant movements of Ethiopian troops at one border or the other. We just hope that unnecessary trouble doesn't get stirred up. We try not to think about it too much and concentrate on our work and our daily life.

If you knew the salaries people get paid in this country, you wouldn't believe it. In fact I could live here my whole life with the money I got from selling my apartment in Barcelona. I don't regret doing that, although my parents didn't understand why I did it. I was too lost, too unhappy. I couldn't go on living in Barcelona like that. I had to leave everything behind and start afresh.

At the clinic and the hospital I've met some really nice nurses. I practice my Amharic with them and gradually I'm getting the hang of it, sort of half mixed with English. Reading and writing is a whole different ballgame … It's so complicated!

Soon I'll start going to lessons because studying on your own is just too hard. Solomon doesn't have any family in Addis and in Ethiopia there's only his sister Aster's family, who are in Awasa, in the south, so we're building a family in our own way. Here, families are not very big and everyone pulls together; everyone can become someone else's family. People are very surprised by a foreigner, or *farangi* as we're called, coming to live in Ethiopia with an Ethiopian, and I've become something of a curiosity. It's usually the other way round: Ethiopians marrying *farangis*, Ethiopians who go to live far away … Or *farangis* who come to help with the development of the country but who end up staying a long time. A few weeks ago I met an amazing woman called Catherine Hamlin. She's eighty-two years old, and she's an Australian doctor who has been living in Ethiopia for forty-seven years doing some extraordinary work. With her husband – who died – she founded the Addis Ababa Fistula Hospital to help save the lives of women who are damaged after difficult childbirth. I'll tell you all about it when I have more time.

What else is there to tell you? I'm hopping about from

one topic to another, I'm in a rush. The office is on the fourth floor of a building in Churchill Avenue. From the window I can see another building being built, with some rather impossible-looking scaffolding rigged up using ropes and logs … And I can also see my car parked up, a second-hand white Volkswagen beetle that's a great little runner. Without a car it's hard to get around the city, unless you aren't in a hurry and can catch the collective minibuses and taxis or walk a long way. The house where we live is very basic but it's in a lovely, quiet, leafy neighbourhood. We have a small garden with a mango tree and loads of bougainvillea which remind me of when I was little, in Mumbai. Solomon didn't want to go back to where he lived with Yeshi, and asked his business partner to find him a new house in the Arat Kilo area. Yohannis is more than his business partner, more than his teacher; he's like an older brother to him. He is part of our little family that we've created. He studied in Scandinavia and is also one of the few that didn't stay abroad, comfortably working and earning money; he's been living in Ethiopia for many years now. His wife is lovely. She's a music teacher originally from Tigray, in the north of the country; she's very beautiful and elegant. I never get tired of talking to her (she speaks perfect English, like Yohannis and so many other people I've met): we sit and drink coffee after coffee (Ethiopian coffee, which is like an infusion, not like ours!). Through her, I'm learning about Ethiopian society and how it works. I'm getting to know some really interesting people. I really admire all the Ethiopians who work every day to try and keep their country going, instead of emigrating to an easier life.

I think I've brought you up to date on just about everything now! As for Muna … I don't know what to tell you. I haven't really stopped to think about her much. Sometimes I ask myself what a sister is. Until I met her I lived without the feeling of having one. I don't remember anything; my first memories are of the convent in Nasik. Anything I might have experienced before that has been wiped from my memory. She says she never forgot me, but why, then, did she take so many years to find me? She explained that she had to wait for the right time to do it, when her life was pretty much complete, that her life had been a whirlwind of films … I suppose she's right. To deal with a difficult past you have to be very strong and secure. You have to wait for the right moment. We've talked a few times on the phone since I've been in Addis. She really wants to invite us out to visit in Mumbai; she wants to pay for our flights. And perhaps we will go soon. Solomon would really like to go to India, to visit the country where I came from. He says that now we just have to go to Cuba, where I've also never been, and then we'll have all the countries covered!

Yesterday I got a really long email from Muna. She told me that in India they've just passed a law prohibiting children under the age of fourteen from working. It will take a few months for it to come into effect and she says that the law doesn't guarantee that the twenty million children already working as domestic servants or in brick or carpet factories will suddenly stop working … But at least it's a step in the right direction. The more I think about Muna's story – going from a slave child to a Bollywood star – the more surprised I am by how my life turned out. How lucky I was.

That's enough for today. I'd love to hear from you. We

must try to keep in touch. You've got no excuse because the computer in your consulting room is fully functioning and you can send me emails whenever you like! Even if it's just a few lines … I'm not expecting an essay like I've just written you.

Say hi to my little patients from me! Write soon.

Lots of love,
Sita

GLOSSARY

Adei Abeba. Yellow wildflowers that grow in the fields of Ethiopia following the rainy season.

Amharic. Official language of Ethiopia. It is a Semitic language.

Auto rickshaw. Means of transport consisting of a motorbike with a small cabin for passengers.

Bidi. Indian cigarettes, usually made from laurel leaves tied with thread.

Bindi. Decoration that is stuck to the forehead instead of the traditional *tikka* powder. The most traditional *bindis* are red, usually in a round or oval shape, adhesive and made from a velvet-like fabric.

Birr. Currency of Ethiopia.

Biryani. Indian dish made from meat, rice and vegetables, among other ingredients.

Chapatti. Bread made from flour and water, cooked over a fire.

Chat. Shrub with small green leaves (*Catha edulis*) that is grown widely in Ethiopia and sold in all of the markets. It has stimulating properties and causes euphoria. It is often chewed as part of traditional customs. It is not prohibited and is exported to neighbouring countries.

Chutney. Type of jam used as an accompaniment to many Indian foods.

Culi. Man who can be hired in India to carry all sorts of packages, usually carried on his back or on a wooden cart pulled by walking along.

Curry. Mix of spices used in the cuisine of many eastern countries.

Dabo. Ethiopian bread, usually round and very thick.

Dhal. Indian dish based on lentils with spices, which is eaten like soup. Poor families tend to eat mainly *dhal* and *chapatti*.

Diwali. Festival celebrated all over India, lasting four to five days, in honour of the deities Rama and Lakshmi. It also known as the festival of lights, as millions of candles are lit. In some regions of India it marks the beginning of the year.

Doro wat. Ethiopian dish consisting of chicken cut into very small pieces, in a spicy sauce. In Amharic, *doro* means "chicken" and *wat* means "sauce".

Dosas. Rice pancakes fried in butter; typical of southern India.

Farangi. The word for "foreigner" in Amharic.

Fukera. Ethiopian music used many centuries ago by tribes to strengthen their morale and frighten their opponents before a battle.

Gabi. Thick, cream-coloured cotton fabric worn by men in Ethiopia, wrapped around themselves.

Gandhi topi. Hat worn by men in some regions of India, like the one worn by Ghandi.

Ganesh. Hindu god in the form of an elephant. The most beloved of all the Hindu gods, Ganesh is the god of everyday life.

Ghat. Stone steps leading down the sacred rivers of India where ablutions and prayers are carried out, as well as laundry.

Golgappa. Indian cake made from flour, hollow inside, that is usually eaten with spicy sauces at any time of the day.

Goment. Ethiopian spinach.

Halal. Arabic, meaning "sacred". *Halal* butchers sell meat from animals sacrificed according to the Muslim ritual, in the direction of Mecca, and letting them bleed out.

Henna. Mixture of herbs that are crushed, boiled and used to decorate the skin, dying it for several days, particularly for wedding celebrations. It is used in many countries around the world, from the Maghreb to the Middle East and Sub-Saharan Africa.

Hindi. One of India's official languages, the major language, although only 20% of the population speak it as their mother tongue.

Idli. Small ball-shaped cake made from steamed rice. It is typical in southern India.

Injera. Ethiopian dish, used as the basis of all meals; a kind of pancake made from fermented *teff* flour (a local cereal), to accompany various stews such as *doro wat* (chicken with sauce) *misr wat* (thick lentil puree), *shiro wat* (thick chickpea puree), etc.

Kohl. Black colouring used as eye make-up in India and other countries.

Kolo. Mix of corn, chickpeas and toasted peanuts that is eaten at any time of the day in Ethiopia. It is offered to unexpected guests and is taken on journeys or long walks.

Kurta. Indian shirt worn by men. Also common in other countries in the region, such as Pakistan.

Marathi. One of the official languages in India, spoken particularly in the state of Maharashtra.

Massala. Mix of spices. Also the name of the Indian dish of rice and meat which uses these spices.

Masala chai. Black tea with spices – in particular cardamom and black pepper – drunk in India.

Mausi. "Auntie" in Marathi. Sometimes used to refer to woman who is seen in this affectionate way, even though they are not a real aunt and have no relationship to the family.

Meret le arashu. "Land to the tiller" in Amharic.

Misr wat. Ethiopian lentil stew. In Amharic, *misr* means "lentils" and *wat* means "sauce".

Namaste. Greeting of the Hindu religion.

Netela. White cotton garment with a coloured border around the edge, worn by Ethiopian women to cover themselves particularly in church (Christian Orthodox).

Oromo. Relating to the Oromo region of Ethiopia, with its own language (Oromo) and a very strong cultural identity.

Paan. Made from betel nut, wrapped with betel leaves and full of spices such as pepper, cloves and coffee beans. Sold in the streets of India, normally close to restaurants. It is chewed and then spat out later. The mouth is stained a deep red colour for several hours.

Pakora. Type of fritter filled with vegetables which, in India, are eaten at any time of the day.

Pappadams. Type of lentil flour pancakes, fried to become crispy. They accompany all meals in Indian cuisine.

Peso. Currency of Cuba.

Puja. Prayers, a Hindu ritual that is carried out several times a day.

Pulao. Indian stew made from vegetables and spices.

Rickshaw. Indian method of transport, particularly in large towns and cities. Consists of a bicycle with a carriage for two people.

Rickshaw-wallah. *Rickshaw* driver.

Rupee. Currency of India.

Sadhu. Hindu religious man devoted to meditation. Most *sadhus* are characterized by being completely naked, with long white beards and necklaces. They live off alms.

Sai Baba. Indian saint regarded as a deity by India's poorest people. His image – a man with a great white beard – is found everywhere in cars, homes, offices, etc.

Salam. Greeting used in many countries. In Arabic, it literally means "peace". In Ethiopia it means "hello".

Salwar kameez. Set of baggy trousers with a tight waistband, and a long wide tunic. Worn by both men and women. Men usually wear light-coloured, smooth cotton; women tend to wear more elegant, patterned fabrics.

Sambar. Very spicy sauce eaten with rice in southern India.

Samosa. Type of pastry in a triangular shape, filled with meat or vegetables and fried. Similar to *pakoras*.

Sari. Dress worn in the Indian subcontinent, consisting of seven metres of cloth wrapped around the body to form a skirt and short blouse. Usually in very bright colours. It is worn in a different way in each region.

Sarong. A piece of fabric usually worn by men in many countries in Asia, including India, Thailand, Indonesia and Yemen. It is like a skirt rolled down at the waist.

Sarpoi. Wooden bed frame without a mattress, found in cafes and outdoor areas, for people to sit and drink tea and rest on. Found in many eastern countries.

Sati. Ancient ritual of India which involved widows committing suicide by burning themselves alive on their husband's funeral pyre. It is now prohibited.

Sera bet. Name of the chefs in the palace of Haile Selassie, in Addis Ababa.

Shiro wat. Chickpea puree which forms part of Ethiopian cuisine.

Sikh. Religion to which millions of Indians belong, particularly in the north of India. Sikh men can be recognised as they wear a colourful turban and a very distinctive silver necklace. The most radical Sikhs also never cut their hair.

Sindoor. Painted hair parting using the same coloured powders that are used to decorate people's foreheads in India.

Sita. The goddess of agriculture. Also the protagonist of the *Ramayana* (the story of Rama and Sita is one of the most popular legends of India).

Tabla. Indian percussion instrument, used to beat out the rhythm in a musical group.

Tella. Ethiopian homemade beer. People drink it in their homes.

Teff. Cereal widely grown in Ethiopia; the basis of *injera*, the most common food in the country.

Tikka. A mark with holy connotations that Hindus paint on the forehead with coloured powders. There are also adhesive versions of all different shapes and colours that most women use to decorate their foreheads.

Urdu. One of the official languages of India, spoken particularly in the state of Jammu and Kashmir, and in Delhi. After the partition of India in 1947, Urdu was the language adopted by the Muslims and is now also spoken in Pakistan.

Wallah. This Hindi word, meaning "man", is added to practically anything to define different professions or activities: *taxi–wallah* (taxi driver), *rickshaw–wallah* (rickshaw driver), etc.

ACKNOWLEDGEMENTS

We started writing this novel in early 2003 and we are grateful for the comments and contributions of all those who have shared this adventure with us. To everyone who has inspired us and who see their names here, we hope you don't mind and that you see it as a small tribute.

Thanks in particular to Ennatu for inspiring so many pages and because without her, the two of us wouldn't have met one July evening in 2002.

Thank you to Ricard Domingo for his essential, unconditional and unwavering understanding.

Thank you to Abera Koumbi for sharing his childhood memories, for his infectious happiness and for introducing us to the history and daily life of Addis Ababa. Our Solomon would not exist without him.

Thank you Abraham Berhe Gebreyesus for being so much more than just the Amharic teacher of some Ethiopian children that are now also in Barcelona; and for his sister Rahel's exquisite *injera*.

Thanks to the Meherkhamb family from Kolpewadi, in India, for welcoming us and understanding us beyond the bounds of language. Above all, thank you for making the effort to understand our way of life. And to all members of the Ghoderao and Sansare families of Nasik, Shaha and Ujani, for keeping the memory so alive.

Thank you Margaret Fernandes, Nirmala Dias and Merlyn Villoz, from the convents Regina Pacis in Mumbai and

Dev-Mata in Nasik, for their hospitality and help, every time we asked for it.

Thanks to Doctors Paloma Rodríguez Mur, Helena Pallaresa and Vicky Fumadó for inspiring us with their work. And to doctor Markos Wudineh for such dedication to his little patients.

Many thanks go to Marina Penalva-Halpin and Martina Torrades at Pontas Literary Agency for their indispensable help and their ever-interesting perspectives. And to Vanessa Intriago for ensuring that everything ran smoothly.

We would also like to thank the support of our editors Ester Pujol, Ana D'Atri and Emili Rosales.

And many thanks as always to our parents, Radhu Ghoderao and Sita Sansare, Josep Miró and Electa Vega, Joan Soler and Teresa Pont, for giving us wings to fly.